THE GODDESS OF MTWARA

AND OTHER STORIES

THE CAINE PRIZE FOR AFRICAN WRITING 2017

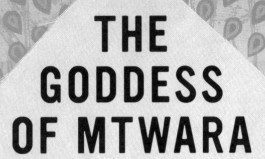

THE
GODDESS
OF MTWARA

AND OTHER
STORIES

THE CAINE PRIZE FOR
AFRICAN WRITING 2017

The Goddess of Mtwara and other stories
The Caine Prize for African Writing 2017

First published in 2017 in Europe and Australasia by
New Internationalist Publications Ltd
The Old Music Hall
106-108 Cowley Road
Oxford
OX4 1JE, UK
newint.org

First published in 2017 in South Africa by
Jacana Media (Pty) Ltd
10 Orange Street
Sunnyside
Auckland Park 2092
South Africa
+ 2711 628 3200
jacana.co.za

Cover illustration: Mkuki Bgoya, Mkuki na Nyota.

Design by New Internationalist.

Printed by TJ International Ltd, Cornwall, UK, who hold
environmental accreditation ISO 14001

FSC symbol

British Library Cataloguing-in-Publication Data.
A catalogue record for this book is available from the British Library.

ISBN 978-1-78026-401-1
(ebook ISBN 978-1-78026-402-8)

Jacana ISBN 978-1-4314-2556-3

Contents

Introduction

Selected from 148 eligible entries from 22 African countries, this anthology contains the five stories selected for the 18th annual Caine Prize shortlist, which was announced in May 2017. The shortlist includes a former shortlistee, Lesley Nneka Arimah (2016), and a story from a Sudanese writer, translated from Arabic for the second time in the 18-year history of the Prize. A £500 prize will be awarded to each shortlisted writer in addition to the travel and accommodation grant to visit the UK in June and July for a series of public events and the award dinner, which will be held in London for the first time, – at SOAS University of London, as part of their centenary celebrations.

The Chair of Judges, award-winning author, poet and editor Nii Ayikwei Parkes, said the shortlist 'reveals the depth and strength of short-story writing from Africa and its diaspora.' He continued: 'There seemed to be a theme of transition in many of the stories. Whether it's an ancient myth brought to life in a contemporary setting, a cyber attack-triggered wave of migration and colonization, an insatiable quest for motherhood, an entertaining surreal ride that hints at unspeakable trauma, or the loss of a parent in the midst of a personal identity crisis, these writers juxtapose future, past and present to ask important questions about the world we live in.

'Although they range in tone from the satirical to the surreal, all five stories on this year's shortlist are unrelentingly haunting. It has been a wonderful journey so far and we look forward to selecting a winner. It will be a hard job, but I've always believed that you can't go wrong with a Ghanaian at the helm of an international panel.'

The 2017 shortlist comprises:

- Lesley Nneka Arimah (Nigeria) 'Who Will Greet You At Home' from *The New Yorker* (US, 2015)
- Chikodili Emelumadu (Nigeria) 'Bush Baby' from *African Monsters* (Fox Spirit Books, UK, 2015)
- Bushra al-Fadil (Sudan) 'The Story of the Girl Whose Birds Flew Away' translated by Max Shmookler from *The Book of Khartoum – A City in Short Fiction* (Comma Press, UK, 2016)
- Arinze Ifeakandu (Nigeria) 'God's Children Are Little Broken Things' in *A Public Space 24* (A Public Space Literary Projects Inc, US, 2016)
- Magogodi oaMphela Makhene (South Africa) 'The Virus' in *The Harvard Review 49* (Houghton Library, Harvard University, US, 2016)

Joining Nii Parkes on the panel of judges are 2007 Caine Prize winner Monica Arac de Nyeko; accomplished author and Chair of the English Department at Georgetown University, Professor Ricardo Ortiz; Libyan author and human-rights campaigner, Ghazi Gheblawi; and distinguished African literary scholar, Dr Ranka Primorac, University of Southampton.

The winner of the £10,000 Caine Prize will be given the opportunity to take up a month's residence at Georgetown University, as a Writer-in-Residence at the Lannan Center for Poetics and Social Practice. The award will cover all travel and living expenses. In addition, the winner will be invited to speak at the Library of Congress in Washington, a partnership which began in 2014 when the African and Middle Eastern Division and The Poetry and Literature Center, in partnership with The Africa Society of the National Summit on Africa, presented Tope Folarin as part of their Conversations with African Poets and Writers series. Since then Okwiri Oduor, Namwali Serpell and Lidudumalingani have all taken part in the African Poets and Writers series and their events are filmed and made available to watch on the Library of Congress website. The 2017 winner of the Caine Prize will also be invited to take part in the Open Book Festival in Cape Town, South Africa, the StoryMoja Festival in Nairobi, Kenya, and the Ake Festival in Abeokuta, Nigeria in 2017.

This collection also contains 11 stories written at this year's Caine Prize workshop, which was held by the beautifully warm Indian Ocean at the Travellers Lodge in Bagamoyo, Tanzania, which proved to be the perfect location to compose short stories. Adjacent to Zanzibar, just across the straits outside our cottages, Bagamoyo was the old capital of Tanzania, with a rich and painful history of slavery dating back centuries. The name itself means 'rest your heart here' or 'leave your heart behind' or, depending on the translation from Kiswahili, 'bury your heart here'. We are immensely grateful to Laurence Cockcroft, Grace Matata, Ayeta Wangusa, Emma de Costa and Demere Kitunga for their useful advice and assistance and to the Carnegie Corporation for funding the workshop. Three of the writers who took part were shortlisted in 2016 and three were local Tanzanian writers (Esther Mngodo, Zaka Riwa and Lydia Kasese); the others hailed from Ethiopia (Agazit Abate), Botswana/Ghana (Cheryl Ntumy), Rwanda (Darla Rudakubana and Daniel Rafiki) and Zimbabwe (Tendai Huchu). During 12 days of peace and quiet the workshop participants were guided by the author and Professor of Creative Writing Mohammed Naseehu Ali (Ghana) and literary agent and co-founder of the Diversity in Publishing Network, Elise Dillsworth (Sierra Leone). It is Esther's second published story in English, 'The Goddess of Mtwara', that lends its name to the anthology as a whole. Mkuki Bgoya designed the extraordinary front cover, which is based on a kanga design featuring teardrops.

Halfway through the workshop the writers visited three schools near Bagamoyo in groups of three or four to speak to and read to the students about writing, reading and storytelling. We are grateful to Charlie Sloane at Nianjema

Secondary School, Nianjema Primary School and Mr Jumanee at Mwambao Primary School for hosting us. The writers were also invited by Mohamed Yunus, who features in *Africa39,* to meet the Bagamoyo Film and Martial Arts group (BAFIMA) who train, film, edit and produce movies nearby. Troy Onyango (Enkare Review and Magunga Bookstore) took time out from the Jalada Mobile Literary and Arts Festival to visit the writers in Bagamoyo, meeting his co-editor Lydia Kasese for the first time in person. The writers also visited artists teaching and studying at TaSUBa (Taasisi ya Sanaa na Utamaduni Bagamoyo), the most prestigious arts college in East Africa.

At the midpoint of the workshop I travelled with Abdul Adan to Dar es Salaam so that he could join fellow members of the Jalada collective at their event at Nafasi Art Space on Saturday 25 March. The Jalada Mobile Festival received a $1,000 donation from the Caine Prize board to deliver donations of Caine Prize anthologies published by Kwani Trust and FEMRITE to senior schools in the five countries visited on their bus, particularly in the Democratic Republic of Congo and Rwanda, where the anthologies had not hitherto been available. It was wonderful to see Caine Prize anthologies on sale in Dar es Salaam and to have the opportunity to introduce the Prize to the audience for the first time.

On the last night of the workshop we were all treated to music by the internationally acclaimed Tanzanian musician Msafiri Zawose at the Bagamoyo Country Club, which was an enormous privilege. Thanks to Nick Walter for organizing the evening and hosting us so fantastically throughout our stay. After the workshop the group returned to Dar es Salaam for an event (on Saturday 1 April) at CDEA's rooftop venue, hosted by the poet Zuhura, in partnership with Zansec, and Soma Book Cafe. Workshop participants Lesley Nneka Arimah, Abdul Adan and Lidudumalingani read excerpts from their 2016 shortlisted stories in English at the Pan African Writers'

Lounge after translations were first read in Kiswahili by Baraka Chedego and Zuhura herself. The translations were commissioned from the wonderful translators Elias Mutani and Richard Mabala, who worked on the Kiswahili in partnership with the writers while they were in Bagamoyo. An interesting discussion about the nuances and challenges of translation followed with questions from the audiences to both the authors and the translators. We are grateful to Raphael Masumbuko, CEO of Zansec, for supporting this successful collaborative multi-lingual public event, which also featured poetry by Musnad Sultan Rubeiyyah and music from Jenson.

We hope that holding the first workshop in Tanzania, providing the opportunity to meet Caine Prize authors, consider translations from English to Kiswahili, and talk about books and writing, will have encouraged locals to keep up to date with all the Caine Prize does each year. Most importantly, we wish to encourage entries from Tanzanian writers, strengthening and supporting local and pan-African literary networks. It is of historic significance that this anthology will be co-published in 16 African countries, including Tanzania and Rwanda for the first time, with Mkuki na Nyota and Huza Press. In addition, the Redsea Cultural Foundation will co-publish the anthology in Somaliland, Somalia, Djibouti, Ethiopia, Eritrea, Sudan, South Sudan and UAE. The anthology is also available in Ghana, Zimbabwe, Uganda, South Africa, Zambia, Nigeria and Kenya through our co-publishers, who receive a print-ready PDF free of charge. It can be read as an ebook supported by Kindle, iBooks and Kobo, and, via a partnership with the literacy NGO Worldreader, some award-winning stories are available free to African readers via an app on their mobile phones. The Prize intends to continue building supportive partnerships with independent African publishers in order to uplift the valuable work they are already doing, reaching more readers and encouraging more writers on the African continent.

The principal sponsors of the 2017 Prize were the Oppenheimer Memorial Trust, the Booker Prize Foundation, the Miles Morland Foundation, Sigrid Rausing and Eric Abraham. The Carnegie Corporation supported the workshop. There were other generous private donations, by John and Judy Niepold, Rupert and Clare McCammon, Adam and Victoria Freudenheim, the van Agtmael Family Charitable Fund and Arindam Bhattacharjee, and vital support was given by the Royal Over-Seas League. Support in kind was received by the Royal African Society; the British Library; Waterstones Piccadilly; Tricia Wombell, Co-ordinator of the Black Reading Group and Black Book News; the Southbank Centre; Gersy Ifeanyi Ejimofo at Digital Back Books and Willesden Library; and we received assistance from interns Jinaka Ugochukwu and Nadina Joy Blair, with support from Asma Shah at You Make It. We are immensely grateful for all this help, most of which has been given regularly over the past years and without which the Caine Prize would not be Africa's leading literary award.

Lizzy Attree
Director of the Caine Prize for African Writing

The Caine Prize 2017
Shortlisted Stories

Who Will Greet You At Home

Lesley Nneka Arimah

The yarn baby lasted a good month, emitting dry, cotton-soft gurgles and pooping little balls of lint, before Ogechi snagged its thigh on a nail and it unravelled as she continued walking, mistaking its little huffs for the beginnings of hunger, not the cries of an infant being undone. By the time she noticed, it was too late, the leg a tangle of fibre, and she pulled the string the rest of the way to end it, rather than have the infant grow up maimed. If she was to mother a child, to mute and subdue and fold away parts of herself, the child had to be perfect.

Yarn had been a foolish choice, she knew, the stuff for women of leisure, who could cradle wool in the comfort of their own cars and in secure houses devoid of loose nails. Not for an assistant hairdresser who took danfo to work if she had money, walked if she didn't, and lived in an 'apartment' that amounted to a room she could clear in three large steps. Women like her had to form their children out of sturdier, more practical material to withstand the dents and scrapes that came with a life like hers. Her mother had formed her from mud and twigs and wrapped her limbs tightly with leaves, like moin moin: pedestrian items that had produced a pedestrian girl. Ogechi was determined that her child would be a thing of whimsy, soft and pretty and tender and worthy of love. But first she had to go to work.

She brushed her short choppy hair and pulled on one of her two dresses. Her next child would have 30 dresses, she decided, and hair so long it would take hours to braid, and she would complain about it to anyone who would listen, all the while exuding smug pride.

Ogechi treated herself to a bus ride only to regret it. Two basket weavers sat in the back row with woven raffia babies in their laps. One had plain raffia streaked with blues and greens, while the other's baby was entirely red, and every passenger admired them. They would grow up to be tough and bright and skilful.

The children were not yet alive, so the passengers sang the call-and-response that custom dictated:

Where are you going?

I am going home.

Who will greet you at home?

My mother will greet me.

What will your mother do?

My mother will bless me and my child.

It was a joyous occasion in a young woman's life when her mother blessed life into her child. The two girls flushed and smiled with pleasure when another woman commended their handiwork (such tight, lovely stitches) and wished them well. Ogechi wished them death by drowning, though not out loud. The congratulating woman turned to her, eager to spread her admiration, but once she had looked Ogechi over, seen the threadbare dress, the empty lap, and the entirety of her unremarkable package, she just gave an embarrassed smile and studied her fingers. Ogechi stared at her for the rest of the ride, hoping to make her uncomfortable.

When Ogechi had taken her first baby, a pillowy thing made of cotton tufts, to her mother, the older woman had guffawed, blowing out so much air she should have fainted.

She'd then taken the molded form from Ogechi, gripped it under its armpits, and pulled it in half.

'This thing will grow fat and useless,' she'd said. 'You need something with strong limbs that can plough and haul and scrub. Soft children with hard lives go mad or die young. Bring me a child with edges and I will bless it and you can raise it however you like.'

When Ogechi had instead brought her mother a paper child woven from the prettiest wrapping paper she'd been able to scavenge, her mother, laughing the whole time, had plunged it into the mop bucket until it softened and fell apart. Ogechi had slapped her, and her mother had slapped her back, and slapped her again and again till their neighbors heard the commotion and pulled the two women apart. Ogechi ran away that night and vowed never to return to her mother's house.

At her stop, Ogechi alighted and picked her way through the crowded street until she reached Mama Said Hair Emporium, where she worked. Mama also owned the store next door, an eatery to some, but to others, like Ogechi, a place where the owner would bless the babies of motherless girls. For a fee. And Ogechi still owed that fee for the yarn boy who was now unravelled.

When she stepped into the Emporium, the other assistant hairdressers noticed her empty arms and snickered. They'd warned her about the yarn, hadn't they? Ogechi refused to let the sting of tears in her eyes manifest and grabbed the closest broom.

Soon, clients trickled in, and the other girls washed and prepped their hair for Mama while Ogechi swept up the hair shed from scalps and wigs and weaves. Mama arrived just as the first customer had begun to lose patience and soothed her with compliments. She noted Ogechi's empty arms with a resigned shake of her head and went to work, curling, sewing, perming until the women were satisfied or in too much of a hurry to care.

Shortly after three, the two younger assistants left together, avoiding eye contact with Ogechi but smirking as if they knew what came next. Mama dismissed the remaining customer and stroked a display wig, waiting.

'Mama, I—'

'Where is the money?'

It was a routine Mama refused to skip. She knew perfectly well that Ogechi didn't have any money. Ogechi lived in one of Mama's buildings, where she paid in rent almost all of the meagre salary she earned, and ate only once a day, at Mama's canteen next door.

'I don't have it.'

'Well, what will you give me instead?'

Ogechi knew better than to suggest something.

'Mama, what do you want?'

'I want just a bit more of your joy, Ogechi.'

The woman had already taken most of her empathy, so that she found herself spitting in the palms of beggars. She'd started on joy the last time, agreeing to bless the yarn boy only if Ogechi siphoned a bit, just a dab, to her. All that empathy and joy, and who knows what else Mama took from her and the other desperate girls who visited her back room, kept her blessing active long past when it should have faded. Ogechi tried to think of it as a fair trade, a little bit of her life for her child's life. Anything but go back to her own mother and her practical demands.

'Yes, Mama, you can have it.'

Mama touched Ogechi's shoulder, and she felt a little bit sad, but nothing she wouldn't shake off in a few days. It was an even trade.

'Why don't you finish up in here while I check on the food?'

Mama was not gone for three minutes when a young woman walked in. She was stunning, with long natural hair and delicate fingers and skin as smooth and clear as fine chocolate. And in her hands was something that Ogechi wouldn't have believed existed if she hadn't seen it with her own eyes. The baby was porcelain, with a smooth glazed face wearing a precious smirk. It wore a frilly white dress and frilly socks and soft-soled shoes that would never touch the ground. Only a very wealthy and lucky woman would be able to keep such a delicate thing unbroken for the full year it would take before the child became flesh.

'I am looking for this Mama woman. Is this her place?'

Ogechi collected herself enough to direct the girl next door, then fell into a fit of jealous tears. Such a baby would never be hers. Even the raffia children of that morning seemed like dirty sponges meant to soak up misfortune when compared with the china child to whom misfortune would never stick. If Ogechi's mother had seen the child, she would have laughed at how ridiculous such a baby would be, what constant coddling she would need. It would never occur to her that mud daughters needed coddling, too.

Where would Ogechi get her hands on such beautiful material? The only things here were the glossy magazines that advertised the latest styles, empty product bottles, which Mama would fill with scented water and try to sell, and hair. Hair everywhere – short, long, fake, real, obsidian black, delusional blond, bright, bright red. Ogechi upended the bag she'd swept the hair into, and it landed in a pile studded with debris. She grabbed a handful and shook off the dirt. Would she dare?

After plugging one of the sinks, she poured in half a cup of Mama's most expensive shampoo. When the basin was filled with water and frothy with foam, she plunged the hair into it and began to scrub. She filled the sink twice more until the water was clear. Then she soaked the bundle in the matching conditioner, rinsed and towelled it dry. Next, she gathered up the silky strands and began to wind them.

Round and round until the ball of hair became a body and nubs became arms, fingers. The strands tangled together to become nearly impenetrable. This baby would not snag and unravel. This baby would not dissolve in water or rain or in nail-polish remover, as the plastic baby had that time. This was not a sugar-and-spice child to be swarmed by ants and disintegrate into syrup in less than a day. This was no practice baby formed of mud that she would toss into a drain miles away from her home.

She wrapped it in a head scarf and went to find Mama. The beautiful woman and her beautiful baby had concluded their business. Mama sat in her room counting out a boggling sum of money. Only after she was done did she wave Ogechi forward.

'Another one?'

'Yes, Mama.'

Ogechi did not uncover the child, and Mama didn't ask, long since bored by the girl's antics. They sang the traditional song:

Where are you going?

I am going home.

Who will greet you at home?

My mother will greet me.

What will your mother do?

My mother will bless me and my child.

Mama continued with her own special verse:

What does Mama need to bless this child?

Mama needs whatever I have.

What do you have?

I have no money.

What do you have?

I have no goods.

What do you have?

I have a full heart.

What does Mama need to bless this child?

Mama needs a full heart.

Then Mama blessed her and the baby and, in lieu of a celebratory feast, gave Ogechi one free meat pie. Then she took a little bit more of Ogechi's joy.

There was a good reason for Ogechi not to lift the cloth and let Mama see the child. For one, it was made of items found in Mama's store, and even though they were trash, Mama would add this to her ledger of debts. Second, everybody knew how risky it was to make a child out of hair, infused with the identity of the person who had shed it. But a child of many hairs? Forbidden.

But the baby was glossy, and the red streaks glinted just so in the light, and it was sturdy enough to last a full year, easy. And after that year she would take it to her mother and throw it (not 'it' the baby but the idea of it) in her mother's face.

She kept the baby covered even on the bus, where people gave her coy glances and someone tried to sing the song, but Ogechi stared ahead and did not respond to her call.

The sidewalk leading to the door of her little room was so dirty she tiptoed along it, thinking that, if her landlord weren't Mama, she would complain.

In her room, she laid the baby on an old pillow in an orphaned drawer. In the morning it would come to life, and in a year it would be a strong and pretty thing.

There was an old tale about hair children. Long ago, girls would collect their sheddings every day until they had a bundle large enough to spin a child. One day, a storm blew through the town, and every bundle was swept from its hiding place into the middle of the market, where the hairs became entangled and matted together. The young women tried desperately to separate their own hairs from the others. The elder mothers were amused at the girls' histrionics, how they argued over the silkiest patches and the longest strands. They settled the commotion thus: every girl would draw out one strand from every bundle until they all had an equal share. Some grumbled, some rejoiced, but all complied, and each went home with an identical roll.

When the time came for the babies to be blessed, all the girls came forward, each bundle arriving at the required thickness at the same time. There was an enormous celebration of this once-in-an-age event, and tearful mothers blessed their tearful daughters' children to life.

The next morning, all the new mothers were gone. Some with no sign, others reduced to piles of bones stripped clean, others' bones not so clean. But that was just an old tale.

The baby was awake in the morning, crying dry sounds, like stalks of wheat rubbing together. Ogechi ran to it, and smiled when the fibrous, eyeless face turned to her.

'Hello, child. I am your mother.'

But still it cried, hungry. Ogechi tried to feed it the detergent she'd given to the yarn one, but it passed through the baby as if through a sieve. Even though she knew it wouldn't work, she tried the sugar water she had given to the candy child, with the same result. She cradled the child, the scritch of its cries grating her ears, and as she drew a deep breath of exasperation her nose filled with the scent of Mama's expensive shampoo and conditioner, answering her question.

'You are going to be an expensive baby, aren't you?' Ogechi said, with no heat. A child that cost much brought much.

Ogechi swaddled it, ripping her second dress into strips that she wound around the baby's torso and limbs until it was almost fully covered, save for where Ogechi imagined the nose and mouth to be. She tried to make do with her own shampoo for now, which was about as luxurious as the bottom of a slow drain, but the baby refused it. Only when Ogechi strapped the child to her back did she find out what it wanted. The baby wriggled upward, and Ogechi hauled it higher, then higher still, until it settled its head on the back of her neck. Then she felt it, the gentle suckling at her nape as the child drew the tangled buds of her hair into its mouth.

Ahh, now this she could manage.

Ogechi decided to walk today, unsure of how to nurse the child on the bus and still keep it secret, but she dreaded the busy intersection she would cross as she neared Mama's Emporium. The people milling about with curious eyes, the beggars scanning and calculating the worth of passers-by. Someone would notice, ask.

But as she reached the crossing not one person looked at her. They were all gathered in a crowd, staring at something that was blocked from Ogechi's sight by the press of bodies. After watching a woman try and fail to haul herself onto the low-hanging roof of a nearby building for a better view, Ogechi pulled herself up in one, albeit labored, move. Mud girls were good for something. She ignored the woman stretching her arm out for assistance and stood up to see what had drawn the crowd.

A girl stood with her mother, and though Ogechi could not hear them from where she perched, the stance, the working of their mouths – all was familiar. They were revealing a child in public? In the middle of the day? Even a girl like her knew how terribly vulgar this was. It was no wonder the crowd had gathered. Only a child of some magnitude would be unwrapped in public this way. What was this one, gold? No, the woman and the girl were not dressed finely enough for that. Their clothes were no better than Ogechi's.

The child startled Ogechi when it moved. What she'd thought an obscene ruffle on the front of the girl's dress was in fact the baby, no more than interlocking twigs and sticks – was that grass? – bound with old cloth. Scraps. A rubbish baby. It cried, the friction of sound so frantic and dry Ogechi imagined a fire flickering from the child's mouth. A hiccup interrupted the noise, and when it resumed it was a human cry. The girl's mother laughed and danced, and the girl just cried, pressing the baby to her breast. They uncovered the child together, shucking a thick skin of cloth and sticks, and Ogechi leaned as far as she could without falling from the roof to see what special attribute might have required a public showing.

The crowd was as disappointed as she was. It was just an ordinary child with an ordinary face. They started to disperse, some throwing insults at the two mothers and the baby they held between them for wasting everybody's time. Others congratulated them with enthusiasm – it was a baby, after all. Something didn't add up, though, and Ogechi was reluctant to leave until she understood what nagged her about the scene.

It was the new mother's face. The child was as plain as pap, but the mother's face was full of wonder. One would think the baby had been spun from silk. One would think the baby was speckled with diamonds. One would think the baby was loved. Mother cradled mother, who cradled child, a tangle of ordinary limbs of ordinary women.

There has to be more than this for me, Ogechi thought.

At the shop, the two young assistants prepped their stations and rolled their eyes at the sight of Ogechi and the live child strapped to her back. Custom forced politeness from them, and with gritted teeth they sang:

Welcome to the new mother

I am welcomed

Welcome to the new child

The child is welcomed

May her days be longer than the breasts of an old mother and fuller than the stomach of a rich man.

The second the words were out, they went back to work, as though the song were a sneeze, to be excused and forgotten. Until, that is, they took in Ogechi's self-satisfied air, so different from the anxiousness that had followed in her wake whenever she had blessed a child in the past.

The two girls were forced into deference, stepping aside as Ogechi swept where they would have stood still a mere day ago. When Mama walked in, she paused, sensing the shift of power in the room, but it was nothing to her. She was still the head. What matter if one toenail argued with the other? She eyed the bundle on Ogechi's back but didn't look closer and wouldn't, as long as the child didn't interfere with the work and, by extension, her coin.

Ogechi was grateful for the child's silence, even though the suction on her neck built up over the day to become an unrelenting ache. She tired easily, as if the child were drawing energy from her. Whenever she tried to ease a finger between her nape and the child's mouth, the sucking would quicken, so she learned to leave it alone. At the end of the day, Mama stopped her with a hand on her shoulder.

'So you are happy with this one.'

'Yes, Mama.'

'Can I have a bit of that happiness?'

Ogechi knew better than to deny her outright.

'What can I have in exchange?'

Mama laughed and let her go.

When Ogechi dislodged the child at the end of the day, she found a raw, weeping patch on her nape, where the child had sucked her bald. On the ride home, she slipped to the back of the bus, careful to cradle the child's face against her ear so that no one could see it. The baby immediately latched on to her sideburn, and Ogechi spent the journey like that, the baby sucking an ache into her head. At home, she sheared off a small patch of hair and fed the child, who took the cottony clumps like a sponge absorbing water. Then it slept, and Ogechi slept too.

If Mama wondered at Ogechi's sudden ambition, she said nothing. Ogechi volunteered to trim ends. She volunteered to unclog the sink. She kept the store so clean a rumor started that the building was to be sold. She discovered that the child disliked fake hair and would spit it out. Dirty hair was best, flavored with the person from whose head it had fallen. Ogechi managed a steady stream of food for the baby, but it required more and more as each day passed. All the hair she gathered at work would be gone by the next morning, and Ogechi had no choice but to strap the child to her back and allow it to gnaw on her dwindling nape.

Mama was not curious about the baby, but the two assistants were. When Ogechi denied their request for a viewing, their sudden deference returned to malice tenfold. They made extra messes, strewing hair after Ogechi had cleaned, knocking bottles of shampoo over until Mama twisted their ears for wasting merchandise. One of the girls, the short one with the nasty scar on her arm, grew bolder, attempting to snatch the cover off the baby's head and laughing and running away when Ogechi reacted. Evading her became exhausting, and Ogechi took to hiding the child in the shop on the days she opened, squeezing it in among the wigs or behind a shelf of unopened shampoos, and the thwarted girl grew petulant, bored, then gave up.

One day, while the child was nestled between two wigs, and Ogechi, the other assistants and Mama were having lunch at the eatery next door, a woman stopped by their table to speak to Mama.

'Greetings.'

'I am greeted,' Mama said. 'What is it you want?'

Mama was usually more welcoming to her customers, but this woman owed Mama money, and she subtracted each owed coin from her pleasantries.

'Mama, I have come to pay my debt.'

'Is that so? This is the third time you have come to pay your debt, and yet we are still here.'

'I have the money, Mama.'

'Let me see.'

The woman pulled a pouch from the front of her dress and counted out the money owed. As soon as the notes crossed her palm, Mama was all smiles.

'Ahh, a woman of her word. My dear, sit. You are looking a little rough today. Why don't we get you some hair?'

The woman was too stunned by Mama's kindness to heed the insult. Mama shooed one of the other assistants toward the shop, naming a wig the girl should bring. A wig that was near where Ogechi had stashed the baby.

'I'll get it, Mama,' Ogechi said, getting up, but a swift slap to her face sat her back down.

'Was anyone talking to you, Ogechi?' Mama asked.

She knew better than to reply.

The assistant Mama had addressed snickered on her way out, and the other one smiled into her plate. Ogechi twisted her fingers into the hem of her dress and tried to slow her breathing. Maybe if she was the first to speak to the girl when she returned, she could beg her. Or bribe her. Anything to keep her baby secret.

But the girl didn't return. After a while, the woman who had paid her debt became restless and stood to leave. Mama's tone was muted fury.

'Sit. Wait.' To Ogechi, 'Go and get the wig, and tell that girl that if I see her again I will have her heart.' Mama wasn't accustomed to being disobeyed.

Ogechi hurried to the shop expecting to find the girl agape at the sight of her strange, fibrous child. But the girl wasn't there. The wig she'd been asked to bring was on the floor, and there, on the ledge where it had been, was the baby. Ogechi pushed it behind another wig and ran the first wig back to Mama, who insisted that the woman take it. Then Mama charged her, holding out her hand for payment. The woman hesitated, but paid. Mama gave nothing for free.

The assistant did not return to the Emporium, and Ogechi worried that she'd gone to call some elder mothers for counsel. But no one stormed the shop, and when Ogechi stepped outside after closing there was no mob gathered to dispense judgment. The second assistant left as soon as

Mama permitted her to, calling for the first one over and over. Ogechi retrieved the baby and went home.

In her room, Ogechi tried to feed the child, but the hair rolled off its face. She tried again, selecting the strands and clumps it usually favored, but it rejected them all.

'What do you want?' Ogechi asked. 'Isn't this hair good enough for you?' This was said with no malice, and she leaned in to kiss the baby's belly. It was warm, and Ogechi drew back from the unexpected heat.

'What have you got there?' she asked, a rhetorical question to which she did not expect an answer. But then the baby laughed, and Ogechi recognized the sound. It was the snicker she heard whenever she tripped over discarded towels or dropped the broom with her clumsy hands. It was the snicker she'd heard when Mama cracked her across the face at the eatery.

Ogechi distanced herself even more, and the child struggled to watch her, eventually rolling onto its side. It stilled when she stilled, and so Ogechi stopped moving, even after a whir of snores signalled the child's sleep.

Should she call for help? Or tell Mama? Help from whom? Tell Mama what, exactly? Ogechi weighed her options till sleep weighed her lids. Soon, too soon, it was morning.

The baby was crying, hungry. Ogechi neared it with caution. When it saw her, the texture of its cry softened and – Ogechi couldn't help it – she softened, too. It was hers, wasn't it? For better or for ill, the child was hers. She tried feeding it the hairs again, but it refused them. It did, however, nip hard at Ogechi's fingers, startling her. She hadn't given it any teeth.

She wanted more than anything to leave the child in her room, but the strangeness of its cries might draw attention. She bundled it up, trembling at the warmth of its belly. It latched on to her nape with a powerful suction that blurred her vision. This is the sort of thing a mother should do for her child, Ogechi told herself, resisting the urge to yank the baby off her neck. A mother should give all of herself to her child, even if it requires the marrow in her bones. Especially a child like this, strong and sleek and shimmering.

After a few minutes, the sucking eased to something manageable, the child sated.

At the Emporium, Ogechi kept the child with her, worried that it would cry if she removed it. Besides, the brash assistant who had tried to uncover the child was no longer at the shop, and Ogechi knew that she would never return. The other assistant was red-eyed and sniffling, unable to stop even after Mama gave her dirty looks. By lockup, Ogechi's head was throbbing, and she trembled with exhaustion. She wanted to get home and pry the baby off her. She was anticipating the relief of that when the remaining assistant said, 'Why have you not asked after her?'

'Who?' Stupid answer, she thought as soon as she uttered it.

'What do you mean who? My cousin that disappeared. Haven't you wondered where she is? Even Mama has been asking people about her.'

'I didn't know you were cousins.' The girl recognized Ogechi's evasion.

'You know what happened to her, don't you? What did you do?' The answer came out before Ogechi could stop it.

'The same thing I will do to you,' she said, and the assistant took a step back, then another, before turning to run.

At home, Ogechi put the child to bed and stared until it slept. She felt its belly, which was cooling now, and recoiled at the thought of what could be inside. Then it gasped a little hairy gasp from its little hairy mouth, and Ogechi felt again a mother's love.

The next morning, it was Ogechi's turn to open the store, and she went in early to bathe the baby with Mama's fine shampoo, sudsing its textured face, avoiding the bite of that hungry, hungry mouth. She was in the middle of rinsing off the child when the other assistant entered. She retreated in fear at first, but then she took it all in – Ogechi at the sink, Mama's prized shampoo on the ledge, suds covering mother-knows-what – and she turned sly, running outside and shouting for Mama. Knowing that it was no use calling after her, Ogechi quickly wrapped the baby back up in her old torn-up dress, knocking over the shampoo in her haste. That was when Mama walked in.

'I hear you are washing something in my sink.' Mama looked at the spilled bottle, then back at Ogechi. 'You are doing your laundry in my place?'

'I'm sorry, Mama.'

'How sorry are you, Ogechi, my dear?' Mama said, calculating. 'Are you sorry enough to give me some of that happiness? So that we can forget all this?'

There was no need for a song now, as there was no new child to be blessed. Mama simply stretched her hand forward and held on, but what she thought was Ogechi's shoulder was the head of the swaddled child.

Mama fell to the ground in undignified shudders. Her eyes rolled, as if she were trying to see everything at once. Ogechi fled. She ran all the way home, and, even through her panic, she registered the heat of the child in her arms, like the just-stoked embers of a fire. In her room, she threw the child into its bed, expecting to see whorls of burned flesh on her arms but finding none. She studied the baby, but it didn't look any different. It was still a dense tangle of dark fibre with the occasional streak of red. She didn't touch it, even when the mother in her urged her to. At any moment, Mama would show up with her goons, and Ogechi was too frightened to think of much else. But Mama didn't appear, and she fell asleep waiting for the pounding at her door.

Ogechi woke in the middle of the night with the hair child standing over her. It should not have been able to stand, let alone haul itself onto her bed. Nor should it have been able to fist her hair in a grip so tight her scalp puckered, or stuff an appendage into her mouth to block her scream. She tried to tear it apart, but the seams held. Only when she rammed it into the wall did it let go. It skittered across the room and hid somewhere that the candle she lit couldn't reach. Ogechi backed toward the door, listening, but what noise does hair make?

When the hair child jumped onto Ogechi's head, she shrieked and shook herself, but it gripped her hair again, tighter this time. She then did something that would follow her all her days. She raised the candle and set it on fire. And when the baby fell to the ground, writhing, she covered it with a pot and held it down, long after her fingers had blistered from the heat, until the child, as tough as she'd made it, stopped moving.

Outside, she sat on the little step in front of the entrance to her apartment. No one had paid any mind to the noise – this wasn't the sort of building where one checked up on screams. Knees to her chin, Ogechi sobbed into the calloused skin, feeling part relief, part something else – a sliver of empathy Mama hadn't been able to steal. There was so much dirt on the ground, so much of it everywhere, all around her. When she turned back into the room and lifted the pot, she saw all those pretty, shiny strands transformed into ash. Then she scooped dirt into the pot and added water.

This she knew. How to make firm clay – something she was born to do. When the mix was just right, she added a handful of the ashes. Let this child be born in sorrow, she told herself. Let this child live in sorrow. Let this child not grow into a foolish, hopeful girl with joy to barter. Ogechi formed the head, the arms, the legs. She gave it her mother's face. In the morning, she would fetch leaves to protect it from the rain.

Lesley Nneka Arimah is the author of *What It Means When A Man Falls from the Sky*, a collection of stories published by Riverhead

Books (US) and Tinder Press (UK), 2017. Her work has appeared in *The New Yorker*, *Harper's*, *Per Contra* and other publications. Lesley was shortlisted for the Caine Prize for African Writing in 2016. 'Who Will Greet You At Home' was first published in *The New Yorker* (US, 2015).

Bush Baby

Chikodili Emelumadu

Somebody is banging on my gate.

At first, I think it must be the wind. I want it to be the wind. The clock on the bottom-right-hand corner of my laptop reads 21.54 and the last thing I need, with a deadline looming over my head, is visitors. Nigerians are masters of the Drive-by Salutation; 'Oh, I was just in your neighbourhood and I said let me come and greet my big sister' and next thing they're there for hours, reciting a litany of ill fortunes which only your imaginary 'forex' can solve. It doesn't matter that I've been home for a year and a half, that my entire savings went into making sure my father was buried properly or that I'm working two jobs to make ends meet. Relatives still think I have pounds stashed away, to which naturally, they're entitled.

The power is out again, and I'm working fast, listening, and watching the dwindling levels of my battery. My generator is only for emergencies. Since the presidential campaigns started, the price of diesel has tripled, thanks to pessimistic marketers hoarding fuel.

'Bang. Bang.' The sheet metal of the gate resonates as if the person outside is whacking it with a stone.

'Na who be dat?' Idi shouts from the gatehouse. His belt clinks and I can tell he's pulled on trousers over his boxer shorts. So confident is he in his ability to speedily despatch the knocker that he doesn't fasten it; he's still clinking as he stomps to the gate. Ever since Idi's new bride joined him from Borno, he's been extra short with unwanted guests, choosing to spend his day off in the gatehouse with the girl than hang out with his boys down the street.

Idi's habits are as familiar to me as my own. For a while, it had been just the two of us in the whole compound. Idi had come with the bungalow, straight from my father's service and into mine. He'd eased my transition back into society somewhat; queuing for fuel under the scorching sun in my clapped-out Volvo station wagon (also inherited), getting the right workers when things broke down (which they often did), and keeping the compound spick-and-span.

The white beam of light from his rechargeable radio-lantern wrecks what is left of my concentration. Words scatter in my mind like flies, disturbed from a bounty of excrement. I've always hated the harshness of battery-powered lamps and I look up, grinding my teeth. Idi stands right outside my mosquito-screened window, calmly plucking at his hairy navel.

'Na madam brother,' he says, in his usual uninflected voice. The lantern points respectfully on the concrete floor outside and his skin is so dark and oily that the light reflects off his bare chest.

'Okwuchukwu?' My brow furrows. 'Open for him, now.'

Idi shrugs as he saunters off, and I know what he is thinking, why he had to make sure before letting Okwuchukwu in.

In the past year, I've seen my brother twice. The first, at our father's funeral, which he attended as though he was an ordinary guest, and not the sole heir of a deceased chief. Okwuchukwu did not contribute towards any costs for the burial; canopies, food and drink and money for the dancers all came out of my pocket. The night of the wake-keeping, he swooped in with a posse of raucous friends, whose sole purpose seemed to be imbibing every drop of alcohol in sight. They sat outdoors, etching patterns in the night sky with weed smoke and partying as if they were facing incarceration the next day. By morning, Okwuchukwu couldn't hold himself up to pour sand over our father's coffin.

People haven't stopped talking about it in the village.

The second time was on a Wednesday, a month ago. I remember because I was supposed to be going on a date that evening, and the guy stood me up. I'd driven past Chizzy's, a popular eatery on campus, and clocked my brother, in his six-foot-five, broad-shouldered glory, surrounded by skimpily dressed students. One of them had plastered herself to his body like a tattoo, fiddling with his belt buckle. Okwuchukwu's car had been parked haphazardly and it had blasted a syrupy R&B, something young that I didn't much care for. I'd gripped the steering wheel and averted my gaze, feeling every inch the staid English lecturer.

A shadow lurches towards the house, breaking my reverie. My irritation increases.

The foolish child is obviously drunk again, I think. But something about his gait, the small, careful, steps of an accident victim, alarms me. My heartbeat resounds in my ears.

'Okwy?'

His silhouette pauses and I can see something is not right. His head is too big; the collar of his shirt hangs around his neck like a noose. I jump up out of my chair and grab one of the kerosene lamps standing in the hallway. Its yellow flame dances, casting wild shadows over the wall. A twist of keys in the wooden door and I'm in the enclosed patio.

'Sister,' says Okwy, smiling at me from the other side of my burglary-proof bars. At least I think it's a smile. Through the green netting it could be a grimace. I hold up the lantern and stifle a gasp, fumbling for the padlock. Tears blur my vision and I am grateful for the momentary respite from the horror in loose clothing, two steps below, staring at me with what seems to be half its teeth decayed.

The lock snaps open and Okwy is falling up the stairs, into me. He exhales, arms wrapped tightly around a bundle held to his chest and instantly becomes unconscious. A terrible odour wafts up from his body; a combination of the rotten-eggs smell of dye pits and the rich moistness of loam.

'Idi!'

Idi slams home the bolt on the pedestrian side of the gate and helps me move Okwy into the sitting room. We lay him down on the sofa.

'Wetin do am?' Idi gestures with his chin.

My forehead creases as I consider that we've just lifted a 30-year-old man who is supposed to weigh 90 kilos, without breaking a sweat.

'I don't know, Idi.'

✳✳✳

In his sleep, Okwuchukwu appears to revert to the baby I adored, once upon a time. My brother's eyes might be sunken in dark hollows but they're still fringed by bovine lashes, brushing against newly-visible cheekbones. His mouth is a pout. In my mind, I see it clamped over my mother's dark nipple, greedily sucking, the milk running out of the corners of his mouth. A lot of the time, he swallowed too quickly and it went down the wrong way. My mother would try to take him off and clap him on the back, chiding him for being such a glutton. Even as he choked, Okwuchukwu would refuse to let go of her breast.

I hated being an only child. Every one of my friends had siblings, more than they knew what to do with. I pestered and nagged until my normally gentle mother snapped one day, 'We're trying our best you know!' which made my lips quiver and a lump of unshed tears sit heavily behind my face. I did not understand why she was so annoyed.

Not long after, her stomach swelled and swelled. She lay in bed, dressed in long, cotton nightgowns, resting swollen legs on a stack of pillows. My mother's face glowed, with an inner light and yet she looked so frail. She reminded me of a princess. In the afternoons when I returned from school, I played pretend that she was Sleeping Beauty and often kissed her to wake her. Sometimes she opened her eyes, but mostly, she just slept and slept.

A few days past my sixth birthday, Okwuchukwu was born. A tiny, warm bundle of beautiful, brown curls. Not for me, the sibling rivalry which plagued my peers. I was totally smitten. And even after he grew up spoilt and revealed facets to his character that I could frankly do without, he was still my baby brother. Selfish, charming, reckless baby brother.

Before I can talk myself out of it, I reach over and brush a hand over his beautiful beard, so out of place on this emaciated self. Okwy mumbles something, snuffling into my hand like a new born animal, seeking warmth. My heart thumps against my ribcage. What trouble has he got himself into this time?

An electronic beep pierces the quiet. Okwuchukwu wakes with a start.

'What is that?' The whites of his eyes take up the entire top half of his face.

'It's just my laptop. The battery is dying.' Surreptitiously, I withdraw my outstretched hand and turn up the wick on the lantern which I'd placed on the floor. Animation strips my brother of the façade of innocence. The amber light does nothing to soften his terrible appearance. His shoulders are drawn inwards over the package he's still clasping to his chest; it's dark, stained in places like rags from a mechanic's workshop. The shirt he has on must have been white at some time, but there are thick, brown lines on the collar and wrists, like smudged crayon marks made by a toddler. A patch of sweat shaped like a light bulb stains the cushions he'd been lying on and his fingernails are crescents of grime. Okwuchukwu licks his lips, scabbed over and crusty in the corners. I pour him a glass of water from the jug on the stool and hand it over.

Okwy exhales and fingernails tinkle against the tumbler as he receives it.

'What time is it?' His voice is hoarse as if he's been crying.

'I don't know. I left my phone in the room when I came out to open the door.'

'Don't you have a clock here? I hear ticking.'

The question comes out desperate, laden, as if he wants me to reassure him of more than just the time. He glances about the room, peering into the darkened corner where my display cabinet of souvenirs stands. I want to ask him to lie down again, because the way his head is shaking on his giraffe neck makes me all sorts of nervous. I half expect it to break off and roll down the corridor.

'Okwy, what the hell is going on with you? '

'Nothing,' he says, sullenly. Then he smiles at me, one of his old smiles that I've seen him wield like a weapon against people's defences. It's a smile that's got him exactly what he wants on many occasions. Only now, he seems to have forgotten the blackened teeth. Despite telling myself not to flinch, I do and his lips come down over them like blinds over windows.

'Sorry, I didn't mean–'

'No problem. Only four more days now. Four more days and I will have all the money I want. I'll buy myself new teeth. Gold teeth. Diamond teeth!' he laughs then quickly sobers. 'You have to let me stay, sister. There is concrete everywhere here. He won't catch me.'

What on earth?

'Are you on drugs?'

'Drugs,' he scoffs, sipping his water.

I take a deep breath, bracing myself. 'Are you sick? You've lost a lot of weight.'

'I don't have AIDS, God! You're just like dad, Ihuoma.'

Okwy grunts when he stands. He paces my living room in the same shuffling motion, which is even more excruciating to witness up close.

'I've always hated this house,' he says.

'It was mum's *idu uno* gift from her father. We lived here for a while before you were born.'

'I know,' he says wearily.

My brother has no shoes on and with each footstep, his

long, curved toenails dig into the carpet, pulling out the fibres with a sickening, ripping sound. 'I'm glad nobody left it to me in their will. I'd have knocked it down. Or sold it.'

Like you sold the others.

'Well, I like it,' I say, defensively.

'It suits you,' he replies. I consider bristling under the implied insult, but his voice is so faint, he could have been talking to himself. 'And it's concrete,' he bares his teeth again.

The bungalow is a modest size – it only takes three strides for Okwuchukwu to reach the end of the living room, but I am proud of what I have done with it; the curtains are cream chiffon, embroidered with purple flowers and ties, made to order, as are the cushion covers of green, purple and pink print. My sofa and armchair are cane, made by King, one of Idi's craftsman relatives, as a thank you for letting him squat with Idi in the gatehouse before he found a place of his own. My house is cosy and welcoming and I love it and can't bear to hear anyone speak ill of it. I don't understand my brother's sudden obsession with concrete.

'I don't think he will come,' he mutters.

Okwuchukwu paces and I watch him with growing impatience. I now know he is on drugs. Isn't the first sign of addiction denial? Part of me wishes I'd been shocked by the realization but my brother is not exactly known for restraint. It would be just like him to try a drug once and get hooked for life. He doubles back around the centre table, ignoring my eyes and stops in front of a reframed photo of our parents, leaning against the bar which I now use as a bookcase. The picture is old; motheaten and water damaged.

'People say I look like him,' he says. Ever the narcissist, Okwuchukwu's eyes find his reflection in the glass.

I shrug, unsure what to say. The person standing before me bears no resemblance to my father. Not anymore.

'What time is it?' he asks again. 'If it's past midnight, then I'm safe.'

'Fine, let me get my phone.'

'No! Wait a little longer. I'd hate for anything to happen without you here to see. I need you to believe me.' He scratches the back of his head. 'After, I will tell you everything.'

'Tell me what? What is "everything"?'

The lantern on the floor flickers and goes out.

'Damn it. I've run out of kerosene.' The other lantern glows dully from the hallway.

'I'll find some candles,' I say.

'It's not the kerosene,' he replies. 'Check it.'

Okwuchukwu's voice floating out of the darkness, quakes.

Rolling my eyes, I let the warmth from the globe guide my hands in the darkness. As soon as I lift up the lantern, I do not need to shake it to know there is more than half a tank left.

'See? I told you,' Okwuchukwu says, breathing raspy and loud. He coughs as he makes his way back to the sofa.

The other lantern starts to flicker.

'It's him. He's coming. But there is concrete everywhere. He shouldn't be able to... ' His voice tails off in a sort of whimper.

I scoot over to him from the armchair and place what I hope is a soothing hand on his shoulder. 'Who do you think is after you?'

Okwuchukwu grips my hand. His palm is rough, spongey like chewed up coconut flesh. He squeezes until it hurts.

'Ow! Stop it, biko.'

He's panting, letting loose a smell of hot sewage in my face. 'Promise me that once it starts, you won't let me go to him. I'll fight you. But you can't let him take me.'

I jerk away. 'Who? Who is coming?' I'm trying not to shout at him. Okwuchukwu either charms his way around things or stubbornly digs in and right now, he is all out of charm.

The other lantern goes out. Okwuchukwu is hyper-ventilating, rocking on the sofa. I clutch him to my bosom, close to tears myself.

'Okwy–'

Something alters and this gives me pause. A silence has

settled on the house. I notice that I can no longer hear the usual hums of life and habitation; no far-away horns from traffic on the express, no generator sets, nothing. It is as though we have been cut off from the world.

A wail rips through the house. My brother goes rigid in my embrace.

The sound is a balled fist, slammed into the gut. It is bottle tops, scraped against pebble dashed walls; the jarring sensation of happening upon a stone in a dish of beans, which wasn't cleaned properly. My mouth fills with saliva, my stomach roils and in that moment I will give anything to shut the noise off.

It is the cry of a baby being tortured.

Okwuchukwu yells.

The crying seems to be bouncing off the walls, building as it travels through the hallway, waves upon waves, making the hairs on the back of my neck and arms stand on end. Okwuchukwu claws at his ears, making guttural noises as if he has lost the ability to speak. The crying grows until it seems to be coming from all around us, seeping out of the floor, pressing down on us from the ceiling. The pressure in the room is the type you get in an aircraft cabin; my head becomes as tight as balloon and my ears pop. Something wet and sticky spreads all over the carpet. It's cold, numbing. When I try to move, I find I can't. I am rooted to the ground. My heart beats in my head, pushing hot blood and adrenaline through my limbs. Everything feels tainted, infected by fear. Okwuchukwu crashes through the coffee table.

'Okwy!'

I cannot hear my own voice above the wailing baby, even though I know I am shouting. I can hear my brother's screams. He rolls on the floor but my legs are held fast and I can't move. Something is burning. The air changes, filling with smoke so thick, I can grasp it.

Just when I think I cannot handle any more, the wailing shuts off, abruptly.

'Okwuchukwu?!'

I can hear myself, so I shout his name over and over but he does not move from his spot on the floor. Struggling against whatever is holding me captive, my legs kick out suddenly and I fall to the floor, freed. The carpet is sticky, sodden. It squishes as I crawl to my brother. Glass cuts into my hands and knees.

The house starts to fill once more with night-time noises.

'Okwy!' I place my ear to his chest but realise it's his back and turn him over. He stinks even worse than before and his heart beats faintly, stuttering inside his ribcage. 'Okwy?' On hands and I knees I feel for the jug of water on the stool and dump it in his face. He doesn't move.

The siren connected to the power grid shrieks and power comes back on. My beige carpet is covered in what looks to be viscera and blood and... soil? I scoop up some of it and sniff. It smells burned, like the underside of an iron tripod pot.

I feel movement behind me and turn. A dark cloud drifts away towards the backyard.

Okwuchukwu coughs, spits. He feels around for the parcel even before he opens his eyes and clutches it to his chest.

'Ihuoma?' he squints at me.

Everything in me is rattling, shaking, as if the nuts and bolts that hold me together are going to come apart. My teeth chatter. Okwy sits up, dragging himself painfully with one arm, to lean against the wall.

'Three more days,' he says. 'Three more days.' There is pride in his voice. Then he bends over and vomits onto what's left of the carpet.

***

Idi is waiting for me outside the front door the next morning. Gone is his usual impassive expression, replaced by a clenched jaw. His flared nostrils tell me he is angry, but his eyes are scared. Terrified.

'That ting wey come na gwei-gwei. Your brother carry am come our house.'

I stare at him. I'm drained from a night spent pulling glass out of my skin and my brother's, cleaning him and dressing his wounds. There's a ringing in my ears. My eyeballs feel gritty from lack of sleep; Okwuchukwu's snores kept cutting off and startling me into wakefulness the minute I nodded off. Twice I was certain he died.

'I no go do gateman if gwei-gwei come again.' He turns and marches off to his house.

Okwuchukwu is asleep on my bed, his entire body exposed in the light of day. My breath hitches in my throat as I survey the wreckage; a dewlap previously hidden behind his thinning beard. I could lift him by his collarbones if I desired. He's wearing one of my bigger t-shirts which stops just under his navel, before the twin peaks of his hip bones and the inky bruise discolouring most of his midriff. The air whistles through the gap in his mouth, where yesterday, he had teeth. My brother's once proud nose, so reminiscent of our father's, seems to have caved in on itself and his eyes…

…are open.

I jump back, embarrassed to be caught in my scrutiny, and straighten my wrapper at the foot of the bed.

'I'm dying,' he says. 'Aren't I?'

I cross my arms over my chest. 'Have you heard of something called a gwei-gwei?'

Okwuchukwu licks his lips. His saliva appears yellowish, gluing his lips together. 'Who told?'

'Idi.'

'Fucking cattle-rearer.'

'Don't be daft, Okwy.'

'I might as well tell you.' He moves, pulls the bundle from under his pillow and unwraps it. I make a face. 'I know, it's really awful, but if it smelled nice it would be easier to steal, wouldn't it?'

'Steal? You stole this? From whom? Ugh! It is disgusting.'

'Not "whom". It's a "what".'

Okwuchukwu discards the outer wrapping with shaking hands, and opens the cloth inside. My mouth drops open, the more he unties it.

'What… is… this?'

'A mat. It belongs to the bush baby. It's what it was after last night.'

'Bush baby?'

'Bush baby… gwei-gwei. It's not an actual baby. It just sounds like one to torture people.'

The mat is a thing of beauty; it is crimson and black and gold, stiff like asoke straight from the loom. Its tassels are fine threads of gold and white thread. My brother strokes it as if it is the hair of his beloved. Just looking at it, makes me suddenly light-hearted. I forget my sense of foreboding. The mat affects Okwuchukwu too; his smile is dreamier, unselfconscious. When he turns to me, it is with the expectant air of a child waiting to be praised. The effect in his old man face is grotesque. I blink my tears away.

'They said if I helped them steal this, they would give me the houses back. I lost all three,' he adds sheepishly. 'I thought the game was a sure banker.'

'You *gambled* your inheritance away?' The gossips got it wrong then. He hadn't made one *kobo* in profit because there'd been no sale.

He sighs and the smell of damp old socks fills the room, carried along on a current of hot breath. I sense him tapping into the reserves of his stubbornness.

'And what happened?' I ask quickly.

'They told me I could get my properties back if I did one thing for them. It was a small thing. There was a man in the forest and I had to find him and get his mat for them. They said they were going to use his mat for *juju*, he was a powerful medicine man. They'd get rich, I'd get my houses back – well, two of them.' Okwuchukwu pauses. 'Only it isn't a man I stole from. It's a forest spirit.' He swallows and his voice takes on a faraway timbre.

'It was so easy. The hardest part was the journey into Ikenga forest. Thirteen hours it took, I timed it first by my watch and then when it got too dark to see, by the light of my phone. The mosquitoes… the mosquitoes! They were as big as bees. I looked under all the *ukpaka* trees as I was told and I did not find the man or his mat or lantern. He was supposed to live in the forest… harmless old hermit. How was I to know?'

Okwuchukwu is talking to himself at this point but I just let him ramble on, while I try to play catch up, to make sense of it all.

'He wasn't at home but there it was, this mat, at the last tree with the hole in its trunk. What was I supposed to do, leave it there? They told me what would happen if I did not come back with it. Everything under the tree as described; the mat and the lantern lit low, and I cannot see anything else the darkness is so thick. Drink's worn off at this point so I am sweating and my mouth is full of sand and my hand is shaking when I bend over to pick it up. Only it starts to reek, my God! I should have let it go then. I should have…' Okwuchukwu's voice trails off and he catches himself as if he'd been about to nod off. He rubs a hand over bulbous red eyes. My brother's fingers remind me of Terminator's skeleton, the knuckles distended grotesquely.

I keep quiet. Inside I am wrestling with my mind.

'Bastards! They told me when I came back, laughing in my face. Of course it had been too easy. The spirit lets you steal its mat, so it can torment you. Seven days it punishes you…' His voice breaks and he clears it. When he wipes his eyes this time, there are eyelashes in his palm. He scrutinises them, indifferent, before blowing them away. 'You survive, you get rich. You don't, you die. What kind of people condemn a man to die over a few measly debts?'

'Can't you just return its mat?'

'No.'

'Why not?! It's simple. You can live here with me, get a job for once in your life. Let those foolish men keep your properties.'

'Do you think I have not thought of that?' Okwy coughs as he talks. He's breathing heavily again and even though I know I should not exert him, all my anger at his happy-go-lucky existence comes to the fore. Three properties by the age of twenty-eight, one a four-storey building packed with tenants and he still manages to blow it all. Our father will be turning in his grave.

'You should have come to me! What are you doing gambling anyway? When did that rubbish start?'

'What else is there to do in this godforsaken town?'

'Then move. Find a job elsewhere and do that.'

'What, like you? Eh? You that went for your masters and came back eleven years later?' Okwuchukwu coughs again and wipes his hand on my t-shirt. It turns slightly grey as though smeared with dirt. 'You left me alone with a widower – what, was I supposed to abandon him too?'

'Please.' I kiss my teeth.

'She was my mother too, not just yours.' Okwuchukwu pounds the bed with his fist and his lips tremble. 'You're not the only one who lost someone. I lost my mum. Dad lost his wife. What is this thing that has always made you think your claim on her is greater than ours?'

I turn away from him and towards the window, staring out into my backyard with its peeling terracotta wall, which seems somehow altered in a way I cannot fathom.

'Jesus, you still blame me for her death don't you?' Okwuchukwu throws his hands up.

'I did not say that.' I shrug. But I am thinking it. She was never the same after she gave birth to you.

'And how is that my fault?' asks Okwuchukwu, not fooled in the slightest.

'Fine, whatever. It's not your fault. I'm the reason you've

not done anything with your life. It's me that drove you to gamble your life away. I'm the one who made you show up to your own father's funeral with a whore whose breasts were falling out of–'

'Don't call her a whore! She's studying accountancy.'

'Great. She can handle the books in the brothel. A promotion.'

'Dad would have wanted me to have fun. You don't know.' Okwuchukwu's eyes blaze. 'You weren't here.'

The accusation stings. 'Return the mat, don't return it,' I retort. 'I don't care.'

I can't believe I'm saying the words even as I speak them. Okwuchukwu doesn't seem surprised by them. He is silent a while, then his lips curl downwards, exposing the wasteland of his mouth.

'There are no returns,' he says, resigned. 'I either last the seven days or I die. All this time it's been living in the forest, starving. Now, it's eating me.' Okwy's tirade comes out speckled with saliva. 'Give me your phone. Where is it?'

I grab it from my bedside unit and hand it over. He taps it, each one more forceful than the last. 'How do you not even have Facebook?' he sighs, tapping some more. 'Look.'

It's a photo of Okwuchukwu as he normally appears; his smile is wide and the camera's flash glints in his well-oiled beard. He has his hands round two girls, a bottle of Heineken sneaking around the waist to his right.

'Check the time stamp'.

It was a week ago. My stomach turns. It hasn't settled since last night and feels tender. I grit my teeth until it settles. I can feel Okwuchukwu watching me, his gaze mocking my unease.

I gulp. 'Why did you think my house would keep it away?'

'Oh. Apparently it hates things like that. Electricity and modern stuff,' he sounds sleepy, as if the act of offloading has weakened him. 'The sprite only comes out in areas close to forests. Dunno why he came... this whole ugly house is concrete...'

A thought occurs to me. My voice comes out slowly, hesitantly. 'Not the back. The man who was building there got into trouble and abandoned the house a few years ago. The real owners of the land knocked it down and it's steadily been going back to bush.'

I walk to the window. That's what's changed in my backyard. The creeping vines coming over from the other side seem to have thickened overnight, choking the razor wire on my fence. Tendrils are growing as I watch, in slight unobtrusive movements, but growing nonetheless. By dusk we'll be overrun.

'We have to move you from here.' I say, filled with urgency. My brother is right.

There is nothing he's done which warrants the kind of death coming for him.

'To where? It hates technology, but I don't think it's allergic to it. At worst, it'll pull the trick with cutting us off from it all again.' Okwuchukwu laughter is a bark, at the end of which he spits out a molar. It's crescent-shaped as if something took a bite out of it. My head swells and goose pimples pop all over my body. My brother opens my palm and places the damaged tooth in it.

'At least you'll have something of me to bury. Don't let that devil chop me finish.'

'Stop talking like that,' I say. 'I am going to fix it. Who are the people you owe? Where can I find them?'

My brother is nearly asleep. 'They are waiting for me to die, so they'll take the mat.

'I'm going to die. We are all dead in our family. Dead... dead.' He snores softly.

I cover him up and go through the kitchen and into the backyard to check the level of diesel left in the jerry cans. The generator will run all night, anything, to make sure the crying monstrosity does not return. Anything to keep my brother safe.

The tendrils snake steadily over the wall.

***

The generator cuts out around midnight. Okwuchukwu wakes up immediately but he is too weak to move from my bed. The baby cries buckle the closed door and even though I've stuffed my ears with cotton wool, it's shrill enough to cut through. My brother clutches his throat, thrashing about on the bed and when I try to hold him, I find I am frozen in place. This time I cannot even call his name – my teeth snap shut the minute I try.

Even though I am prepared, I'm still shaken. My hair drips with sweat in its ponytail and I feel as though my brother's stink has imprinted itself on me. Okwuchukwu moans but doesn't open his eyes anymore. I lift his head to put a sip of water down his throat. He's dry and light like stockfish.

***

Someone is rustling around my gate. The time on my phone reads 05.06 and the sun's rays are staining the sky's cheeks with a rosy blush. I tie my wrapper and grab the keys from the kitchen.

'You are leaving?'

Idi turns around. The fear in his face dissolves my belief in everything turning out alright. I'd hoped I would fix Okwuchukwu's screw up, somehow; find the guys, see a *dibia*, anything. I have never seen Idi afraid of anything. My *maigadi* is feared and respected among his boys – many migrating to our town from his village on his say so. Now…

He turns and says something in Hausa to the shadow behind him. His wife looks up from underneath the print cloth draped over her head and shoulders. She nods and opens the gate. Outside, a pick-up truck idles.

'I no do gate-man for gwei-gwei house.'

I don't know what to say. I don't think I am capable of speech.

Idi sighs. He touches my forearm. I don't think he's ever

touched me before. Loneliness thrashes my soul. From the gesture, I know my brother is going to die. The extent of loneliness is staring me in the face.

'I can't bury another family member,' I shake my head. 'I can't.'

Idi glances behind him. He can't wait to be gone and I don't blame him. I smell of death.

'Kakan say, the only time gwei-gwei leave you commot be say, if you fight am.'

'Fight him? How can I fight what I don't see?' And then there was the small matter of always being too paralysed to move.

Idi looks embarrassed. 'Na to naked yourself. You go dey naked fight am. Only person wey no want im property, na im fit fight gwei-gwei.' He shrugs. 'I no know. Na wetin I dem tell me.'

I have to fight a forest spirit that nobody can see, naked.

Idi says sadly, 'Gwei-gwei too strong. E go chop una. I no fit stay.'

I nod. I understand that he can't bury a family member either.

***

I put my affairs in order. The advantage to not having much is that it only takes me three hours. I don't bother sending an email to the university – they'll probably find a replacement from the hordes of unemployed graduates doing the job rounds.

Okwuchukwu is still breathing; a moist finger under his nose dries, in record time. He is burning up and his flesh is greying.

'I double dare you not to die,' I whisper in his ear, imitating the game we played as children. I clean him one last time, dress the weeping sores. My bedsheets are soaked. If I survive, I'll have to burn the mattress.

I don't bother with clocks or lanterns this time, just strip off my clothes and wrap myself in the mat. It's as if I can no longer smell the odour, which is a good thing. I'll need all my wits.

As soon as the muting feeling creeps into my house, I stand and brace myself. Behind me, Okwuchukwu gasps in his sleep and from his mouth, a baby begins to screech.

Chikodili Emelumadu is based in Nigeria. Her work has appeared in *One Throne*, *Omenana*, *Apex*, *Eclectica*, *Luna Station Quarterly* and the interactive fiction magazine, *Sub-Q*. In 2014, Chikodili was nominated for a Shirley Jackson award and is working on her novel. 'Bush Baby' was first published in *African Monsters*, edited by Margrét Helgadóttir and Jo Thomas (Fox Spirit Books, UK, 2015).

The Story of the Girl Whose Birds Flew Away

Bushra al-Fadil

Translated by Max Shmookler

There I was, cutting through a strange market crowd – not just people shopping for their salad greens, but beggars and butchers and thieves, prancers and Prophet-praisers and soft-sided soldiers, the newly arrived and the just retired, the flabby and the flimsy, sellers roaming and street kids groaning, god-damners, bus-waiters and white-robed traders, elegant and fumbling. And there in the midst, our elected representatives, chasing women with their eyes and hands and whole bodies, with those who couldn't give chase keeping pace with an indiscreet and sensual attention, or lost in a daydream.

I cut, sharp-toothed, carving a path through the crowd when a passer-by clutched his shoulder in pain, followed by a 'Forgive me!' Then a scratch on a lady's toe was followed with a quick 'Oh no!' Then a slap to another's cheek, after which was heard 'Forgiveness is all I seek!' So lost in dreams I could not wait for their reply to my apology.

The day was fresher than a normal summer day, and I could feel delight turbaned around my head, like a Bedouin on his second visit to the city. The working women were not happy like me, nor were the housewives. I was the son of the Central Station, spider-pocketed, craning my neck to see a car accident or the commotion of a thief being caught. I was awake, descending into the street, convulsing from hunger and the hopeless search for work in the 'cow's muzzle', as we say. I suppressed my unrest. The oppressed son of the oppressed but despite all of that – happy. Could the wretched wrest my happiness from me? Hardly. Without meaning to, I wandered through these thoughts. The people around me were a pile of human watermelons, every pile awaiting its bus. I approached one of the piles and pulled out my queuing tools – an elbow and the palm of my hand – and then together they helped my legs to hold up my daily depleted and yearly defeated body. I pulled out my eyes and began to look... and look... in all directions and to store away what I saw.

I saw a blind man looking out before him as if he were reading from that divine book which preceded all books, that book of all fates. He kept to himself as he passed before me but still I felt the coins in my pocket disappear. Then I saw a woman who was so plump that when she called out to her son – 'Oh Hisham' – you could feel the greasy resonance of the 'H' in your ears. I saw a frowning man, a boy weaving an empty tin can along the ground with his feet. I saw voices and heard boundless scents and then, suddenly, in the midst of all of that, I saw her. The dervish in my heart jumped. I saw her: soaring without swaying, her skin the colour of wheat – not as we know it but rather as if the wheat were imitating her tone. She had the swagger of a soldier, the true heart of the people. And if you saw her, you'd never be satiated.

I said to myself, 'This is the girl whose birds flew away.'

Her round face looked like this:

Her nose was like a fresh vegetable and by God, what eyes! A pharaonic neck with two taut slender cords, only visible when she turned her head. And when she turned her head, I thought all the women selling their mashed beans and salted sunflower seeds would flee, the whole street would pick up and leave only ruts where they had been, the fetid stench of blood would abandon the places where meat was sold. My thoughts fled to a future I longed for. And if you poured water over the crown of her head, it would flow down past her forehead. She walked in waves, as if her body were an auger spiralling through a cord of wood.

She approached me. I looked myself over and straightened myself out. As she drew closer, I saw she was holding tight to a little girl who resembled her in every way but with a child's chubbiness. Their hands were woven together as if they had been fashioned precisely in that manner, as if they were keeping each other from straying. They both knitted their eyebrows nonchalantly, such that their eyes flashed, seeming to cleanse their faces from the famished stares of those around them.

'This is the girl whose birds flew away,' I said.

I turned to her sister and said, 'And this must be the talisman she's brought to steer her away from evil. How quickly her calm flew from her palm.'

I stared at them until I realized how loathsome I was in comparison. It was this that startled me, not them. I looked carefully at the talisman. Her mouth was elegant and precise as if she never ate the stewed okra that was slowly poisoning me. I glanced around and then I looked back at them, looked and looked – oh how I looked! – until a bus idled up and abruptly saved the day. Although it was not their custom, the people made way for the two unfamiliar women, and they just hopped aboard. Through the dust kicked up by the competition around the door I found myself on the bus as well.

We lumbered forward. The man next to me was smoking and the man next to him smelled as if he were stuffed with onions. If the day were not so fresh, and were it not for the girl and her talisman and their aforementioned beauty, I would have got off that wretched bus without a word of apology. After five minutes, the onionized man lowed to the driver: 'This's my stop, buddy.'

He got off and slammed the door in a way that suggested the two of them had a long and violent history. The driver rubbed his right cheek as if the door had been slammed on him. He grumbled to himself, 'People without a shred of mercy.'

The onion man reeled back around and threw a red eye at the driver. 'What?' he exploded. 'What'd you say?'

'Get going, by God!' I yelled. 'He wasn't talking about you.'

As the bus pulled away, the onionized man's insults and curses blended with the whine of the motor. As if the driver wanted to torment us, he continued the argument as a monologue, beginning, 'People are animals...' He blamed the matter on human nature, such as it was, and railed and cursed until we hit a pothole in the main road. The bus hopped up like a frog, croaking until he floored the gas and it bolted forward, roaring 'Zamjara zamjara' like some wild animal.

The cruel movements of the bus began to hurt my back. But when I looked over at the girls, I figured they must have taken the shape of their seats, as they did not seem to be in pain nor was their flesh being shaken from the bone. Finally we arrived. They got off and I followed, unable to hear their footsteps over the sound of my own hooves, audible to all. I nearly reached for my ears. Had they grown longer? I trailed behind them. This was not the Sudanese way and, before I saw them, I would always walk alongside my fellow pedestrians. Yet they seemed to be walking to the rhythm of my thoughts, so I said to myself, let them walk ahead. The rhythm should lead the tune anyway. They walked in front, a music of excessive beauty, and I walked behind, confused and off-beat.

Then suddenly they spun round, beautiful, their faces coloured with an ornate rage.

The older said, 'What's with you? Why're you following us?'

'No, no, my cousin,' I said, trying to loosen the strings of their fury. 'I already have someone just as beautiful as you. And anyway I am not the kind to chase after beauty in the streets with a rifle.'

'We've heard that a thousand times!' she said.

'You don't believe me. I was trying to say that I already have a girl. I love her and she loves me and my camel loves her she-camel.[1] A thousand times I've come to her angry and left with a smile, as if she lived in some sort of joy factory. This morning, I left so full of her that people catcalled me in the street.'

Instead of laughter, a pure melody slipped out of the throat of the girl whose birds flew away. Then we fell silent.

My mind turned to the memory of my beloved. What a devilish afreet she was![2] So sure of herself, that girl, so confident. Once, when the summer was at its most intense, she said to me as we were returning from a concert: 'My grandmother was so beautiful that Suror himself used to sing to her.'[3]

---

1   A well-known couplet from a poem by the pre-Islamic poet al-Munakhkhal al-Yashkuri (580-603).

2   Afreet: a mischievous, otherworldly creature of Sudanese mythology.

3   Al-Haj Mohammed Ahmed Suror (1901-1946), one of the founders of modern Sudanese song.

'Suror and the other singers were slowly crushed by the Haqiba poets,'[4] I told her, 'until they began to moan and cry and oscillate as if enchanted by the melodic rounds and dirty words.

'What do you mean?' she asked.

'Their poets are like butchers selling women by the pound. When a man goes down to the butcher's shop, he hears a voice singing and hollering "Breast! Breast! Cheek! Cheek!" So he rifles through the selection of female parts, turning over those bits that please him while the voice draws his attention to the beauty of those pieces he may have missed. He leaves after buying a breast with onion or a flank garnished with arugula, and those who have guests would buy a whole rump.'

My love said, 'Knock off that dirty talk and pull back your tongue. Have you forgotten that Khalil Farah was one of the singers?'[5]

She left me speechless. That must have been my daydreams returning because when I looked around I could not find a trace of the girl whose birds flew away nor her sister.

I turned my senses into a tracking device. My ears became two microphones, my eyes two cameras, my nose a chemlab and my tongue a newscast. The device worked perfectly, unlike the products made in our factories these days. From there I monitored the situation like a mouse following the movements of its age-old enemy in order to protect itself. But then the girl's radar picked me up. I quickened my step, afraid she would insult me, but she ran behind me, saying, 'You've been tormenting me. What do you want?'

'Nothing,' I said, 'except to see you. To sing of you and dream of you! There's no need for pain between us. There's no doubt that it's a one-sided attraction, for I'm enamoured of one like you but I feel in front of her a certain... inferiority.'

---

4   The Haqiba school of song and poetry appeared in Sudan in the 1920s, advocating modernization and promoting the erotic in poetry.
5   Khalil Afandi Farah (1894-1932) – an anti-colonial Sudanese poet and activist.

The girl laughed and scrutinized me, as if seeking to identify what it was that was strange about me, and so I persisted:

'Made of red blood, are you? And was your heart a single rose struck by tragedy after tragedy until it folded back upon itself?'

She laughed again and my heart felt the soothing snow of contentment and joy.

'A poet?' she asked.

'So they say,' I said, adding: 'Who told you?'

'We've heard,' she said.

'And who's with you such that you address yourself in the plural? Why, your face is light and your voice light and you a mirror suspended in my tears illuminated, and so I cry.'

'Beautiful,' she said dryly. 'I had misunderstood you but now the truth comes out. You know the young men these days, so inane and brazen.'

'But dig deep and you'll find precious metals not found on the surface,' I said. 'My friends are more numerous than the ants and most of them understand and are understood.'

The girl whose birds flew away skipped ahead out of joy. Her form wavered until she disappeared, the sweet ring of her bells still in my ear. The image of her eyes remained in my mind, growing bright then dim then bright again, her face still nourishing my memory with joy. Her birds flew away. Away. Away.

And just like that we became friends. For an entire month our meetings continued in the streets: skipping, laughing, discussing – without reaching her true depths – and fearing she had only touched my surface. And so, one Wednesday, I asked her:

'Who is that little girl on your right?'

'My sister,' she said. 'I need her when we're walking in the markets. She protects me from the evil of the cars.'

'A talisman?' I asked.

'What?' she said.

'Like a charm or a spell. She protects you from envious

eyes, no?' Then I said to myself: But if death has already sunk
its claws in, no talisman will help. I stared in the faces of
the two beautiful girls for a long moment. The younger one
shrunk away, her strength drained like an ox at the water
wheel. No doubt her endless chores had made her grow old
before her years. I got on board the bus with them again. The
passengers' eyes, like glass saws, flew over the thighs and
eyes and faces of the young girls. I turned. All around me, the
passengers' mouths gaped like empty salt dishes. Their eyes
had taken flight, leaving two holes in every face. My glasses
may have held back my eyes, but they could not hold back
my innate curiosity and the deep pleasure I took in statistics:
On their bodies I counted a total of 99 round eyes. Strange, I
thought, to add up to an odd number, until I looked around
and saw a man with only one eye.

I returned home angry and rummaged through my papers
until I found what I had been looking for. I resolved to
return immediately. It was already midday. The sun was
wide awake and I was furious. I found the bus door flung
open like a gaping maw and entered. It was like Noah's Ark
inside. Every face imaginable. All kinds of peoples. Once
seated, it was easy to slip into distracted daydreaming. I sat
down and released my strong-hooved stallions from their
stables to gallivant through the fields of my imagination
and fantasy.

It was as if I had lost my voice. As if it had evaporated. My
worries barked and yapped at me but neither my own two
eyes nor anyone else's woke me. I was the son of the heaping
portion, the steaming dinner plate, but they filled me with
despair instead of millet and milk. In return, I filled others
with joy, for my fate was miserable while theirs was better
(and good for them!). It was as if I had been created to ensure
their survival and they survived to torment me.

And yes, I am the comatose son of sleep, the son of long
anticipation and unfulfilled promises. A beloved I have in

memory and longing only. Someone like me only hopes for someone like her. And someone like her would never be satisfied with someone like me. So who am I like? *You cow,* I said to myself, *you beast. Man stuffed with disease, with bacteria, with transformations and shake-ups, with ascents and long, tumbling falls. Women searching for happiness clamour around him only to find suffering under the whip. Those searching for a friend he treats as an enemy; and around him gather those women whose birds have flown away – and yet, there is nothing around which he clamours. And despite all of this, he claims that he is one who understands, who is aware, who has chosen to pick a fight and rebel.*

I returned to my state of despair to find myself still on the damned bus, the people around me butting heads and locking horns, the men refusing to relinquish their seats to the women, the women not sparing the men a single curse from the dictionary. I needed to get off before Bagheeti Station and, when I did, I saw before me a train of humanity propelled by curiosity towards the hospital. My own curiosity was no less than theirs but perhaps I was more arrogant. I rode the wave of the crowd after I had exhausted every expression and exclamation of surprise.

'What's going on?' I yelled, but my question was lost in the din of similar questions. Several interpretations came to me, each independent of the next, pulling together certain details and disregarding others. The responses of onlookers did nothing but catapult me forward, toward the source of my curiosity. I was swept away by the crush of the people around the vortex, closer and closer until I screamed –

'Blood!'

It was as if a razor had cut the light from my eyes. As if I had died. A bloodbath. A bath whose dye was blood and impact. The talisman stained with blood and terror. And the blood of two girls just like them – the dye of henna. Blood on their hands like murderers, and on their legs like the murdered, and elsewhere, everywhere, such that you could not tell from where it was seeping. I said out loud: 'Must've been a traffic accident, no doubt.'

'No way,' yelled an agitated man with a rounded face.

'What, then?' I asked myself.

I turned with the rest of the gaping onlookers to a calm-voiced boy. 'They were on the beach,' he said. 'Twisted just like that and unconscious. A heavy-set man found them and went to the police station.'

'It was a traffic accident!' I screamed.

My neighbour, who happened to be among the crowd, turned to me. 'Have you gone mad?' he demanded. 'A traffic accident on the beach? What the hell does that mean? A boat collided with them? Or perhaps a fish jumped from the water and smacked into them?'

A traffic accident, no doubt, I said to myself. Then I turned towards the wide avenue, calling out in a laughing scream, a sobbing, playful sermon: 'No, no, no. No! Her birds flew away! Her birds flew away! Her birds flew... flew... flew...'

Some of the passers-by glanced at me, shaking their heads, and then, certain I was mad, they turned away.

'Flew... flew... flew.'

A man stopped his car. His jugular bulged with laughter as he asked me, 'What flew off?'

'Her birds...' I replied.

The driver laughed until the tarmac shook and the car stalled and emitted a cloud of fumes. He restarted the engine and disappeared.

Flew... flew... flew... Could it be? It must be that some force took them to that place. Some sort of deception, some trickery. Did I not see the terror and fear on their faces? The terror of the talisman and the shock of the girl whose birds flew away? No... she landed... landed... landed.

Around me a crowd had gathered. They were all staring at me as if I were responsible for the accident. I nearly screamed at them: 'They flew away! She flew away!' But the tarmac spread before me and so I began to walk. And walk and walk. That terrible day! I did not reach the well-spring of my dreams, nor my house. The river was closer and the eyes of the lovers there more reassuring. So I decided to go there, perhaps to cleanse myself or lay my head in the darkness of their pupils and sleep in their solid whiteness. *He filled my void and arose from sleep to fight what had been ordained for me.*[6] As long as the innocent birds were struck with stones and selfish desires, they would continue to land in such ugly places against their will, in patches full of violence and hate.

Translated from the Arabic by Max Shmookler, with support from Najlaa Osman Eltom.

Bushra al-Fadil has published four collections of short stories in Arabic. His most recent collection *Above a City's Sky* was published in 2012, the same year that he won the Altayeb Salih Short Story Award. Bushra holds a PhD in Russian language and literature. 'The Story of the Girl Whose Birds Flew Away' was first published in *The Book of Khartoum – A City in Short Fiction*, edited by Raph Cormack & Max Shmookler (Comma Press, UK, 2016).

---

6 A partial line from the praise poem of al-Mutanabbi (died 965), dedicated to his patron Sayf al-Dawla.

God's Children Are Little Broken Things

Arinze Ifeakandu

We are the miracles that God made
To taste the bitter fruit of Time.
Ben Okri, 'An African Elegy'

I

You met in your second year. At the stadium one cloudy evening when you played against his department. He was not a player, he was too small to be one, even though you knew that bigness wasn't the stuff anyway. But he was so small, so fragile, you were dead sure he had never kicked a football.

He reminded you of Dave.

You walked up to him at halftime and told him he reminded you of someone. The way he smiled, his eyes lingering briefly on your sweaty chest and then on the ground, made you certain that he was one of them. Dave was one of them too, and he had almost put you in trouble.

I wanted to tell you that you reminded me of someone, you said, with what you knew was a weak smile, and then you were gone.

You lost the game to his department. On your way home, you called Rachael and told her you loved her so much did she know that? She giggled over the phone and you told yourself again that Dave had almost put you in trouble, Jesus!

You met him again. At Christ Church Chapel where he

played the organ so well on Mothering Sunday, the entire church was filled with a tender light, the women burst into tongues in the middle of hymns, and the chaplain for once didn't say, First and last verses only. You couldn't believe it, that his legs could strike the pedals so strongly. He did not look fragile on the organ.

After the service you lingered around the door of the choir room, until he came out and said, Hey.

Hey, you said, scratching your head and glancing at the floor. That was great, what you did up there.

T-thanks bro, he stuttered. I wasn't sure at first, b-but then...

And you learned that day how well he could talk and not bore you. (Later, he would tell you that he had been afraid you would walk away again, so he'd talked and talked.) You exchanged numbers, and you whistled on your way home, skipped by the roadside like a little boy, so full were you with giddiness.

But you did not call him. He called you, twice, first to know how your day had been. You said, Fine. The second time he called, he told you that his piano instructor was OCD, the man didn't give him any breathing space, and you said, Really?

Yes, he said.

After that, he stopped calling, and you did not call either. Not until the night Dumebi texted you that Mum and Dad were quarrelling, could you please call them now? You were asleep when the text message came in, and when you woke up at midnight, you had 11 missed calls. You tried to call her back, but she wasn't answering. You started to dial Mum's number but then stopped. Then you dialled his number. His voice was rough: Hey, Lotanna.

You sat on the bed, running your fingers through your hair. Hey, Kamsi, you said. Didn't expect you to be awake.

I'm rehearsing my exam pieces.

I see.

Then you told him everything, how every time Mum and

Dad would quarrel, even though it was in low tones, the entire house seemed to reverberate with their bitterness. How it hurt you in the chest so badly you couldn't breathe; shit, you couldn't breathe. Then, because he was so quiet, you said: I'm not even sure why I'm telling you this. I hope I didn't disturb you.

No, no, he said. N-not at all.

Okay, you said, and then asked how he was doing, and what were the pieces he was playing?

The next day was Saturday. The girls from your department had a football match with the girls from his. The match was already on when you came, and you walked straight to him after shaking hands with your friends. He folded his arms across his chest, smiled so widely it made you happy simply standing there, saying, How'veyoubeenbro?

You sat with him on the racing track. He was wearing three-quarter shorts and an Arsenal jersey, the hair on his legs and arms black and curly against the light brown of his skin.

You have nice legs, you said. Let's run.

He said no, weakly, but you pulled him up, called him lazy and laughed at his pout. He did not run a hundred metres before he stopped. He bent over, his hands on his knees. You walked to him, laughing. His classmates were laughing: Mozart, you dey fall hands oh. He was panting. He collapsed on the track and lay on his back.

Lazy, you said, smiling down at him. Is this how you do your girlfriend?

He arched an eyebrow, stared at you.

You did not hold his gaze, merely chuckled. And then you sat on the ground beside where he lay.

II

You thought of him often. Stalked him on Facebook, squinted at every update ancient and modern, and told yourself that you found him interesting. Simple. Sometimes, you would lie in bed trying to visualize Rachael from last time. Her lips, what did they taste like the last time? Lemon mint? TomTom? What would his lips taste like? Like TomTom too? Or like nothing.

You told him Rachael was the best thing that ever happened to you. Told him she saved you.

From what? he asked.

You won't understand, you said.

You were seated on a step at the stadium, watching the sun, once white, fade into a calm yellow, and all you could think about were his hands, how they tapped rhythms on his knees as he tried to get the words out of his mouth. You wanted to take them in yours and rub them until they were warm, and then blow on them, in circles, until he giggled.

Don't conclude so quickly, he said. But I understand if you don't want to tell me.

You put your hands in your pockets, stood up. It's getting late, you said. We should start going.

You had noticed certain things about him. Little-little things. How his stutter became obvious only when it was cold or when he was emotional. And how when he told you about his relationships he looked you bold in the eyes, teasing, Does my story make you horny? Though he tried to sound flippant and cool, the shyness still billowed in his voice. And how he liked to sing whenever he was in the bathroom, you often heard him screaming, *ekuro la labaku ewa...* and it made you laugh because he sounded so much like Justin Bieber screaming *baby baby baby oh*. Nobody sang Davido with that kind of voice.

One morning, he came to your house and flopped on the bed face down. You were seated at the table, trying to make sense of your History of Nigeria lecture notes. You watched him for a while, and then you asked, What is it?

When he stared at you, his eyes were red. His lips quivered. I h-hate e-every. One o-of them. I've met, he said.

What happened? you asked.

He grabbed your bedsheet, bit his lips so hard, you thought he would draw blood. I. Told him. No, he said. I t-told him. No.

He covered his face with the bedsheet. He was shaking terribly.

You sat beside him on the bed and held his hand, rubbed it gently. He was still shaking. But as you rubbed and rubbed, he began to calm down. You rubbed and pressed, rubbed and pressed. Better? you asked. He nodded, sniffled.

Who was it?

Kent, he said.

All his friends had funny names: Kent, Klay, Vinny. Like names on body-cream bottles – Kent, Light & Lovely. I thought you were just friends, you said.

He nodded, blew his nose. Your stomach felt full of hot anger. I want to bathe, he said.

Later, he refused to dress in front of you, yelled, Stop! at you when you teased him about acting like a girl, why couldn't he dress in front of you? And, as you sat on the veranda, waiting for him to be done, you shocked yourself by how hard you wanted to punch Kent.

It was in the days that followed that you learned the definition of the word *gentleness*. He was delicate, always lying in bed eating plantain chips. Sometimes, he woke up in the middle of the night kicking. You learned to hold him close, to press his head against your chest and whisper, It's okay, I'm here. It's okay.

You called Rachael and told her that you couldn't wait to return home for the holiday, you missed her so damn much. But the truth was, your heart beat too fast when his head rested on your chest. And you wanted too much to bury your nose in his neck and sniff the talcum powder he wore when going to bed. And then, every time you saw the tears in his eyes, making them look silvery in the darkness, you wanted too much to tilt his chin up and kiss him hard and gentle.

Exams came in July. Nsukka had this funny weather: sometimes it rained all night, and you had to wear a sweater and socks as you read. You asked him to bring his keyboard to your house. No, you didn't mind the noise, you could cope.

He smiled and said thank you.

One night it rained so hard, it sounded like pebbles hitting the roof. You shut the windows, but the wind still filtered in. You stopped reading and eased into bed beside him. You had to spoon against him because the blanket was small. Your nose was on his neck, and you whispered, Kamsi, are you awake?

Yeah, he said. I want to practise the Sam Ojukwu piece for my exam, but I'm feeling so lazy.

He adjusted slightly, his back warm on your stomach. You held his hand and pressed it, then pressed your nose so closely to his neck, you could smell him, clean as air, through the talcum powder. When your hand eased under his sweater and rubbed his stomach, he whispered, I thought you would never decide.

Decide what? you asked, moving your hand upward and upward, until you found his nipples, two tiny hard grains. He stifled a giggle (you would learn later that he did that often when he was turned on, stifle a giggle, so that it sounded like a snort). He tilted his head backward to look at you, and you pressed your lips, tentatively, on his. He tasted almost of nothing. You sat up, helped him out of his sweater and inner shirt, put your hand into his trousers. Your eyes closed. Your lips and tongues dancing. He had given himself up so easily, so gently, and then all of a sudden he was shaking. I c-can't do this, Lotanna, he said.

You had his hands pinned down, his legs wrapped around your waist. You leaned forward. Just relax, you said. Relax.

No, he said. His legs around your waist slackened.

Come on.

No, he said, shaking his head.

For a while you towered over him. Then you rolled over and lay beside him, staring at the dark ceiling, your hand on your forehead.

Was this what happened with Kent? you asked.

No, he said quickly, like he had been expecting the question.

I d-don't like K-kent. I didn't even want to k-kiss him.

I see.

The next day, after your History of Nigeria exam, you said to your classmate, Pascal, I have this babe who was hurt, and it's affecting her sex life badly.

Pascal nodded. She no wan' give you, eh?

Something like that, you said. Pascal was the perpetual lover boy in class, he had to know some stuff.

Give it some time, he said. Keep trying, small-small. No force am oh.

God forbid! you said. I no fit try that one na.

Later, you searched on Google. You had said the word in your head, *gay*, and had typed it. And now that you needed someone to talk to so badly, there was nobody who would certainly understand.

III

The first time you quarrelled, it was because he did not tidy the room after he returned from school. You returned home that evening to the sound of Beethoven's 'Für Elise'. (You were beginning to know the names of his favourite pieces.) The room was dim; the only light came from the dying sun. The bed was unmade, your clothes scattered on it just like you both had left them in the heat of last night. The room still had the air of morning rush – two empty cups sat unwashed on the cupboard. His schoolbag lay open on the floor. You picked it up and hung it, together with yours, on the wall beside your clothes rack.

Normally, when he was on the keyboard, you did not talk to him. But today had been bad, and the sound of the keyboard felt like someone was sticking pins into your ears. You returned since afternoon, you said. How could you have left this room like this?

He played two more notes of the music, and then there was utter silence. Lotanna, he said. Good evening.

Why didn't you tidy the room?

I was rehearsing for my recital, as you can see, he said. He sounded rebuked, confused. But there was also a hint of testiness.

You stood in the middle of the room, watching him fiddle with the collar of his polo shirt like a child.

You began to pick up things. He stood to help you, but you said, No, please, and took the rag from him. He stood there, watching you. Then he took his schoolbag and left the room.

All through the evening, you stood on the veranda waiting for him to return. The evening turned from orange to blue and then to grey-blue, but he still did not return. When your lodge mate, Henry, put on his generator, you rushed to charge your phone, waited until a bar came on, and then dashed out to call Kamsi. The voice came through, soft and sweet: *The number you're calling is currently not available...* You boarded an okada to his house. He wasn't there. You returned home and sat on the veranda, waiting.

You wanted to tell him about the phone call you got at school today. How Dumebi had sounded like she had been crying all day. Mum was going mad, she had said. Mum was hurling things at Dad, the television was on the floor now, broken, and Chisom was crying, and she, Dumebi, was crying, but Mum wouldn't stop – Mum was going mad. You wanted to tell him how, when you called Mum and she did not pick up, you felt all these tiny insects crawling in your head. How when, hours later, Mum called you, she did not sound mad at all. It's your father again, she said. And this time it's with my friend's daughter.

How her voice sounded nasal and tired and shaky.

You wanted to tell him it's called *transfer of aggression*. That you'd had a bad day. But he did not return that night, nor the next day, nor the day after. And you did not tell him.

The next time you quarrelled, you flung words at each other. Quietly, so that the neighbours wouldn't hear. He wanted you to end it with Rachael, and you called him selfish. He said, No, it's you who is a liar, stop fooling the girl.

You told him, See who's talking, you knew I had a girl, and you still came to me. He snorted, I didn't come to you, dude, stop lying to yourself. You bit your lip hard and called him a fucking child, and he looked at you with tears in his eyes and yelled, I am not a child! He flung a pillow at you and stormed out of the room.

You lay in bed. The ceiling spun so fast it was about to fall on you.

IV

He liked to say this prayer:

> God, grant me the serenity
> to accept the things I cannot change;
> courage to change the things I can;
> and wisdom to know the difference.

He said it on mornings when there was no lecture rush. He sat on the chair in front of his keyboard, his hymnbook open before him, his Bible closed. His hands clasped in a praying posture against his chest, and his eyes closed. He muttered the words softly-softly. You woke up those mornings to watch him. Sometimes the sun drew fine lines on his face, and his lips became redder, his skin brighter, his aura more childlike.

V

It was on the day of your last exam that you heard that Mum had fallen in her restaurant and had to be carried home by some of her customers. You rushed home after your exam, threw some clothes into your travel bag. On your way to Peace Park, you called Kamsi. I won't make it to your piano recital this evening, you said. My mum fell sick.

Where are you now? he asked. I'm c-coming.

He met you at the motor park. W-what happened? he asked.

They said it's hepatitis B, you said. I don't even know what the hell that is.

He sat beside you on a bench. You both watched the hawkers and agboros. Most departments were through with their exams, and the park teemed with students. Something serpentine crawled in your stomach. You'll still travel tomorrow, right? you asked.

Yes, he said. My b-brother will meet me at the airport.

Okay, you said, moved closer and held his hand, you were trembling so badly.

You need a sweater, he said. It's going to g-get cold by the time you approach Kano.

I have a sweater in my bag, you said. He had his hand in yours, hidden from view by the way you both sat so closely.

You had never said it to anyone before, but now you told him, how sometimes you were afraid that Mum would die suddenly, just like her mother, and then you wouldn't be able to buy her all the cars and clothes she didn't have now. It's like mourning someone many years before their death, you said.

He squeezed your hand. Everything will be fine, all right?

All right, you said.

Moments after he'd left, you stared out the window as your bus ambled out of Peace Park, ignored the girl seated beside you who wouldn't stop giving you the eye, called Dumebi to ask how Mum was faring. Nsukka glided past, rusty roofs and red dust, the evening turning grey-blue so quickly – Kamsi's recital should be on now. You blocked your ears with earphones. The song was Asa's 'So Beautiful.'

VI

Only three months, and Kano looked changed and new. You opened the window and devoured the sight. The sun shone remorselessly bright. Houses, tall and short, ugly and beautiful, stood side by side. And people. So many people. People who didn't care whether you said good morning to them. People who were I-don't-care like that. *Ba kwomi.* That was the word: *I-don't-care.* Nsukka had reminded you of another word, *solitude*, with the town's dusty red roads and old houses scattered between farms and bushes. But Kano, big ancient Kano, Kano of merciless sunniness, Kano of wide-road and coffee-smelling Bompai, Kano of slang-and-decay Sabon Gari. Kano reminded you of the word *be*.

In Sabon Gari, the air smelled of decaying refuse. The roads had holes like bushmeat traps, the houses were like discoloured matchboxes strewn around by adventurous children. And so many people speaking Igbo and Yoruba and pidgin. And no okadas.

Yes, army pursue okada, Chisom said, searching your bag for the toy car you had bought him.

Why? you asked.

Boko Haram, he said. Boko Haram use okada to bomb.

You reclined against the sagging sofa and noticed without trying how the living room seemed so small, so square, so artless, with the fading blue walls covered with pictures bearing everybody's stories, from Mum and Dad's wedding to Chisom's first birthday; and how the neighbouring house blocked much of the light.

At the hospital, Mum could barely talk. She lay in bed, too bony to be Mum, Mum who had always been described as full. You sat on the bed and touched her hand gently. The room smelled of cleanliness; it was remarkable, how this hospital managed to keep the hospital smell away. Dumebi sat on a mat spread on the floor, her legs stretched out in front of her. A man in a too-ironed Ankara stood up and said, Brothers and sisters, the devil came to steal, to kill, and to destroy. He waved a huge black Bible in the air, spoke with an authority like he could kick open locked doors and storm dark rooms and make them super bright. As he spoke, everybody hummed; it was like he was pulling them with an invisible string. Even Mum grunted. When he said, Rise, *rise*, let us pray, *pray*, the room filled with voices high and mighty, and you stood reluctantly, worried that a nurse would storm into the room and yell at everybody to fucking shut up, they were too damn loud.

Later it was just you and Dumebi and Mum. She smiled, her eyes tired. When she said, How is school, in a voice so thin and cracked, something inside you broke.

Dad came in with Chisom. He shook your hand and asked, Nwoke, a naeme kwa? You left the bed and sat in a chair. Dad sat on the bed beside Mum, saying something softly to her. She nodded now and again, and once you caught a smile on her face, and the broken thing in your chest began to collect itself.

Leave that thing, now! Dumebi said to Chisom, who was trying to get the bottle of Lucozade Boost on the refrigerator.

I want to bring it for Mummy, he said in his three-year-old voice. The way he stood on tiptoes, struggling to get the bottle, looked comical. Before you could rush to help him, he had already taken the bottle. He turned and faced all of you, smiling.

Oya, go and give it to Mummy, Dumebi said, but Chisom rushed to you, screaming, Lota, open for me! You were all laughing (Mum smiled), he was damn cute and comical, standing there thinking he had fooled everybody. Later, when you described this scene to Kamsi, you told him how it made you feel hopeful, how suddenly the world was capable of tenderness.

VII

Rachael sat curled on a sofa in her living room and cried. You emerged from the bathroom and found her crying.

She tossed your phone to you. You picked it up, noncommittally, flicked it on. Kamsi's text message glared: *I'm listening to Davido right now, and I'm thinking of that night we went to Flat and the Klin Promo car was playing 'Ekuro' and you said you'd kiss me behind the old buildings if I dared. Miss you, man.*

You flopped on a sofa and stared at her. Last night when Kamsi had sent the message, you had read it over and over, had searched for hidden meanings. And you had forgotten to delete it like you did the others.

Who is Kamsi? she asked, sniffled. Who is she?

She's my course mate, you said, then added quickly you'd stop seeing her.

You sat beside her, held her, let her struggle until she relaxed.

That evening, when Kamsi called and told you that he had finally arrived in Kano, could you come to his house at Bompai, you said no. You were a little sick, you said. You needed to rest.

Who was that? Dumebi asked.

My friend, you said.

Kamsi?

Yeah.

She nodded, gave Chisom a mild slap on the bum – Stay one place, let me wash your armpit – and said to you, You lied to him.

You shrugged. Well, sometimes it's necessary.

She hoisted Chisom out of the plastic bath and proceeded to wipe his body with a towel. I can't lie to Obika, she said. He'll not talk to me for weeks if I do.

Digressing, you asked, What's up with you and Obika, sef? I've not seen him since I returned.

Oh, he travelled to China, Dumebi said. He should be back next week. She paused, helped Chisom into his pyjamas, then, without changing the colour of her voice: He wants to bring wine to Dad; I agreed.

You laughed. But she wasn't laughing. She meant it, she really meant it.

You are serious, you said.

Do I look like I'm playing? She patted Chisom's head and sent him off to watch TV with his friends – If you dirty your body you'll enter the bedroom and sleep. You watched him run off, his gait shaky, like the breeze would carry him away.

What about school? you asked. No more JAMB?

She chuckled. JAMB, kwa? JAMB that I have passed how many times. Where is the admission? I cannot continue to wait for university, biko.

You couldn't get her. You had waited three years before you got into the university, changed your course choice from law to political science and then finally to history and international relations. She had waited just two years, and there she was, complaining. Like, seriously?

She scoffed. Biko, don't forget that I am a girl. My time is short.

You stared at her. But you're just 19, you said.

She shook her head. Me, I have decided, she said, turned her face away from you. Besides, I'm tired of all the quarrels in this house.

VIII

The night before you returned to Nsukka, you said bad words to Dad. It wasn't that you couldn't have kept quiet. It wasn't that you couldn't have swallowed the phlegm. But as he stepped into the living room that night, laughing at something Chisom had said, you couldn't understand.

You had been seated on the bed at the hospital, playing a game on your phone, when Mum had said, You see how heartless your father can be, eh?

You had stared at her. O gini?

She shut her eyes. Her cheeks looked sunken, and her cheekbones jutted out luridly. She said, Just look at me, lying here like this, and he can't even show some respect, small respect.

She was crying. You placed your hand on hers. Mum, what is it?

Where did your father sleep last night?

You had assumed that he had slept over at the hospital with Dumebi. I don't know, you said, suddenly uncomfortable. I thought he slept here?

Here, kwa? Your father, your father left me here and said

he was going home to you and Chisom. Only for me to hear this morning that he was seen coming out of that useless girl's house.

Who told you? you asked – you did not know what else to say – but Mum had already shut her eyes and was shaking her head slowly.

The anger you felt roamed, hingeless. You weren't sure if you were angry because you knew it was true, that Dad had slept at the girl's house, or because someone had brought the news to your sick mother. So that night, when he stepped into the living room, laughing, you said, You're heartless.

He looked around the living room, behind him, above him. What?

How could you do this to Mum? How?

The way he stared at you, mouth open like he was going to say something, you wanted to stop, to apologize. But your heart burned like you had hot charcoal on it, and your tongue tasted like bitter lemon. The words poured out like hot water. And then he was saying, Nwoke, nwoke.

You had almost forgotten how tall he was, how you looked so much alike, with the same broad shoulders and the same sleepy eyes and well-kept goatee. It stared you in the face like a child's taunting, this resemblance, sticking out its pinkish tongue at you.

You walked on into the looming darkness. Through Abedie and Sanyaolu Streets where the sound of Hausa music filled the night and keke napeps covered everywhere, and you remembered your days in secondary school when one night, on your way to Dave's house, a dirty-looking lady stopped you on Abedie Street and spoke florid Hausa, and when you gaped at her, she tugged impatiently at your arm and asked, You wan' poke? You wan' poke?

I no wan' fuck, you had said to her, dragged your hands away, and ran.

You walked to France Road. France Road with the

streetlights beaming orange light. France Road with locked-up shops at night and with rushing cars at day. France Road with Dave in a room of his own, chatting on 2go all day and hooking up with hunky guys, short guys, fat guys, men guys. France Road that led to Bompai and Airport Road. France Road that led to Kamsi and Rachael.

You turned around and began to return home.

IX

The first moments at school were awkward. You staring at him, he staring at you, and the room suddenly still and silent. He had texted every day. Called every day. Had wanted to see your mother and your siblings. Had wanted you to meet his twin brother, Kosi, and his parents if possible. But every day after Rachael cried you had bounced his calls, deleted his text messages mostly unread. And now you were back to school, and he was standing at your door, and you were staring at each other.

How is your mother? he asked finally.

She's getting better, you said.

Okay, he said. I returned yesterday. Couldn't get to you. I c-came to get my keyboard.

You watched him throw his music books into his bag. And then some clothes he had left behind before traveling. Watched him lift the keyboard. Watched him walk out of the door. We'll see later? you asked, and he shrugged and walked away.

X

Every evening you called Rachael and told her you loved her so much, did she know that? She giggled – it was what she wanted to hear. And every evening you sat on the veranda and stared into the street, hens and a few people walking lazily by, and hoped that something would fall from the sky and break the silence in the house. Sometimes you walked down to Flat because it wasn't so quiet there. Not once, not twice, you'd picked up your phone to call Kamsi. But not once, not twice, you'd stopped yourself.

You had never believed that you could love this way, your entire being absorbed in something in the air like that; that you could want someone always near you so badly it consumed you, so that when you were apart, it felt like torture.

People happen to people, Rachael once said.

Kamsi happened to you.

Then, one evening after football training, you found some students and a lecturer from your town's union at your door. You hadn't attended their meetings since eternity. You opened the door and let them in. The light from your rechargeable lamp cast tall shadows on the wall. The union secretary, a lanky guy in sociology, spoke like a character from *Things Fall Apart*, and you wanted to tell him that your heart was beating too fast, you could have a heart attack; that proverbs were cliché, and that this generation, your generation, spoke in monosyllables: She. Died.

And then he said the words, Your mother died this evening.

You watched the shadows and nodded like an agama lizard. Everybody was saying sorry, and it was like something was killing you slowly.

When everyone left, the lecturer took you in his car and drove you to Jives. You sat at a table for two. He ordered two bottles of Hero, said, That's the new drink for men.

Jives was open air, students and lecturers lounging around tables. The speakers were blaring out some fast song, and a handful of people were dancing.

Lecturer said, When my mother died 12 years ago, I was 20. My father was already dead four years.

He had a flat nose and small lips and dirty eyes. He drank from the bottle and watched you with his dirty eyes. Then he said, And all I could think about was how much she had suffered. And also how I was going to take care of my younger siblings, all four of them.

He drank again. But somehow, God helped me, he said. Our last born will be doing her convocation next month.

He paused, stared intently. You stared away, at the people dancing.

Where do you worship? he asked.

Christ Church, you said.

Do you have a relationship with God?

Church was routine. It had always been routine. And God was just there: at Holy Communion on Sundays when the choir sang your favourite hymn, 'Abide with Me'. And 'relationship' was what you had with Rachael, with Kamsi, with your teammates.

I don't know, you said.

He laughed, shaking his head. You chuckled. You don't know, he said, his eyes wet with mirth. I think it's God you can talk to now, really. It will help. And, you haven't touched that bottle since.

You raised the bottle to your mouth, and the image that never left your eyes was of Mum lying there, shaking her head slowly.

On your way home you asked him to drive you to Lemon Villa. A few minutes, and you were standing in front of Kamsi's door, listening to muffled strains of guitar music.

You knocked. Once, then twice. Tentatively. Who's there? he asked.

It's me, Lotanna, you said.

You heard the clicking of bolts, and then he stood in front of you, a near-silhouette in green shorts and a white singlet. Mum died, you said, swinging your arms like you were in Sunday school and he was your Bible recitation instructor.

Oh my God! He covered his mouth with his palm, eyes bulging. Then he stood aside and let you in. He shut the door. When was it?

Today, you said. This evening.

You sat on the bed, and he sat beside you. For a while you were both quiet. His wall clock ticked, the walls more green than lemon in the whiteness of the electric bulb, the rug red and soft under your feet. And the room smelled of Kamsi, that mix of talcum powder and nothing. And then you told him how you had called Dumebi and wished you had not because her grief inflamed your own, how you had ignored your father's call until the lecturer asked you why, and how Rachael had called to say God cares. Does God really care?

I hope he does, Kamsi said. Otherwise what's the use of everything?

You stared at him and he stared at you. Then you touched his face, tilted his head up and kissed him hard and gentle. You heard the grunt at the back of his throat. You were a little tipsy from drinking Hero. But not too tipsy to feel all the things that you felt at that moment: relief and love and that heavy, drumming sensation in your chest that always exploded in tears.

XI

At first, he did not tell you about the boys who had threatened him. They said they would have beaten the gay out of me, he said. But that I was so cute they'd have a little fun raping it out of me. Doesn't that sound gay to you?

He laughed, like that sounded funny. He was seated on the bed, his chin on his knees drawn to his chest. He was trying to sound unfazed.

It had been going on since around the time you travelled for the burial, he said. This is not funny, you said. I think we should report it to school security.

He laughed. And tell them what? Please.

But how did they find out about you, sef? You don't even look gay, for Christ's sake.

How does one look gay, Lota? They even said what's the size of your macho boyfriend's thing. I think they're just freaks.

You grabbed your phone and began dialling a friend's number.

What are you doing? Kamsi asked.

Calling some of my teammates. They'll deal with this.

And what will you tell them? Please forget it.

You cut the call, flopped on the bed, and covered your face with your hands.

XII

You told him you wouldn't be returning to Kano for the holidays; that, since there was a strike going on, Lagos or Enugu would make sense, you had relatives there. He looked at you and said, It's about your dad, right?

At Mum's funeral, Dad had tried to tell you how it felt like sinking and sinking, and you had told him, coldly, that you never knew he was a poet. The day you broke up with Rachael, telling her you needed to concentrate on school, he had called you into his room and told you a long story about how all that time your mother had been his number one, how even though he couldn't help it, seeing some other women, she had been the one he truly loved. He'd said, I'm telling you this because you're becoming a man, and that evening, you went to Rachael's house and told her you had to end it.

Kamsi said, I think you should let go. He's your father, after all.

Whatever, you said, and continued folding your clothes into a travel bag.

Kamsi held your hands, gently pressed them to his cheeks. Then he began to blow on them, in circles, his eyes fixed on yours. The room was suddenly still, the air calm and waiting. You felt like a child stealing milk.

Wait here, he said, his eyes lighting up. He rushed into the bathroom, returned to the room with a new razor blade.

Let's have a blood covenant, he said.

Don't be silly, you said, laughing.

Yes, I'm silly, he said. Let's be silly together.

XIII

In the mornings when you watched Enugu from Aunt Oge's balcony, you saw calm, orderliness, something large and grey hovering over the faraway houses. August. The air in the mornings was cool, a little wet, not wet-wet like in Nsukka, and not dry and brittle like in Kano. You stood on the balcony in your singlet and boxers and stared.

This morning you were standing there, staring, when a yellow taxi pulled up by the gate. When the passengers alighted, you were speechless – Dad in jeans and a baseball cap, Chisom looking bigger, and Dumebi carrying these two small bags, her stomach the shape and size of a football. At first they looked a little clueless, and then Chisom looked up and saw you and started shouting, Lota! Lota!

You did not tell me! you shot at your cousin, Somadina, as you both rushed downstairs to the door.

Mum said it was a secret, he said.

At the door, Chisom jumped on you, laughing. And Dad said, Since the mountain has refused to come to Muhammad… He smiled.

Welcome, you said, after a slight pause, and took Dumebi's bags.

Somadina drove everyone around Enugu – Dumebi, Chisom, and you. There was something vainly ambitious about Enugu City. A tidy city if you drove or walked through the right places; messy and rowdy if you walked or drove through the wrong places. Enugu with the wide roads and do-not-litter policy, and pretty housing estates, and ShopRite, and young people watching their villages suddenly transforming into something big and glittering. Maybe Enugu wanted to be like Lagos. Or compete with Lagos, even.

Enugu glided past you. You nodded when they asked a question, but nothing you did could pull you out of the dark hole into which you were sinking. You heard Somadina say something to Dumebi about his friend Binyelum. And then there was Chisom tugging at your arm.

Leave him alone! Dumebi snapped. He's not happy to see us. And then, to Somadina, she said, You mean Binyelum is really leaving the seminary?

You whipped out your phone and sent a WhatsApp message to Kamsi: *Hey love.*

You were not sad or anything. You just didn't feel right.

Dad had not left his business in Kano to simply visit his sister in Enugu. He came for something, and later that evening, seated alone with him and Aunt Oge in the living room, you felt like a trapped animal.

Aunt Oge said, You must forget all that has happened, life must go on.

But how can I forget? you wanted to ask. Like, maybe I should just press a button in my head and say delete?

Lotanna, Dad said. You cannot continue to run like this. You have to return home.

He said, We can start afresh.

He said, I'm sure your mother is in a better place now, and she'll want us to forgive, so that we can all meet her again at that place someday.

All these in Igbo, which you could not speak in a situation like that. Because you had very few Igbo words. So you kept mute, kpim. So you just stared at the flower vase on the table. So you just tapped your bare feet on the floor.

Later, you called Kamsi.

Someone else picked up. Lotanna, right?

Yes, you said. Good evening.

I was going to call you, young man. Now, listen, don't ever call this number again, ever, or else…

You cut the call while he was still talking and stared at your phone.

Dumebi wanted to know what was wrong. Was it Dad? Were you sure it was just Dad?

Yes, you said. I'm sure.

Then you have to sort it out, she said. Sharp-sharp.

I'll do that in my own time, you said. He should respect that.

But every night, you slept with that heavy thing in your chest that rose up and up, until it choked you, until it strangled out a sob from your throat.

XIV

You are in Nsukka. Everything looks worn, fading. You walk to the stadium, still incomplete after all these years, and sit on a step on what should be the spectators' stand. It is getting late, and the bodybuilders are packing and leaving. A flock of herons have descended on the football field, where the harmattan haze covers everything.

You met in this same stadium where you sit now, watching the herons and the late-evening joggers. You used to return here often, both of you. He used to tease you about checking out the bodybuilders, which made you laugh.

Which reminds you of Dumebi in Enugu asking how long you had known.

You sure this Kamsi guy didn't convert you? she had asked. Because, from his pictures, I'm sure he could convert even the Pope.

You had laughed. So you don't think I'm handsome enough to have been the one.

Vanity, she'd said, rolled her eyes. What about Rachael?

You shook your head, stared at the street below, cars flooding the night with yellow lights.

I don't get this, she kept saying. What will people say? What would God say?

Since when did you start caring about God, Dumebi? you asked, and she chuckled and said, I be God pikin, abeg.

You still expect him to show up at your door at any moment.

After his friends came to your place, you called Dumebi

and told her. I kept waiting for him to return to school, you said. I even dared it and called his number, but it was switched off. I didn't know, Dumebi. I didn't know.

You walk out of the stadium. It is getting too dark, and soon bad guys will come here to smoke, and you don't want to be there when they arrive. You put your hands in your sweater's pockets to keep the cold away. The harmattan haze is so low, you can't see the world ahead of you. You walk and walk and walk. Slowly, like you are walking with someone. Listening to their footfalls.

You create dreams in which he comes and talks with you. You talk and talk and laugh and laugh, and it feels like you are stretching a fractured arm, testing it. When you wake up the room is so fucking cold.

You want to ask him, Why?

And, Did you think about me?

And, Why didn't you just endure like everyone else?

You walk into your room. There is no power. You light a candle, and everything else becomes shadows.

You call Dad. He sounds surprised: Lotanna?

A si m ka m malu otu i di, you say.

Oh, thank you, he says. A na-eme kwa?

Ee, a na-eme.

Tonight, you dream that he walks into this room. He is wearing his Arsenal jersey and green shorts. He lies beside you and says, What happened to you, Lotanna? You look so broken.

Arinze Ifeakandu was the editor of *The Muse* at the University of Nigeria, Nsukka, where he studied English and Literature, graduating in 2016. In 2013, Arinze attended the Farafina Trust Creative Writing workshop and he was shortlisted for the BN Poetry Prize in 2015. 'God's Children Are Little Broken Things' was first published in *A Public Space 24* (A Public Space Literary Projects Inc, US, 2016).

The Virus

Magogodi oaMphela Makhene

You ask how it was when this thing started? Well. Have you ever seen a late summer flock, before flight? I mean, yes, I was there. But what you're asking of this ou kerel is like naming the very Book of Names. It just always was. Unless you read Genesis. Then you know that in the beginning were the children of God. The serpent's seed spawned also from the beginning, but from disgrace, which still marks the bobbejaan making themselves Baas nowadays. And it's the same between the simple kaffirs out here and the big ones that speak with you only in English.

Do you know I once heard a man who'd gone out there on some line of business, way out there – to some bush country in Africa, where civilization never made it past the birth canal – anyway this man told me life was so cursed out there they even have a sort of rabid disease that attacks you merely by speaking its name. I mean, if that's not God having something to say, then I don't know what.

But back to your question. Yes. I remember. We were used to a certain kind of visitor then, after the fall of the Republiek. Americans mostly. Some Australians. They all came here looking for something, something snuffed out wherever was home. To tell you the truth, I think a lot of them came here to puff out their chests, to look at old verkrampte Boers like me and feel themselves a more upright man. The rooineks were the funniest. They would stand behind the cameraman, stepping back there between takes, on the prowl for this thing they have in the head about the veld and the Boer:

irreligious kaffir-enslavers that we are, ploughing an open sea of arid farmland, blowing our nose through thick skin on bare fingers.

Then would come the questions. Statements really, alluding to our dying language and hopeless cause.

–A stand-alone Boer Republiek? they would repeat.

–In South Africa? they'd ask again.

No, jou dom donner! In the moist warm farts of your Royal Highness. Dries Van de Duidenstee got so uptight with a reporter like this once, he marched the Englishman and his crew to the border of our town without even a water bottle between them for the whole trek back to the nearest dorp, forget back home. We didn't see a visitor like that again for another while. Not until the Steenkamps sent an emergency signal, calling in for help. They thought they were under attack.

You will laugh now when you see the man mistaken for an attacker, but it was nothing to laugh about in those days. The bobbejaans were out to finish the last white indigenous tribe of Africa, farm by farm. And there was nothing to stop it. Nothing. So we armed ourselves. Just like the old days. And we learned our people who the enemy was. How to finish him. We weren't laughing when we heard the Steenkamps' signal, my friend. Not with that news about Bertie Bezuidenhout already. About how it went with his family.

Bertie Bezuidenhout's hands weren't wide enough to go around a sack of mielies, but believe you me when I say it – that little undertaking of a man had oxen blood sweating through his pores. The other boys used to tease him when they all started smelling themselves, but young Bezuidenhout was already the quiet sort. He would just lean against the wall, thin arms crossed over chest, saying less and less out his mouth as his opponents grew longer and boxier beside his frame. It took maybe three or four dom kops a good and wholesome donner before word spread wide among even the older ous: Bertie Bezuidenhout was nobody's eight-toed tortoise. He had pure unfiltered Afrikanerdom beating through his heart. He could take any man.

And unlike the others, Bertie came home. He found him a capable girl in Potchefstroom and fetched them here – on the same land the Bezuidenhouts have tilled since our grandfathers' fathers lost heart at the Slag van Spioenkop. Bertie extended the old house to make room for his family. He even added a flushing outhouse for the competing rugby teams his farm hands seemed hell-bent brooding. That's just how Bertie Bezuidenhout was. A Christianly good man, as the Dominee would say.

He was only 29 when those bastards wasted him. Cowards, these assassins. Five men to one. Laying low in tall grass like dogs. Bertie on his knees in the Lord's House. Mouth open wide – receiving the Holy Body, while those dogs stole onto his farm. A growth on Bezuidenhout land. First they did to his earth what they later did with him. Tied down in the dirt we found him. Ploughed into soil. We found Bertie Bezuidenhout's panga standing right there, next to him, feeling very sorry for what had been done with it. His garden boy ran out soon as he seen Bertie's truck back from Kerk, tried to warn Bertie, Turn around Baas, not safe here. Turn around. But the tsotsis were quick, the land already surrounded.

At least he didn't die on his knees, we said, seeing two of the dogs lying there, one of which we finished ourselves. Lying, lifeless. In wait. Waiting for police who always come only after, to stand around.

–Ja, the policeman said, Almal dood.

–No, says Bezuidenhout's wife. Not Bertie.

But he was going home. Unsoiled in his spirit. We found him with the Holy Body still in his. On his tongue the Dominee had placed it. Bertie Bezuidenhout had swallowed the entire thing whole. Unbroken. His wife and klein kinders were with him to his end. Watching.

The man the Steenkamps mistook for an attacker turned

out the first cyvivor, as we call them now. We went from
dismissing him as a crazed American bloated on too many
McBurgers, to something of a never-ending Vakansie Man.
Then, eventually, after news reached us in the papers,
we took a real interest in this Cyberwar Refugee. But the
cyvivors always resisted that name. Sounds too much like
Africa, I suppose, even though the government said Africa,
having never really been inter-webbed, is the one true refuge.
There are lots more safe towns they said, but without the
creature comforts the cyvivors crave. And further, way out
there. Up, past the hippos of Limpopo, past Zim, Vic Falls,
the man-eating crocs of Mozambique, beyond all that. Real
bushman country. And I told you already what is what, in
those deep jungles farted straight out a blind bat's bum.

Leon Steenkamp – who ran away from his land, leaving
his poor vrou with a man then taken for an attacker – later
told us the story he got from this American. It went like so:

The man was from America. I already said. From one of
its big cities where people live in skyscraper buildings so
that your kitchen and toilet don't have any windows and
your neighbour can be a man living with another man, as
his wife. Leon Steenkamp didn't ask our American friend if
he lived in such arrangements, had such neighbours. If he
knew what filth they did. But we of course get a general sense
from things the TV says, from similar nonsense on the radio.
Steenkamp did ask him what kind of gun he favours, since
we all know carrying is a natural fact of his culture. The
American was a funny one though. Steenkamp told us how
soft putty he got around a simple 9mm even a child knows to
handle. Leon Steenkamp was so tickled he cocked the empty
pistol to his own head – it was only in fun – but not before
the American took off, into the dark, without even a proper
Goeie Nag.

The thing Steenkamp asked when he started this story
was how much we knew of viruses. Well, many of the kerels
didn't like this at all. They took it as insult, asking a farmer

who carried the tribal memory of rinderpest in his stoop, a man who nursed his kraal through bluetongue virus, lamsiekte, Rift Valley and everything else in between; asking such a man, What is the meaning of a virus? It was just the last of Steenkamp's nerve.

–What is a virus? Lennie Jaeger yelled. It's the three letter certificate your daughter brought home from her high living, my friend.

Of course, Steenkamp's face reddened, but he just tucked his warbling wattle into his chest, managing a slight flare of his nostrils. It was cruel, Jaeger dragging up the dead girl.

When she grew her womanhood, we all pretended a healthy boredom. But on Sundays during prayers or weekdays, watching girls' matches sullying the rugby fields, we all wondered with our eyes how grazing the back cleavage of her knees would feel.

She returned home to die. Killed by ferocious gossip or the ugly and fleshly things they say she did in big towns. That shut Steenkamp right up. But you know how it is with a leopard and his spots. It wasn't long before he found something new to know about. That man just has a way with living skin – he always crawls under its weight. So you can understand Jaeger's callousness. Not undeserved. It just sped up the curdle in Steenkamp's story. He spoke simple and quick after that. But I read it in the papers what Steenkamp was trying to say:

American authorities have issued a statement urging the public not to panic. The situation is under control. The City of New York remains without water. The city's Department of Environmental Protection confirmed attackers gained root access to their computer systems and issued a series of commands, essentially shutting all water valve chambers throughout the metropolis. A spokesperson could not be reached for further comment or to provide an estimate of how soon New Yorkers can expect running water.

It was a regular shit show out there. I mean, you read these things wanting to shake your head and suck your teeth a bit, feel a decent level of sympathy for these sorry bastards, but instead you ended up with stiff laughter choking through your throat, imagining the world's so-called superpower being run by generals who considered a few weeks' toilet pile-up a legitimate war attack. Imagine where we'd be if General de la Rey or Paul Kruger cried war against the Brits every time a few chamber pots overwhelmed our nostrils, or if the Brits orchestrated a giant enemy pile-up so high even the Oranje Rivier refused to swallow.

Of course, cyvivors didn't like this kind of talk. No, my friend. Not one bit did they like it. To them it was full-on war, this thing. And it is true they were thirsty during these water holdouts. I heard a man say he paid a scary sum to a petty overlord for a few litres from the local park, when their money still meant something. His wife then boiled that pisswater for their baby, who couldn't do on strict rations.

Another early cyvivor looked like a tender little girl recalling how the cyber-drought shut his family restaurant down.

–Four generations, he whispered.

A great-grandfather started the eatery in his great grandma's name, using this oumagrootjie's recipes. On the last day of service, the little water they had was knocked over accidentally.

–We cooked that shit in wine, he said, thumping the table with big, useless hands. Bottles and bottles of fine Italian wine. Never tasted anything better. We tried fighting back. But there is no fighting an enemy you cannot see. Nothing you can do but walk away... We walked away. Four generations and just like that – he snapped his fingers. We upped and walked away.

Into Africa.

They came almost by truckloads after that first Steenkamp American. Smuggling themselves into Mexico and hijacking docked cruise ships. Bribing pirate carriers, some UN flights even. The Italians and Spaniards, we hear, even reverse engineered the Mediterranean fucked-fish-in-a-rowboat route. I mean, picture that on the high seas – a bunch of sunfried Diegos and Ave Marias sardined into a sinking raft, praying their way from Sicily to Libya. It really was as late summer flock – each one pecking about, as if forever – until every one seemed to understand through some giant cobwebbed birdbrain: winter is here, only flight will save us.

By then, nobody found these first world refugees in Africa queer. Especially not with all the bribecrack they'd brung – heirloom seeds sewn between hemlines, Cuban tobacco leaves and medicine packs glued under second shoe soles. Even rare carpets and diamonds stuffed into soft children's toys. That shameful spazashop, the one Coenie's widow barely propped up even while sitting on all the money three husbands left behind, finally found some legs to stand on. The old maid was even talking about adding an addition to the place.

–An addition? I asked, What would you sell in an addition, Tannie?

A milky glare followed that question, so I knew to take my tobacco from the counter and head straight out the same door I came.

The next time I'm in the shop, the widow has lined the shelves with glass jam jars wearing silly hats when regular canned All Gold would do just fine. Black coffee can't be plain good brew anymore, it has to be God's own beans imported from the killing fields of Rwanda. I know better than to ask the skelm old vrou, What is all this kak about? And is it just me wondering what is what with all this birdfood? With the cheeky prices?

That's how it was in the beginning. A temporary inconvenience, we told ourself. A now open and just now-now finish pitstop, while these First Worlds sorted theyself out. Or at least that's how we thought things were, until it came out, and I can't remember who pulled the snot out the rot, but it came out Steenkamp should have bliksemed that American with his kak-stories first chance he got.

Remember how Steenkamp found him farting around his plaas? How he spoeked the jiggle out Leon Steenkamp's arse so that Steenkamp hit the panic button and ran off for help, fat flying all over the place? Well, my friend, turns out that's all the time it took for the American to make his move on Steenkamp's wife. That old visvrou might as well've sprouted bird wings on her fishscales, so full she became of this American's nonsense – this and that he could do for they land, stars and such he could grow with his hands. She was half near trading Steenkamp's farm for Mr America's applesauce and pie in the sky. Of course, we didn't know this then, when we first showed up at Steenkamp's farm, guns at the ready.

You should have seen Steenkamp, still panting from the effort lugging hisself, now-now realizing the thing he just done to his wife: leaving her standing there with what very well could have been a blerry kaffir with a gun; now also catching the thing on her face that asked without speaking, What man are you, Leon Steenkamp? What manner of man fetches others to call man, to do for his wife what he can't hisself?

–There, Leon points, pointing out the foreigner. That's him. Shoot him!

We laugh seeing Leon's supposed attacker, hold our guns at ease. Steenkamp eventually shakes Mr America's hand, orders his wife pour us a round of spook and diesel.

Speaking of action, there was finally enough to this cyber thing to actually grow a hard-on. Our town was overrun with sissies, moegies that imagined living with a week's pile-up hardship. But suddenly, we started getting volk a man could understand. A power grid blew up, killing thousands of civilians within the hour. The big guns was beginning to doubt a bunch of ululating beards hiding under turbans could pull off a remote-control war on the US and her bedfellows from some cave in What-not-stan.

Fingers wagged. Korea? Syria? Khomeini? Who else counted for a Terminator? China? Russia? I didn't know all the what is what, but I do know my one plus one: youngsters in a pride take their chances when the alpha shows weakness. I never seen a musthing bull take kak from a dying olifant. Babylon was a plump worn whore, ripe for the taking.

Chinaman mastermind or not, real volk were dying real deaths in the cyberwars. Piet Niemand and his family took in a girl whose life dissolved in waters that drowned her house. A flood ran straight in from a dam enemy malware raped. The water swam off with her mother. And she was one of the better ones. The fog-heads that came after her were worser than anything I seen on the South West-Angola line. And those were some blerry bosbefok ous. Situation Normal All Fucked Up, we called it – SNAFU.

Back then, back in the 80s on the South West Africa border line, we had one ou couldn't get a word out of him that wasn't singing. And all kindergarten rhymes. Those of us felt sorry enough learned the funny nonsense he'd sing:

Mary Had A Little Lamb – Armed enemy approaching
Humpty Dumpty Sat On A Wall – Ambush ahead, landmine
Two Little Birds Sitting On A Tree – Civvie spies out sussing
Old McDonald Had A Farm/And On That Farm He Had A…
Gook! Civvies hiding gooks

I admit, there was something vroulike about him. Smith, they called him. Ian Smith. Always managed to eat from his dixies with both the fork and the knife. Patted his mouth clean with a small white square he hand-washed nights, even out in the bush. The desert dyed it that pus-rust colour which bled through sunsets; sunsets that seemingly choked the sky they were so overwhelming. Like swallowing dust.

But you could always leave it to Smith, seeing something there was nothing to see. Saving a grace, where no man lived. I got into more than one fight with the thicker skulled parts of the platoon, defending Smith. The cheapest kak was the obvious – punishing him for his Rhodesian namesake's busted nuts. Crooning about the monkey parade Smith handed Rhodesia to. President Canaan Banana! That's who the kaffirs elected when Ian Smith cowered. I mean, what sort of illiterate half-bakes? You can't even cook up such kak. A President Canaan Banana? But that's what the kaffirs wanted. So our Ian Smith, poor ou, became the cow's arse in all these laughing farts about Ian Smith selling out old Rhodesia, Ian Smith bending over for a black banana.

–Raped by the Black Banana, they'd taunt a already bush-fucked Smith.

He'd try ignore. Was all he could do. But me, it bothered me. Stirred rattling dis-ease in me. It couldn't be because I was just. I'd be lying if I thought myself just. Plenty goodly Christian volk wouldn't speak to me still today, I suspect, accounting who and what I was, back at the border. And who could blame them? It wasn't that. More the madness of the thing. Posting a blerry stampling of manhood like Smith into the border, not barely a man-child. It bothered me in the strange way things come outside you and you don't have words for the things, just feel their rage in your fist, taste their thick thirst, seeing blood. They knew to leave Smith alone on my platoon, but I couldn't say what happened after his callback to another unit. Couldn't say what Smith made of it all, if he made it out at all.

The bush fucked you. Made you FUBAR. Somehow, all of us – we was totally Fucked Up Beyond All Recognition. Did I dream, sleeping?

No sleep five days straight.

I'd lie under nights, closing my eyes that were theirs, but they refused closings. Stiff eyelids died unshut. I couldn't close them. Shut my ears, face in elbows. Heard strange cry. The bush enjoyed this. Making jackals laugh. Vultures sing.

Breakfast was ostrich eggs. They threw in stale brake shoe biscuits that morning. Chomped down. Read Ma saying she'll write. Told Pa to say, to write, Bly Sterk My Seun, and to say also she'll write. The letter arrived 336 hours ago. Folded. Refold.

Read the familiar writing, dribbling yellow yolk on the same page Ma eyed over Pa's shoulder: Ma standing over Pa, tin-teacup in hand. In the kitchen. Wearing that pale green pinafore with frilly shoulders, deep pockets. Stroking Pa's neck. Trying not to worry. I'll write, she says. Tell him I'll write. Smell the cinnamon under her nails, lingering in her pores from the melkkos on the table. Pa spoons a mouthful. Plops the milky custard on this paper. Finger the stain where I fold it again. Place under my thoughts. Lying awake.

–*Whu-whu-whuuu...*

–*Whu-whu?*

–*Whu-whu-whuuu*

What is that? Ostriches deep gobbling out there?

A small nomadic herd used to circle our farm. Ma hated full moons. They'd come out, the ostriches, pecking about. Naturally, we kids wanted out too. Chasing wild ostrich. Have you ever done that? I catch one as I wake, grateful for first sleep.

You got used to it. To dust lining your gum. Elephant virgins on bread, no butter. You even got used to taking a shit in go-karts, the ou in the next buggering you for a fag. It was put to us that we were making advances on the rooi-gevaar, that twenty-man dugout pile ups and lust in our nuts was worth it. We were winning the war.

But Listen, Kommandant said. Luister. Rooi-gevaar is dangerous. It is a wild, unwieldy thing. You have to get it into your head. You will be fighting the enemy, but with good kaffirs on your side. You will be fighting with black South Wests on your side. They are natural trackers, natural bushfighters. Our blacks must help us track the enemy. The black man is not your enemy. I looked to my left then tried out for the right. We men from my unit stood listening, mealy-mouthed at Kommandant.

It was a first. And for me, the last. The quarters were

small. Two open showers. Twenty-four men. One mess hall. Twenty-four men. Around the camp on quiet days. Keeping guard overnight. There was nowhere else to put them, so there we were: all twenty-four bodies stripping naked. Soaping. Washing off soiled blood. Twenty-four mouths moving, chasing down dog biscuits with the same disgust and relish. All our arses plastered to the go-karts when cooks fucked an order, so we all, each of twenty-four, suffered as a unit from leaky gypo guts. It rocked us, understanding this thing. Who was us? Who was them? The terrorists was secreted in the land. A man could understand that. Our job was to finish them. Wipe the land clean. Of rooi gevaar – commie alert. Of swaart gevaar – black terrs. But. And nobody can stand there now, saying I got weak. But struzebob. God as my witness. My blacks – the blacks in our unit – it was because of them. Land and duty were no longer simple things.

I see now the 80s was simpler. Looking back I see black and white. Any blind fool could show you that. But this thing these First World know-alls have they dicks smothered in? Viral computer infections blowing up dams? Root commands raping entire intelligence systems? What does a soldier suppose, to fight such a thing? How is a man supposed to protect his property – vrou, farm and kinders – except to pack it all in and leave? You left no choice but you pull the plug. Literally. That's what people who know more than even the know-alls are now-now advising the States and the States' chommie-countries. But you know what houtkop is – hard headed. They still talking Situation Normal, Under Control; not from how we seen it. Every day, the cyvivors. They keep coming. Droves of them – human droplings out Babylon's rear.

And what started small – the cheeky spazashop prices, the harmless halfway stop our town became, even our Samaritan welcome and goodly cheer – seems to me a growing cancer. Can't step out a day without hearing another story of cyvivors outsmarting a Boer his entire farm – flock, stock and bride. At first, a fur coat traded for a little patch of earth, then suddenly the kraal also for some hardy heirloom seed the foreigner hisself once tended, until entire farms switched hands for a few cases of rum, some rare ammunition and a kak promise, leaving Boere families squatters in their own fatherland. The situation is bad. Made worse by spineless Boers arse-creeping 'round the refugees.

Even Johannes Van de Merwe, I heard him say he don't mind them. But Johannes, I say. You mean to tell me you can't see what's really going on?

–Like what? Says Johannes.

So I drop it right there, counting him out of the laarge.

I know what's got the balls of good men like Johannes. It's not just the flash of fur and nifty little shiny things. The cyvivors came spinning all sorts of sugared smoke and technicolour dreams they'd build for the goodest Boers. Just lend us an ear, it started. Okay, now share us your wife. You're a good man, but if you want that pie in the sky we're baking, if you really want the kind of special kak only our glittered promises can afford, let's talk about this land. You know we may have lost everything, but these seeds we brung, they like magic beanstalk seeds. We can grow this thing together. In a single year, your yield could triple.

And the Johannes Van de Merwes of this world – good, Christianly dense man that he is – it wouldn't occur to his likes to doubt. To read the signs. Van de Merwe I know for a fact signed papers making his land they silly experiment. Like the big-dicked manchild he is, he goes around believing these cyber-fucked Americans want what's best for his land. That they share his dream. I even hear they promised him, if they can ever flush their shit again, a trip to the lights and lunacy of New York.

Van de Merwe thinks he's the only one heard of New York? The only one dreamed of another life? That's just the problem with the Van de Merwes of this world. They never seen it coming when it comes. I knew a luckless bastard like this once. Left him right where I found him. At the border.

Enoch Omugulugwombashe could tell you feral stories buried in the bush. Secret things, laden in the land. Just looking at dirt, he could tell. Sifting sand between fingers, he'd point out evidence of a scorpion the night before, a wood dove that dawn or where a pompilid wasp drugged and buried a dancing white lady spider after impregnating her with wasp eggs. He once showed me fresh spoors on the track. Pointing, he detailed to a hair – the sex, size and weight of a kudu. Knew exactly what it was feeding on, how far to expect before reaching it. I wasn't surprised at the fat bok we braaied that night, feasting for a change on sweeter meat than tin stuff and water-fed dog biscuits which swelled into porridge.

Enoch was our tracker. A natural tracker. Natural bushfighter. He told me he was a schoolteacher before the war came. Spoke clean Afrikaans, English and German even. Also his kaffir taals. I kept my distance at first. But in the bush, like I say, a man is only as strong as his unit. And Enoch grew on you.

Out on our jaunts tracking gooks, you couldn't even tell who was who. With my Black is Beautiful smeared on good and lekker, and Enoch already born in camouflage, all you seen is four eyes above, sixty and four teeths below. Even on days off sometimes I'd wear the black face, just for shits and giggles with the phuzas at the local shebeen.

Once, we was driving supplies between camps. Me, another bloke and Enoch. The gooks planted landmines everywhere, so you drove off-road. I don't remember why, but we wasn't in a casspir that time. Anyways, there we is. Me and these two ous. We'd just flushed a Terr-stronghold out, so we expected the enemy about, on defence.

We come to a clearing with no shoulder. There's nowhere else to go but inside the road. So we steady the vehicle and drive. Slow. Kick up some dust. Enoch is our eyes and ears. A natural manhunter with a nose like a dog. Sniffs landmines out like a Soek-steek-stok on steroids. More than once Enoch shifted my arse in gear, saving me from a blast even as I fingered that Soek-steek-stok into the ground. Anyways, we are going-going, nice and easy on the road when sudden as sin, Enoch calls for a piss parade. We tease him – the bladder of a knocked-up visvrou on this one – but come to a stop. He dismounts to let his leak. I light up and have a piss myself. Driver still at the wheel.

Without a word, Enoch walks back to me and motions I finish. Danger, he whispers, Make fast. Obvious, I cradle my gun. No, he shakes his head, Not Terrs. He waves me with his hand. I follow. Standing in our path – body lifted, head high to the heavens, all dressed in neck flap now spread wide – is a black mamba. Jirrre-God! I bite my tongue. A foken blerry snake? Seeing the serpent, its black mouth hissing death, I know we could be done. Even if the Tampax Tiffies came quick with the meds, a man has under a hour before that venom expires him. Just my blerry luck, I think, reading the moggie epitaph:

Killed In Action. Fell To A Bush Snake.

Enoch motions again, Get in the vehicle. I hop in. Keeping hisself facing the devil-snake, Enoch walks back. Painfully slow. I tell the driver by now, so he starts the engine. Still, the snake standing. Enoch turning. Finally inside.

What happens next is we drive forward, toward the snake. But instead of grinding the mamba, rubber to reptile, Enoch insists we curve around its path, a wide girth to the snake. The driver is reluctant, and I'm getting annoyed. But Enoch persists, We don't kill mamba, he says. Bad luck. Killing mamba? Very bad luck. We hiss and we tease. Kaffirs and their witchcraft. Enoch laughs also. Strange, isn't it? How funny it was – just three ous in a bakkie, laughing stupid along the border.

Enoch had three little ones. Still remember they names. Helvi, Martta, Maria. His dream, he told me, was going home after the war, getting God to finally bless him with a son.

I didn't have kinders. But I knew what it was for a man to bring his family to you out in the bush. So I told Enoch the one truth with any meaning for me. He is the only man I ever tell my dream.

I wasn't supposed to. Pa would have blixemed me if he found out. News they were coming spread mouth to mouth. Even Dominee seemed to know what day they would be in our town and the sordid things this promised for his flock. So we were warned. I snuck out only because the herd needed tending winter nights. I put on my stepping-out Sunday shirt and slacks underneath the weathered coat I always wore. Hoped nobody noticed instead of veldskoene, I'd repolished my school shoes all afternoon. I slipped out after dinner, as expected, but in place of the kraal, I headed for the big tent.

It was windy. And true to our town that time of year, a cold night. I gave the man all my money saved from odd-jobs and he handed me a ticket. Inside the tent the show was already on. The painted elephants and talking monkeys we had plenty of in those parts, I wasn't interested. The funny little dwarfs were so weird you had to laugh. You have to remember television wasn't a thing for us back then. All we knew was the radio and even that kept everything Dominee-dusted.

We didn't know exotic, never mind you freakery. The bearded fat vrou so space-eating she had to be carted to stage enticed our wonder, her roly-poly arms and legs threatening to tip the wheelbarrow. The snake charmer with his strange song deserved our applause, we thought. And those mooilike girls with naked bellies, dancing like inside them lived a snakepit – they alone would have been worth my money. Except, I seen that night this man they call Ring Master.

He had on a tall impressive hat and those bowtie suits with a big smooth waistband. He held his stick very sure of hisself. Without him the whole thing would have crumbled. It was stupid, I knew it even then. As soon as I seen him, he was my dream. Pa would've moered me. But when I told Enoch my plan to head for die Kaap or Jo'burg maybe, after we left the border – that I wanted to wear a tall hat and learn the circus – he didn't laugh at me. I was shy about it, he could see. But still. He made me feel the stupid thing I wanted was maybe not so stupid. Why not put the Kommandant and his snakes in your show, he teased?

Kommandant fetched live ones out in the bush every chance he got. Stuffed them in a plastic bag he hung in the sun. The writhing bastards were kaput without fail by 1200 hours. From heat exhaustion or lack of hydration. I don't know. We clinked beer bottles, laughing to this. To life after war.

After the war, the fighting went on. We pulled out from the border, but you know how it is with kaffirs and their tribal wars – like a spineless beast chasing its tail.

Here, back home, things slowly grew stranger. Hairy. Fucked up, beyond any and all recognition. On the final end of the Republiek, in 1994, I remembered the thing the Kommandant had spoke: The black man is not your enemy. Nobody said this when we were discharged, unthanked for our service. Our leaders made their dealings with kaffir kings, while we were left standing under the flag, trying to fly marred colours. The black man is not your enemy. That's how the leaders justified handing our fatherland to the enemy they learned us, the same enemy they fetched us to the border to finish. None of it made any sense. And when you stood up to ask how this thing should be remembered – what were we doing at the border? That rainbow kak was forced down your throat. The same ubuntu gobbledygook these American cyvivors and related refugees are now-now singing to better pull the wool over our eyes.

Of course, everyone would rather deny it, pretending the likes of this old Boer a conspiracy theory, but the ordinary truth of the fact is that while this cyberwar goes on, confusing the world, American cyvivors and they friends is busy colonizing the last white indigenous tribe of Africa. Why you think these cyvivors is here, kidnapping our land? Why you think they fill the shelves in our shops with food a Boer can't pronounce, and force Afrikaans out of our kinders' classrooms because there's so goddamn many of them, suddenly here to stay?

Yes, my friend. The Americans is here to wipe us. I wouldn't be surprised if the African National Cronies is behind the whole thing with them. Paying the Americans, even. People think I'm going foggy in the brain, pointing out the obvious. I hear they monkey chatter, whispered behind my back, but you mark my words. And I'll tell you another thing. There will be no cyvivor-style walking away from here. Our names is written in the ground. Like I said that day to Johannes Van de Merwe: We will be fossilized in this here earth. It drinked our fathers' blood. Our fate is this land.

Anyway that's not what you really want to know, asking all innocent and official how it all started. You're here arse-creeping for what happened that day. About what is its why.

Well, it was just another braai at the spazashop celebrating our tribelessness. Nobody marks Van Riebeck Founders' Day anymore. Or remembers how, on the Day of the Vow, the Lord made good His covenant with us, delivering the Zulus to our oupagrootjies' barrels. Instead, we are hostage to everything foreign-born, pulling out all stops for they blerry Bastille Days and heathen Halloweens. And since the new addition, and what with her enabling customers, the old widow feels herself way up in the sky – a fat kite, flying thin on they high life.

Everybody came from our town and beyond. The Big Five already sizzling on the grill: Boerewors. Porkchops. Chicken. Steak. Mutton cuts. Enough Castle beer to row these blerry cyvivors back over the seas. Even some respectable and lethal mampoer – the widow still brews it on the sly. We make normal kak-talk, How's the wife? Which Springbok is gonna moer what's left of the All-Blacks? What new direction is the government pissing in these days?

Somebody taps my shoulder, like we did in Standard One. They duck they head when I pass a look back. Grown men playing games. I turn round. But it's a mooilike lady when I seen who it is. Up from die Kaap, she says. Smiling. Real friendly. Welcoming tits in my face. I smile back. She's some Boere's daughter. I've seen her around. But they grown up so quick. Trying to remember, whose daughter is this? She's talking-talking:

–Brought somebody I want you to meet, Oom. She says.

Wish now I'd said no.

–This is Themba

Or cleared my throat maybe, just walked away...

–Themba Ngcobe.

I extend a hand. He's standing right beside her.

–He was there also, Oom.

–There?

Where, I want to know?

–Told him about you. How you were also at the border.

I feel the man's hand. It isn't hard like a soldier, like what you expect. Not smooth either. Deep ridges run there, like Kimberley's Groot Gat is carved in his palm. I let go his hand, but can't with his gaze. The girl keeps yakking, saying things I know just undressing his eyes: Gook. They stare back at me. Gook. Her voice trails into wind, sweeping up around us.

Gook, The wind answers.

'Foken Terr.' I hear myself shouting, barking so loud dust bites down my tongue. The eyes stare back at me. Accusing eyes. Inside this Themba Ngcobe are Enoch's eyes. I tell myself that's kak talk, Enoch died many years ago at the border. But I keep seeing him – Enoch staring back at me with unbelieving eyes. Already dead eyes. Or deadened.

That day at the border, Enoch's eyes begged for no plea. Prayed no mercy. Seemed only to mirror me my own unblinking fear. Staring through me. Kommandant stands akimbo, beside me. The entire platoon, twenty-two men – a bosbefok large – stand around us.

Enoch had been a man of the Bible. Learned me verses he knew in German. During contact with the enemy, it calmed me, speaking them. Inside my head, I'd say them to myself. Hear Enoch correct me. Tea-re, he'd say, slow. Gurgling the re.

Und ich werde die bösen Tiere aus dem Lande vertilgen, und das Schwert wird nicht durch euer Land gehen. And I will give peace in the land, and ye shall lie down, and none shall make you afraid: and I will rid evil beasts out of the land, neither shall the sword go through your land.

When I asked Enoch, Why? Was what Kommandant said really true? How could he betray us to the Terrs? How could he betray even me? Enoch brung me his family again: Helvi, Martta, Maria. And his wife. He said he couldn't watch them bow they heads forever in they own land. Couldn't let us do with them and they children's children what we'd done with his father, his father's fathers. I listened because I thought he'd say I'm sorry. That Kommandant must be blerry bosbefok calling him a enemy spook. After all the times he saved me? The many mines he saved us? But Enoch spoke nothing of sorry. Denied niks nie. And when he brung up the wife and his daughters, that he couldn't be a man watching them bow they heads like his mother and his father, I feel my head fog up again. The bush fucked with you, made you feel you almost understand why Enoch made hisself a poison in your own platoon. Kommandant shouted the order. My hand shook. Enoch watching my eyes flood, blank, drown.

I didn't hear myself speak the German Bible. Enoch was so close he heard me. Before I pulled the trigger, I tripped on the same word I always did. Tea-re. Enoch corrected me. His eyes remained fixed on me, even after. They refused to close.

The man with Enoch's eyes, Kimberley's Groot Gat mined into his palms, says nothing when I walk away. The Boeremeisie he came with, the one with a healthy chest, she calls out. I walk past my car and the others' cars. Turn down old streets. Streets walked all my life – the known world I returned to after the border. I pass the same leafless kokeboom that surely witnessed my birth from this earth. Remembers the founding of our town, how naked bushmen received my ancestors underneath its shade. I pass the few houses. Lights on. Hear alien tongues spoken inside Cape-Dutch homes. I reach my house eventually, begin the effort of stilling myself. Kommandant used to say power is not aggression. It is control inside calm. I sit. The television watching. Lights still off. Heat gathering in my palms. Before I finish reciting, remembering the verse, I wall my hand against my mouth, rushing for the toilet.

Magogodi oaMphela Makhene's work has appeared in *Ploughshares* and Elie Wiesel's *An Ethical Compass*, and has been recognized by the NYU Reynolds Program for Social Entrepreneurship, the Elie Wiesel Foundation for Humanity and the Truman Capote Fellowship at the Iowa Writers' Workshop, where she earned her MFA. Magogodi is a recipient of the David Relin Prize for Fiction and is currently working on a collection of interwoven stories exploring the inner lives and loves of ordinary South Africans. She is a proudly Soweto-made soul. 'The Virus' was first published in *The Harvard Review 49* (Houghton Library, Harvard University, US, 2016).

The Caine Prize
African Writers' Workshop Stories 2017

Fidel

Agazit Abate

1. I should have known that it wasn't going to work out when he told me that he suffered from chronic constipation. While I don't know about the regularity of Fidel's bowel movements, especially after the advent of his intestinal issues, I believe now that it was a sign from God when my guy revealed that he struggled with releasing his excrements. It is impossible to be truly free and therefore any kind of suitable partner if you cannot, with a certain degree of regularity, liberate your bowels.

The worst part about it is that he did nothing to cure his condition. In comparison, I'm not going to make a list of all of the things that Fidel did to find solutions to his problems. My guy only remembered his ailment when he was in discomfort. Even then, he ate meat whenever he could get it, loved pasta for dinner and wouldn't touch gomen. If I pushed him hard enough, he would agree to swallow telba. But generally, he put himself at the mercy of a troubled gut, perpetually waiting for shit to happen.

2. A person doesn't end a relationship over constipation alone. Reason number two, we stopped kissing. If I knew that the last time we kissed would be the last time, I would have paid more attention to it. In truth I can't remember what the last time felt like, how long it lasted, where or even when it took place. He was a good kisser though. Kissing was never our problem. I stopped kissing him because I wanted to spare him the anguish of a cold.

When he had a cold, he didn't stop kissing me. He offered; I kissed him anyway. I made ginger tea and swallowed honey that night, but I kissed him still. It wasn't so much that I wanted to kiss him, but more that I didn't want to not kiss him because of a cold. Two months later, when I began to feel a scratchiness in my throat and when he leaned in to kiss me, I turned away and, like the selfless martyr that I am, said, 'I think I'm getting a cold. I don't want to get you sick.'

He frowned, tightened his eyes and asked, 'Are you sure?' It was the kind of 'Are you sure?' that really meant, 'Please stay away from me'.

I affirmed and we sat down in our separate chairs facing each other at our favourite café instead of sitting side by side as was our habit. Aside from that and the fact that we weren't holding hands, everything else about that day was perfectly normal. I told him that my car was still with the mechanic and complained about the long lines waiting for a minibus. I shared my bewilderment at a woman who very confidently said 'weraj ale' less than a block after the previous stop. He blamed the intensity of the sun for her not wanting to walk 30 metres to her destination. I maintained my disapproval. He told me about his day. Work at the office was busy, he debated whether to eat at his desk or have lunch at a restaurant across the street from the bureau. He decided to go to the restaurant. He spoke about a man who was at the café before I arrived who told him that he is working on inventing a reminder app that beeps deadlines and partners you with people who can help you complete the tasks on your to-do list.

Two days after the day that we stopped kissing, Fidel died. I can't say that I was surprised. He was 90 years old with well-known health problems. I always knew that Fidel's death would be a defining moment in my life. I watched news programmes on TV, listened to the radio and read online articles waiting to hear the perfect words to sum up an extraordinary life, words that show that history has done much more than absolve him. Radio hosts spoke of Guad Fidel, the improbable revolution, his support of African liberation movements, his friendship with Mandela, the scholarships he provided for Ethiopian students to study in Cuba, and sometimes noted his alliance with Menge. One programme interviewed a professor at Addis Ababa University who used to be a member of Ihapa and who speaks like he remains a member of Ihapa. Still, he talked about the importance of the Cuban revolution as an inspiration for the student movement and recalled a revolutionary anthem,

Fano tesemara

Fano tesemara

Ende Ho Chi Minh

Ende Che Guevara

It was a respectable remembrance, but nothing came close to what I was looking for. It is possible that, in Fidel's perseverance, he outlived the people who would have best memorialized him.

In other news, what I thought was a cold ended up being allergies. He stopped kissing me because of dust. He believed that I had a cold, and I am the one who told him to stay away, but still, I had to leave him. There was no way that I could properly mourn Fidel while in a relationship with a man who would stop kissing me for fear of the sniffles.

3. There was nothing profoundly wrong with his reaction to Fidel's death, nothing contrary to how any self-respecting Third World subject would react. But, like everything else about him, it lacked feeling.

'Did you hear about Fidel Castro?' he asked.

'Yes.'

'He was old, but it's sad. There are no leaders like him in the world.'

'There are no men like him any more.'

I wanted to say that men today stay away from love for fear of a cold, but I didn't. I let him have his time of mourning. It was pretty standard, an average reaction really. He didn't cry. I didn't expect him to. He said it was sad, but he wasn't sad. He suggested the extent of the loss, but couldn't articulate the measure of a man. He posted 'hasta la victoria siempre guad Fidel' on his Facebook page with the same picture that many of our common friends posted of Fidel exhaling cigar smoke. I clicked like. It's what you do, public displays of mourning or celebration, whatever the situation calls for, to show what side of history you are on.

I fell in love with Fidel when I was 15 years old. My older cousin was studying at the university and took me with her one day. She left me in the library and, as I began looking through the books, I saw one called 'Radiant Gems of the World'. I opened it because, although the title suggested that the book was about gems, the cover picture was of a white man standing under a tree. In fact, it was a book about gems that included very few black-and-white pictures. Before I could close it, something fell to the ground. It was a picture of Fidel with his arm raised up seemingly addressing a crowd. I later learned that Che was in the original picture and it was taken by Alberto Korda after the victory in 1959. On the back of the picture was a barely legible handwritten note.

My love,

A reminder of what is possible. Until we win, Ethiopia forever.

Martha

13 April 1976

That was it. I took the picture home. Fidel was in my life, he lived and the world was full of possibilities.

After I heard the news of Fidel's death, I left the house to take a walk. A crazy man on the street yelled, 'There is no

truth in this world! In a world with no truth…' 'Aleweledem!'
I responded out loud. He looked at me like I had pushed
him off the stage of his own theatre. I returned his stare,
wanting to see what he would say next. Aleweledem. I read
the book in secondary school. I don't remember the details,
but the idea of not wanting to be born in a world without
truth appealed to me at that moment. I wanted to speak
to him, to ask him if he was referring to a world without
Fidel. He didn't seem interested in having a conversation
with me. I waited, thinking that he could give me the
answers that I was looking for, but then I remembered
that he is a crazy man. Crazy men in the streets don't like
women and always have one big rock at their disposal. I
continued walking.

4. We met five months ago at an outdoor daytime party.
He was with a group of his friends and I was with Meme.
I noticed him before he noticed me. He is conventionally
good looking in that, even if you were not attracted to him,
you could agree that he was attractive. He's tall, has broad
shoulders and a beard. I know how that sounds, but I am
almost certain that my attraction to facial hair has nothing to
do with Fidel, and women generally like tall men.

We made eye contact and he walked over to me. 'Konjiye,
can I get you another Ambo?' It was a joke; one Ambo is big
enough for one person. The opening line wasn't so original,
but he was cute and when he said it he had a half smile, chin
down and eyes up. I thought he was endearing.

We spent three hours together that day. Meme stayed
with us and so did his friends. They were funnyish and did
guragenga, tigringya and eskista to hip hop. He was also a
good dancer. Fidel didn't know how to dance.

In the five months that I was with him, I must have been
introduced to at least 50 people. Most of these were random
introductions. He would honk to a neighbouring car, 'nefse,
selam new?!' Then turn to me, 'he's a close friend, his brother

is Aster's neighbour and he once went to the same wedding that I did'.

With him, everybody was a close friend, but his were friendships based on chance, debt and favours. Melak works at Jupiter Hotel but has a side business selling car parts. Mohammed works at the AU, has lots of money, a wife and two girlfriends. Danny has two sino trucks hired out for imports to Addis and one moving truck that is available for friends. Aman works for Ethiopian Airlines and can check in your overweight luggage for free. I'm not sure what Elias does, but he gets discounted habesha bera in bulk through friends of friends. I can continue like this for at least five more close friends. If I took notes, I would be able to recall more. In school I always thought that it was easier to remember stories, much harder to remember lists.

In our time together, he revealed that he was friends with half the population of Addis, but never told me one story about a friend that alluded to love. He told me what they did for a living, sometimes how they met and always how they were useful. He never fought with his friends, or with anybody for that matter that I know of, and they spoke to each other only through random encounters or when they needed something from each other. They relied completely on the currency of convenience.

When asked by a journalist once about Che after his death, Fidel responded, 'I dream of him often'. A love letter in five words: I dream of him often.

5. I once told him that I dreamed my dead grandmother was flying in the sky with eagle wings asking me to come to Casablanca with her. He told me that he wasn't sure if he had dreams because he could never remember them. My grandmother used to say: 'Beware of men who don't dream. If they don't dream during the night, they are sleeping during the day.'

6. He takes selfies. I know it's not the worst thing that a person can do and no real reason to leave a relationship, but he takes selfies and Fidel died. It's a combination that is essentially untenable. Also, more than the selfies, it's the way that he looks at himself while he's taking the selfies. He squints his eyes as if blinded by the sun, inflates his chest and, unfortunately, I've seen that at times that there is also pouting involved. Sometimes he posts the selfies on Facebook; a selfie was once his profile picture. It's too much, I can't continue talking about this.

I can't explain how I could have let this happen and why I let it last five months. I don't mean to say that he is a bad guy, but lines were crossed. Sometimes it's good to move in spaces outside of your comfort zone, but a person can only take so much. I'm sure that being 28 years old and single with no marriage prospects in sight increased my openness to pursuing the relationship. At 28, I am right on the precipice of not being acceptable for a woman to leave a man for reasons that could be deemed frivolous. In truth, 28 may be too old, but that's okay too. Especially because the greater truth is probably that it is never okay for a woman to leave a man for reasons that could be deemed frivolous. In any case, Fidel is dead. I did what needed to be done.

Meanwhile, while my guy's taking selfies, Fidel asked that in the event of his demise, no streets be assigned or monuments built in his name.

7. When Fidel died, I didn't tell my guy the depth of my mourning. I didn't want to talk about Fidel with him and I didn't think that he would understand anyway. I'm trying to remember our conversations during the time that we were together. He wasn't interested in politics, history or art. He talked mostly about what he saw in front of him and about what he wanted in the future. He was saving money to build a ground plus three in CMC.

He spoke about nothing and I spoke about less. Our

conversations always glided on the shallow end of the water. Early on in the relationship I tried to share with him thoughts other than what happened during the day, but it seemed to be too much work for him. I think I began to say less because it was tiring for me as well. If I shared some of my more unusual thoughts, he would somehow shut me down with his disapproval. I am complicit. Had he known who I was and what I was really thinking, he would have ended things before I did. In any case, his 'friend' makes money by supplying women to international visitors, but when I told him that hearing the drums at church made me want to do eskista, he looked at me like I had forsaken the Lord.

8. In 1956, Fidel and the 81 other 26 of July movement members set sail on the *Granma* for a journey from Mexico to Cuba in order to begin guerrilla warfare against Fulgencio Batista. On the last night of the journey, a man fell overboard. The men searched for their comrade but could not find him. As the leader of the movement, Fidel told the men that they would continue searching, that they would leave no man behind. They stayed, endangered the mission, and found their brother.

One day we were driving on our way to dinner and we saw a car stalled on the side of the road. The driver was clearly agitated, leaning against the car talking on the phone. My guy looked and of course realized that he knew him. It was Zele, his close friend who had once helped his brother get a job and whose cousin used to go to secondary school with him. I suggested that he pull up in front of him instead of behind him so as to not exacerbate the already-heavy traffic. He kept driving. 'It looks like he's on the phone and probably has help on the way. I know you're hungry. Let's just go. I don't think he saw me.'

9. I think that I need to reiterate the loss of touch because it's not only that he stopped kissing me, but that he stopped holding my hand that day as well. There was no outbreak of a deadly and contagious disease. No signs of leprosy that I know of. It was allergies masquerading as a cold. I had no illusions that this was a fikir eske mekaber type of relationship, but when you stop holding hands due to a cold, there can be no hope for longevity. In truth, there should be no desire for longevity. It was too easy for him to disconnect, too easy to give in to fear and withhold affection. Sonia Sanchez said: 'There are things sadder than you and me. Some people do not even touch.' We were the saddest thing.

10. Five days after Fidel died, I left him for all of the reasons that I have mentioned. I could say in detail what happened when I broke up with him, but it was predictably uneventful. Sometimes when things come undone, they do so quietly. He was as absent in the breakup as he was in the relationship. He began to argue when I mentioned that he had stopped kissing me. 'You told me not to kiss you.'

I reminded him about the hand holding and almost began the 'we're just different people' bit, but I could see that it was a waste of time. It was over before it began. He quickly lost his energy and gave up. The constipation, I'm sure. I did mention Fidel's death. Not because I thought that he would understand, but because I wanted him to know what was at stake, that at one point in his life, there was a chance, a slight chance, for him to be loved by a woman who could break up with a man over the death of Fidel. I wanted him to know that Fidel died and we lost a whole world.

After I left him, I went to the café where we had stopped kissing. I sat on the patio and ordered a double white macchiato and a slice of banana bread. The sun was hot and the breeze was cool. I was watching the cars pass by when I saw it: a lone donkey running through the street. In this city, donkeys move slowly – they carry the world's burden on their backs and they always have an owner. I had never seen a liberated donkey and had no idea that they could move so fast. When I saw that donkey running with purpose past the driving cars, I knew that Fidel lives and that I had made the right decision.

Agazit Abate is the daughter of immigrants and storytellers. She lives in Addis Ababa, Ethiopia.

The Secret Language of Vowels

Abdul Adan

Dear Saltanat

I understand the unexpectedness of my letter. Please do not tear up this note. This isn't a love letter. In fact, I am no longer in love with you or anyone else. I wouldn't accept you now if you came running to me this minute. The missive you hold is about things a lot greater than that which could possibly have materialized between us or any two people. It is about the unspoken tragedy that, whether you believe it or not, is happening, has happened, and will happen to a number of people in this bleak world.

Every human being, say the civilized laws in this world, has the right to a decent life, and no human may enjoy abundance while others toil in hardship next door. Do not get me wrong lest you drift off into thinking that I have somehow been relegated to capitalism while the rest of you feed off the fruits of true socialism. I feel fortunate that I don't live under the former, but experience has also taught me that I do not belong in the latter. I belong in a world that allows everyone to create their own language. Not where one has to inherit the ways and tongues of one's parents.

I do not like your socialism. It is not for me. Yes, I said it. Feel free to show these words to everyone. Believe me, if Beria were alive today, I would encourage you to inform him of my blasphemy. I do not care one bit. He wouldn't do anything worse to me than what I am undergoing now. Not a single person, including those awaiting execution in crowded filthy cells, is going through the life I have been condemned to live.

The worst part about this is that I had no role whatsoever in the predicament I found myself in. If I had a hand in it I would be less depressed, for at least I would get to take comfort in the old adage about reaping what one had sown. There's comfort in the knowledge that your problems aren't entirely exclusive to you, that others somewhere have experienced or are experiencing the same thing, that the option of employing tried solutions, even temporarily, is available. Not so in my case. I have yet to meet a single person in this country with a problem similar to mine. I have asked around: in shops, hospitals, public squares, schools, and even among shepherds in the steppe. I can tell you right now that there's no one, possibly in this whole country, who thinks they share my curious predicament.

Now, just because one is unaware of a problem it doesn't mean it doesn't exist. It is like the devil that thrives among those who dismiss his existence. Just because you don't believe in God, it doesn't mean he won't call you to account in the next life. Yes, I said that too. Go shout it from the rooftops. Like I said, what can anyone possibly do to me at this point? I can feel your curiosity as I write this letter. You want to know what it is that has emboldened me so much. Me, the coward of cowards. I, who refused to participate in a freestyle contest in Almaty for fear of a long-dead Beria. Be patient, sweetheart. My struggle surrounds you wherever you go. You just aren't paying attention. It's in the words you speak, the books you read, the songs you listen to, and pretty much your entire engagement with the world. Yes, nearly everything around you holds some detail to do with my suffering. Even the signs on shops and buildings.

I won't torture you any further. My problem is simple. It's the cursed E. Remember when I rejected the beautiful and talented Aqerke and chose to pursue you, even though she was superior in every sense, as per your own admission? Remember? You seemed totally in disbelief then, throughout my pursuit. You kept asking about Aqerke, and whether, should you accept me, I would change my mind all of a sudden and replace you with her. You felt unworthy of the attention of one good enough to reject Aqerke, of all people. Forgive me if I am taking undeserved liberties with your narrative, but I felt it was obvious. Of course, this was way before you ran off with that fortunate fool Marat Sasykbaiuly. Anyway, long story short. I rejected Aqerke because of her name. Yes, her tedious, languid name that should have been declared illegal if there was such a thing as empathy and equality in this world.

You probably think me mad, like many have already. I suggest you use more of your imagination in understanding this. Remember that African story we read in our final year. You loved it, didn't you? Guess what? It was more than a story. The writer didn't randomly come up with the characters' names. He was speaking to a deeper truth about human language. We laughed at the names and language of the underground creatures in that story. But what didn't occur to us then was that the very rules used by that alien race to choose names are also necessary among humans to a lesser degree. I have reread that story at least ten times since. You've forgotten its title, haven't you? 'Chiukyulew' it was. Imagine if the title character's name was Saltanat? Would any one of his race survive repeating that name? He said it himself. Their fish mouths would tear at the edges if the vowel 'A' appeared anywhere in their language. As you very well know, there are good reasons why birds have hollow bones and zebras are striped. My tragedy, unlike Chiukyulew, is that my problem is shared by a very special few among our species. This is a near death sentence. There's no one to help me. No one to sympathize with me. Our world is filled with people too dishonest to admit their problems.

It is impossible that I am the only person who experiences mild nausea every time my name is called and who almost falls over on his face whenever the 'ke' suffix is added in the third-person form.

No, this is not an elaborate joke meant to arrest your attention. In fact, the last thing this could possibly be is a joke. So sit up, wipe your eyes, and pay closer attention to what I am on about. This is the last letter you will read from me. Ever.

Perhaps before tiring you with the details of my unique affliction, I should answer some of the questions you have raised in the past with regard to those unexplained moments of pointless decisions. I suppose you have always wondered why, at freestyle contest in Qorday, I exchanged my expensive trophy for an old Dombra that barely worked. To understand that behaviour (which by the way you called totally insane) you would have to consider the trophy. Now, what does its name have in common with Aqerke? You got it. It was the cursed E. A Zhetigen is just hurtful to me as Aqerke, and it was a matter of safety that I got rid of it at the earliest opportunity. I will remind you again of the mini-stampede at the Aitys tournament that was held in Zhambyl Ata's honor in Taraz in which a little boy named Serik Jeksenbaev died. I was in attendance and myself escaped by pure chance. I watched the poor boy get trampled. He had his right knee trapped between two women and fell on his face before a crowd of oblivious and sweating youth made him one with the ground. Believe it or not, Saltanat, (how I envy you for your name!) the boy died hours before the stampede. His fate was sealed by the end of the first session. His soul had already broken at the waist and was just in the process of severing itself from him completely when the stampede occurred. If he'd been my son, and assuming I had a name that sounded somewhat like yours and still possessed the knowledge I do now (an impossibility pretty much), I would not have brought him along in the first place.

There's no doubt that we have the most poetic language in the world. God knows why he burdened us with this language. The hidden treasures of power in the day-to-day words we speak are limitless. We, however, are oblivious to it, unfortunately! I have heard a saying that with great power comes great responsibility. We are an irresponsible nation because we don't have any idea what power lies in our kymyz-laden breath. The drunken whim overtakes the poet in the middle of a battle and the rhymes invade his head in their mysterious detail so that he dangles somewhere between the actual treasure and the oblivious world, a state he mistakes for artistic rapture. No. It isn't. It is precisely at the most pleasurable of moments that the poet should desist from the vowels and schemes his rhymes had taken, and change its direction, upright, sideways, or whichever way that doesn't break the soul of a Serik or an Aqerke or several others who were unfortunate enough to be afflicted with this monstrous vowel. As adults we have been desensitized so much that even in the rare moments of awareness, such as when, in a respectable gentleman's after-dinner speech, a horrible curse word escapes his tongue in a parallel space to the actual speech, we are too shy to take note of it. We ought to heed these moments and warn others of the dangers that lurk in the spaces surrounding us, spaces that are just as real as our own. In such spaces, an artist could speculate, languages were formed and decisions made as to which tribe or nation will speak which.

I still remember some of the lines from Marat Sasykbaiuly's battle against Aigul Nurzhankyzy. Yes, your husband had a role in the little boy's demise. The unfortunate boy, who was burdened with a dominant E vowel in the first syllable of his name and subsequently with its demonic suffixes the 'Ke' and the somewhat feminine 'Ten', had heard every word uttered by your husband. If I had been observing him I certainly would have noticed his winces from stomach cramps as his soul bent out of shape and, as Marat persisted further with his merciless 'ketkendiktens' and 'ketpegidiktens', began the process of severing itself from his body. I can't count the number of times I have heard sudden shrieks from babies with names like my own whose ignorant mothers caused them sharp sudden pains by shouting to acquaintances across the road that Mierbek or Aielder had left for Bishkek-ke. You see, if Marat had compassion the size of a dust particle, he surely would have known that sticking to one vowel for an entire ten-minute recital is not only in poor taste but is painfully boring for younger listeners. As for whether he knew the harm caused by his countless Ketkendiktens and Ketpegendiktens, I will give him the benefit of doubt. Remember though, obliviousness to a problem doesn't render the problem non-existent. The same goes for the man in whose bed you sleep. He's a murderer like any other. But enough of Marat's great crime. This letter isn't about him.

I was about six years old when I became aware of my affliction. I was asked by my teacher to sing Abai Atta's 'Kozimnin Qarasy' for guests on Parents' Day. I had sung the song many times before then, but it had always been as part of a crowd of children. It didn't occur to me until that day that I had never really sung it alone. A half hour or so before I was due to sing, the teacher called me into her office for some quick practice. She was aware that we all knew the song by heart and had sung it countless times. So there was no cause for worry. She just wanted to hear how I would sound on my own and to smooth away any rough edges at the last minute. As you know well, 'Kozimnin Qarasy' is in verses of four lines each, with 'A' as the dominant vowel in three of them. I sang the first two lines well, and actually enjoyed it. The third line, however, to my teacher's surprise, seemed to cause me plenty of difficulty. I didn't forget any word or mispronounce anything. Nor was I off tune. All was well in the conventional sense. What happened was that, as soon as I got to the line that said 'Batpeidi ishtegi', I felt a sharp, slicing pain in my abdomen and, immediately after, an invisible hand seemed to push me forward, encouraging me to fall. Once or twice I tripped, so that my teacher worried I might be fainting from anxiety. She had me recite the second verse, and the same thing happened at the line populated by the cursed vowel. But, like a new smoker, the pain ceases after several attempts and the damage continues undetected.

In the famine of 1931, a Shymkent-ten family of five from the Kereit clan were found dead just outside Almaty. Their bodies were all in the same position. A young shepherd on horseback reported seeing them fall face forward at the same time. The neatness of their fall fooled the shepherd into thinking they were engaged in some obscure choreographed ritual. Now, Saltanat Talgatkyzy, how often do five people of the same family collapse at the same time and die like that? Pay attention. The family was comprised of Erkinbek the father, Aqerke the mother, their two sons Berik and Medet, and their two-year-old daughter Zhibek. That family was burdened from the start by belonging to the Kereit clan. The least they could have done to assuage the damage was to choose any of the wonderful A-dominated names such as Talgat, Bagdat, Almas or Baglan for their children. But, curse his ignorance, the father found it romantic to marry an Aqerke and further to suffocate his kids with numerous Es, and the subsequent suffixes served as the final nails in their coffins. Every time I had fallen, even in those instances when the force of the spasm would tilt me backwards, I had, to my own surprise, fallen with my face forward. You see, this is what this vowel does. It points one's entire being downwards on one's face. If you didn't understand Kazakh and heard the words 'Kelgende' and 'Barganda', wouldn't the first form an image of a tall drunkard tripping forward just before a fall? And wouldn't the latter embody a fat, short man walking with his arms swaying away from his body on both sides? Be honest with yourself, Saltanat Talgatkyzy.

I fear I could be wasting precious time attempting to explain the nature of my affliction. Apart from the hardships I have undergone because of this cursed vowel, I am otherwise a healthy man. My issue with the vowel, as I have already stated, isn't simply with its sound. If mere sounds were the issue, I would be like numerous others with the much simpler problem known as misophonia. No, I am not misophonic. It isn't the sound of things that bothers me. I have no problem with the jiggle of keys, the squeaks of rusty screws, the scrape of sandpaper on wood, or any of the other sounds people usually complain of. None of these bother me one bit. My issue goes a lot deeper, as you have by now understood. I don't want to see my life bend out of shape by the time I am 40. My soul is already strained. If you had made a good decision ten years ago and settled with me, you would have seen the dim reddish line that has formed around my waist and which continues to darken. I do not need to be a genius to know that my soul is almost cut in half, and that the dark line around my waist is simply a material manifestation of that fact.

Harsher than all this, harsher even than my miserably bent life, is the realization that I live in a terribly cold world. People whose hearts are as hard as rocks – if not harder, for some rocks crack so that springs can emerge from them, and doesn't the Qur'an say that among them are those that fall off mountains out of fear of God? Yes, stones commit suicide too.

About a month ago, I went to the local commissar's office to enquire about a possible name change. I was told to go home and come back in four days for an appointment with the Commissar. I wish I could tell you the wait was worth it. The Commissar's office is not what it was made out to be. It is a drab little room that is full of pigeon shit and dust. The man was no better himself. He sits there like a giant egg and laughs at his clients' every word. I arrived at his office at about seven o'clock in the morning. How I wish I arrived two hours later! I was so scared about missing my appointment that I left Uzynagash at five in the morning. By six I was in Almaty and, as there was nowhere else to go, I smoked a cigarette with the Commissar's office guard and waited. Tragically, it was exactly at the cursed hour of seven when I walked into the building. I knew, right then, that my chances of accomplishing my mission were very slim. Nonetheless, I took a chair by the door and waited for the People's Commissar.

When we spoke, he laughed, scratched his belly, smoked a cigarette, and, after a long pause, punctuated by sudden giggles for no reason at all, wrote a little note and sent me to Citizen Services on Lenin & Gogol streets where I came face to face with the cruelty of man.

In the long hallway leading to reception stood a tall Russian with a bony face, and at the far end stood another, who looked just like the first, except for his red beard. I ignored the tall Russian (who was on my left as I walked to the reception) and headed straight to the bearded man. He examined my note, read through the codes drawn by the Commissar, and, with a smile and a shaking of his head, motioned me towards an old chair. I waited an hour, one of the longest in my cracked life. My waist continued to ache as, in the office behind me into which the bearded Russian had disappeared, ripples of laughter kept popping out through the holes in the window. I could hear the bearded sucker, may his father's mouth be screwed, say such things as 'Let him be Maxim? I guess he could do with a Maxim so long as he can hold his vodka!' His comrade laughed even harder, and presently there was the sound of wood against the floor as he pushed the table away to stand up, trying to match his friend's joke, but Lord, no! The brute pushed the door ajar and peeped my way, all the while smiling. I didn't look at him. After another hour of more laughter, they summoned me and, not wanting to waste much time, said that my reasons for a name change were of a most peculiar nature and that, no provisions pertaining to the said application existed in the law as yet. The white-eared brute then winced and asked if I didn't mind being a Maxim. Enough said. You'd think it would have ended there but no. The sadists had to rub it in with a note in my mail box saying: 'If you are at war with your own language, that is your fucking problem.'

Back in Uzynagash I made myself a hammock and pulled my shapeless soul into it, hoping that, in the disorderly posture I assumed, my body and soul would reconcile, if only for a short moment. Alas, I was wrong. My soul misunderstood my body's message and proceeded to detach itself even further, much more abruptly this time, so that, suspended there in the hammock with my two legs dangling on either side of myself (mimicking the image of broader and more upright vowels), I allowed myself to be. I had had enough. The soul, though, wasn't about to go anywhere. It sent me a sharp message, letting me know that the way forward wasn't to render my body shapeless but rather to head back to the root of the problem – the bloody E.

But how? The office of the people wouldn't change my name. I decided to help myself the only way I could – by asking the people of Uzynagash to call me Aqylbak instead of Erkinbek, which would mean my suffixes changing accordingly. Little did I know that the people of Uzun Agash were a bored folk waiting for the first interesting thing to come by. The first crowd of men, some butchers and a friendly neighbor, started off arguing with me, claiming that my new name made no sense. Who were they to give sense to my name? I was happy to suggest an entirely new name, including the radical Kyzbolsin, provided they would use it. No, no one gave me that option. My neighbours forced sense into my name, removing the first syllable entirely and adding an extra 'qa' at the end, so that I had now, in a metaphorical sense, been reduced to a Baqa. Knowing that you grew up in Taraz, I need not explain Kazakh words to you. Saltanat Talgatkyzy. For the next two weeks, I endured endless mockery from my neighbours and their children. Adults are insistent on calling me Baqa. When I confronted Bauyrzhan

Zhumabaiuly, your former dombra teacher, he dismissed me with an outward shrug and said: 'Don't blame me for giving you what you've always wanted. If you stick an object into yourself with your own hands, you know best how to pull it out.'

You are probably surprised by the length of my letter. Forgive me. I have to write as much as I can, for this is the last thing I will ever write. Yesterday the villagers mocked me again, along with their kids, because I happen to have been carrying around a zhetigen on my two shoulders for a week now. Yes, a zhetigen, of all things. There comes a time when you, just before your demise, become one with your disease. This is such a moment for me. For my last week, I thought it wise to embrace the cursed vowel and see its limits, with all its various horrors. Last zheksembi I left for the furthest duken with my zhetigen and deliberately walked with my face downwards, in defiance of all I had feared until then. I had thought I wouldn't reach my destination, with all the Es about my person, in the zhetigen I carried and the day of the week within which I shook the beast's fangs. I did not see my soul leave me, nor did I fall face forward at any time. The only result of my audacious stunt was that the outline of my soul's struggle around my waist became even more pronounced, spelling unheard-of tortures.

This, compounded with the unfriendly jeers of my fellow townsfolk, is why I must do the unthinkable. Now, no mad man will call an act of self-termination unthinkable. This is just one of the proofs that I will carry out this act at seven o'clock with complete awareness of all that it entails and what follows thereafter. I will not wait till I am 40 and watch my soul, and by extension my entire life, bend itself out of order. I will expedite its journey and see my soul off before it gets mutilated beyond recognition. And mutilated it must be, if I let things continue as they are. Trust me, I do understand that murder is murder, even if the victim is the self. But there are moments when even the meekest among us must yield to the forces of order and unleash the dragon within.

Have you heard the story of the meek angel? It happened in Noah's time, right after the floods were released. The angel was reclining on a rusty cannon (the same one later used to destroy Sodom and Gomorrah) halfway between the earth and the sky when he observed one of the condemned men from Noah's people holding onto a piece of wreckage to stay afloat. His meekness notwithstanding, the angel casually flew to the spot and eased the wreckage from the man's grip, saying, 'Go on, son. Drown, for thy Lord's will must be done.'

Similarly, I must force my meek self to perform this special task, a noble one at that. Not many people can claim to have literally saved their own souls from certain mutilation.

To that end I will clear my back room in the morning, sweep it clean, sing 'Kozimnin Qarasy' with emphasis on the third line of each verse and then get to the task of saving my soul. If I fall asleep while preparing for the deed, I am certain to see hundreds of people run downhill over a grassy slope and disappear right before their feet make contact with flat ground.

It's almost six now. I must conclude my letter soon. I need to get my space ready. In a few minutes, I will place my mutilated zhetigen across the room and write 'Levrenty Beria' on the wall above it. Did I tell you that my grandfather Erden made zhetigens before he was dragged off by Beria's men in 1941? There you have it. Levrenty Beria killed the zhetigen making Erden, grandfather to Erkinbek! I don't want to leave any doubt as to who killed me. Believe what you may, but the cursed vowel is my real killer. I will show that in the boldest way possible by tying the strings to the roof beams in a U shape. I won't hang to death. The first person here will find my corpse dangling in a falling position. Both my feet will be on the book shelves behind me, and my neck will be supported by the zhetigen strings in the manner of one held back from a terrible fall. The imaginative are allowed draw invisible bubbles of the Ke and Ten suffixes in front of my lips in mid-air. There will be a note hanging on my neck. The words will read 'Here fell Erkinbek, grandson of Erden, a victim of the cursed E'.

Please let it be known that I don't intend to have my corpse washed. You will find enough money in my old dombra's belly. Please use it to transport my body all the way to Shymkent. You may have all the books in my backroom, as well as the precious khobz that Erden Atta left me. You've always wanted it, haven't you?

I can feel my soul preparing itself for a journey outward. No doubt my soul will forever be grateful for this morning, for this soul-saving moment in which a great deed was undertaken. People have been rescued from many dangers, but not many eternal souls have been rescued from eternal mutilation. Earthly rescues are temporary, and won't ever hold a candle to a brave act done to save one's soul from eternal mutilation. I will now get to what must be done. Please tell your husband to care about the less fortunate. Inform him about the power of his work. Share my letter with the poets of Zhambyl Oblast. Keep the special wincers and scratchers whose lives are afflicted with this vowel in your mind. With this, I must take my leave.

Yours forever

Erkinbek Zheksembaev

Chronicler's Note

The chronicler would like to correct the great Erkinbek. Kazakhstan's famine, in which over a million Kazakhs are said to have perished, occurred between 1932 and 1933. My great friend Erkinbek was off by a year. However, the reader is advised not to dismiss our hero's recollection based on a mere chronological inaccuracy. The translator, to his credit, retained the original Kazakh words 'from Shymkent' as 'Shymkentten'. Notice the added 'ten', representing what in English would be the 'from' preposition, and consider along with it the second syllable of Shymkent and its significance for our unfortunate hero. *The chronicler has been able to find phrases which might have caused unwarranted hardship for our hero (or shall I say our hero's soul?) such as Shymkentten kelgendikten or its negative form, Shymkentten kelmegendikten. Sometimes a ketkendikten or ketpegendikten would worsen his state, after which certain upright words like Aitpay and Barmay would restore his comfort temporarily. It was discovered too, by the chronicler, that only about a third of our hero's letter appeared in The Secret Language of Vowels.*

Through extensive searches in the most obscure places, I succeeded in finding a publisher's contact and accessed the rest of the letter. The bulk of his message has pretty much been rendered in the short excerpt that was shared but there were also details of great entertainment value for the intelligent reader. Once a school of migratory birds came flying his way and, to test the power of the vowels, he sang the folk song 'Sary Bidai' (yellow wheat) and observed their flight tilt to a gentle downward turn by the end of the first verse, only to revert again to their original angle when he got to the chorus.

It is not my intention as a mere chronicler to paint our hero in one way or another for, while I admittedly hold him in very high regard, the reader is free to make his/her own conclusions. I recommend, however, that his letter be read with an open mind as though he were speaking to each of us directly. In obeying his request to be honest with myself, I have opened my pores to his highly original thesis and absorbed it all. I expect to be forgiven for comparing this most profound testimony with certain childhood whims of mine. Once my elder brother, who often made observations like my own, wanted me to deliver an envelope to one of four young strangers in a room a short distance away.

'Give it to Yusuf. You will recognize him when you see him.'

Truth be told, without having ever met the Yusuf in question, I entered the room and, after a quick scan of the faces, walked right up to Yusuf and delivered the envelope. Now, how was it that I recognized him? Could this possibly have something to do with Erkinbek's life thesis? My brother, a curious fellow if ever there was one, had to ask how I recognized him, at which point I answered casually, 'I just looked for a Sundusi face'. Sundusi isn't a word in our language, or in any other language we spoke. Yet my brother, just like I recognized Yusuf without having ever met him, recognized the word immediately. The only difference, he said, was that his word would be 'Bukusu'. The appearance of U in both of our words is significant not only for the way in which the easy U is utilized by Chiukyulew's race but for the way in which their faces invoke the honest vowel.

Our hero seemed unsure to what extent the rules of Tukulu's people could apply to humans. I will go further here, if I may be allowed. It applies perfectly, just within reasonable limits. We are way more complex than Chiukyulew's race and cannot have our names and language dictated by the shape of our faces. In our case, harmful sounds, vowels, do most of their damage through immaterial means. I am a devout believer in the idea that we shouldn't pick our names randomly. Names, with their vowels and consonants, are powerful vibrations and no parent should approach the task of naming carelessly.

The African story discussed is by Danal Badu, one of several young writers from the Horn of Africa who won a trip to Moscow, sponsored by the Soviet government in 1954. 'Chiukyulew' was probably first published in Pravda's supplementary summer issue of 1956, and republished decades later in the underground Kazakh resistance journal The Koshpend alongside Esengali Raushanov's counter-revolutionary poems 'Sholpan Zhuldyz Tugansha' (Until Venus Rises) and 'Perushteler men Qustar' (Angels and Birds). Raushanov would also become the 13th director of Zhazushi Publishing, the first being the late Saken Seifullin. Erkinbek Zheksembaev and his classmates most likely read it in The Koshpend issue of November 1982. The chronicler has read the story and drawn similar conclusions to Erkinbek's own.

Chiukyulew, the main character, is three feet tall. His hairless head is vertically long, sharp at the top and flat on both sides. *Nearly every feature is sharp and pointed, including his shoulders. His country, Tukulu, lies somewhere beneath the Kenyan coastal city of Mombasa, somewhere above the earth's burning core, and their gravity is upwards, explaining the upward pointing features of that race. The King's name is Pyunsufu, and nearly everything has got U as the dominant vowel in their names. It's both illegal and dangerous to attempt pronunciation of the A vowel in that kingdom. Their fish-like mouths risk tearing at the edges if such a stunt is attempted. I suppose what Erkinbek meant to say is that humans are similarly torn, not at the mouth but in such unseen dimensions of the self, such as the soul and their lives in the abstract. It is the chronicler's belief that artists are once in a while let in on bits of such secrets as were concocted in the massive space described by Erkinbek, spaces where decisions are made as who will speak which language. By the same token, one may further assume that one's language could be at odds with one's own soul, like people destined in that space to belong to one nation but who, by no fault of their own, find themselves in another. Such was the case of a young gentleman who learned a new language on the other side of the world from his home country and could swear that he had spoken that language fluently at some point in the past that he couldn't quite place.*

Abdul Adan was born in Elwak, Somalia, grew up in Kenya and later immigrated to the US. In 2014 he moved to Kazakhstan where he studied Kazakh and taught English. His fiction has appeared in *Kwani?*, *African Writing*, *Jungle Jim*, *Scarfmag* and elsewhere. He was shortlisted for the Caine Prize in 2016 and won the Miles Morland fellowship later that year.

Shells

Lesley Nneka Arimah

A girl was walking on the beach and encountered a spirit who asked her to collect 32 perfect shells. The girl was young, seven, and thus in awe of the spirit but also in possession of an unbridled curiosity, that plague of parents everywhere that had them fielding constant 'whys'. Why, the girl asked, and the spirit, who had never encountered a person who dared ask such a thing, smote the girl and turned her into a crab and three days later a hungry bird consumed her.

The spirit then encountered a fisherman and asked him to collect 32 perfect shells. Unfortunately, this fisherman was an extremely superstitious man, the butt of many jokes of his fishermen peers for how many times he would dip his net in the water before casting, and the exact spot where he'd kiss the prow of his boat. So, when the spirit spoke to him, he prostrated himself then promptly died of a combination of anticipation and fright.

The third person the spirit encountered was a young woman who did not believe in spirits and so his command came to her as a suggestion that, hey, she was on vacation and wouldn't it be fun to see if she could find 32 perfect shells? She strolled the beach, dragging her feet through the wet sand in an impromptu pedicure and tracking the shore for nice-looking shells.

After picking up a beautiful conical shell only to discover it occupied with a spongy little body and flinging it into the water with a scream, the woman stuck to flat shells. She found eight the first day – varying sizes and colors, perfectly ridged with no chips or cracks. She sent a picture of them to her sister and her younger twin brothers. They were the only ones who knew of the recent heartbreak that had her vacationing alone. One of the twins sent back a picture of fingernail clippings arranged in the same manner as she had the shells. The young woman laughed, feeling almost better.

She found ten shells the next day, followed by a poor find of one on the day following, but by the time her vacation came to an end there were 32 perfect shells piled on the table in her hotel room. As she packed to leave, she debated over whether to take them with her or to return them to the ocean. She would have to leave something behind and chose at the last minute the rolled-up souvenir t-shirts she'd got for the twins. They were off at university, surely with access to many other t-shirts, and she'd make it up to them later.

In the lobby of the hotel she left a note in the suggestion box about the uncleaned state of her room as housekeeping hadn't shown up in days. She didn't draw the connection between the appearance of the shells and the maids' refusals to enter her room. If so, she would have returned them to the sea.

Why 32? Her sister asked via text, and the young woman thought about it for a moment and decided it was because she was turning 32 in 32 months, and something about the symmetry of it appealed.

Once home, she had the shells mounted on corkboard and framed and she admired the wild beauty of it, the many sizes and textures, each shell unique and interesting and perfect. It's something *he* would have liked and even now she had to resist the urge to send him a picture, had to remind herself that she was the one who'd left and could hardly reach out now.

She fell back into the pattern of her life: work at the bank, happy hour with friends, the occasional get-together at her place where everyone admired the shell display except for one acquaintance who found it creepy, don't you think, that each hollow curve had once held a living thing and isn't this practically a collection of little gravestones? She was not invited back.

After a time, when the shell collection had lost its newness, transformed by time to just another decorative item in her apartment, the young woman noticed that two of the shells were missing. She checked behind the couch above which the shells were hung and then behind all the furniture, but the shells had simply disappeared. The collection was still pretty, but skewed by the loss and appeared just a little bit off. Looking at the picture of the frame the young woman had sent, her sister said it still looked okay and she should just leave it up.

But one week later, when a third shell went missing, she couldn't take the off-centeredness of the image, how it now listed to one side, and took the frame down to store in a closet. The same closet where she kept the box of his stuff that he never came back to get, even when she offered to drop it off at his place or with a mutual friend. Maybe she could take it to his other girlfriend's place, she'd snidely said in the voicemail she'd left those many, many weeks ago.

It seemed appropriate that the shells and the box of his things would share the same space as the vacation had been to his home country and she'd cancelled his ticket out of spite and gone by herself anyway. She was supposed to have met his family and had been happy and excited to do so until she'd met Girlfriend #2, whom her sister took to calling Skanky Spice, who had already met his parents months before, and did that in fact make the young woman Girlfriend #2?

She wished she had brothers. She'd have them waylay him one night and bring her his two front teeth and then she'd be able to sleep soundly knowing he'd only be able to charm another woman with his smile after a serious investment in dental work. She kicked the box for good measure and shut the closet door and didn't notice as the shadows closed over the shells that yet another one had disappeared.

She began feeling anxious, as though she'd left an iron or

the stove on or had forgotten to pay an important bill. The feeling never left, no matter how she checked and double-checked every appliance in her home and sifted through her painstakingly organized receipts. Something always fluttered at the edge of her mind as though she caught sight of something out of the corner of her eye and jerked her head only to find an empty space.

I think I'm going crazy, she told her sister. Older by six years, her sister had been like a mother to the young woman.

You just need to get out of the house. When was the last time you went out just to go out?

The young woman thought about it and wanted to say Never, but that seemed too pathetic a confession to make. She'd never been the sort to make friends and didn't have anyone she could call up for drinks or to hang out at her place just because. He had been her only friend, until.

She said as much to her sister and could hear her roll her eyes over the line.

You need to toss out his crap, just put the box in a dumpster or, better yet, set the damn thing on fire like in *Waiting to Exhale.*

Laughing, the young woman walked to the closet where the box was stored, knowing she'd never throw it out, but needing to look at it anyway. She hadn't opened it since she'd first packed it up and it had become a sort of talisman. He would come for the box. He would apologize. He would beg her to take him back. He would never stray again. She was closing the closet door when she glanced at her souvenir. There were only 14 shells.

The young woman spun around at the soft sensation of a hand passing over her head in ghostly comfort, but there was nobody there. Taking deep calming breaths, she asked her sister if she'd ever heard of dissolving shells.

No, her sister said, I mean shells stay in the water for decades and don't dissolve. Why?

The young woman scrolled through her phone, looking

for the first picture she'd sent to her sister just to make sure she wasn't losing it. Sure enough, one of the missing shells had been among them, a cream-colored one with cheerful peach stripes. She paused on the next picture. Fingernails. Something about the image made her palms itch. The young woman told her sister she'd call her right back, grabbed the shell collection and went to her computer. She googled 'disappearing shells' and came up with tons of results of endangered shellfish and the dying coral reefs and other such uselessness.

After digging through twenty-something pages of search results she searched again, this time adding the filter of the country where she'd vacationed. The first result was a link to a blog post that read: DON'T PICK UP THE SHELLS!!!!

Heart in her throat, the young woman picked up the phone to call her sister before she remembered that she was an only child. She looked at the frame and swore she caught one wink out of existence. Now there were 13 shells.

The young woman turned back to the slowly loading blog page to see an impenetrable block of text. Someone had a lot to say about shells.

Before you start reading, know that the shells will continue to disappear. There is no way to stop them that we can see.

The young woman looked at the frame; there were still 13.

Second, it's always there, watching you, you cannot trick it. I am down to three shells, but I started this blog at 18 shells, or maybe I started earlier, I don't know, but 18 is where I switched to the computer. It doesn't know how to work computers properly, it's analog. Check your phone for clues, check your emails, there's something it missed. BUT FIRST type up everything that exists in your life right this minute. Do it before anything else.

The young woman checked her phone, to see a missed call from a number she didn't recognize. She called back and a woman picked up, her voice low and comforting. The woman at the end of the line swore no one in her home had called then excused herself and hung up. The young woman scrolled through to find another missed call by that number, then a record of a ten-minute conversation that had happened not two hours ago. Same number.

As far as my wife and I can tell, you just forget and then the world forgets, too. Cindy didn't go to the beach resort with me, but thank god she noticed the shells. (Edit: I wrote this last week and it's the only reason I know that I once had a wife. I have no memory of her, I don't miss her, there is no longing, she was simply never here.)

The young woman become frantic, the phone an oracle she investigated for answers. She scrolled through her pictures, stopping at the ones she couldn't remember. Evidence of the gaps. Evidence of the unique and interesting memories that had been taken from her.

She opened the notes app on her phone and began mapping the constellation of her life on the page. Her personal inventory included a job, an apartment, a vehicle, an ex she never (but also always) wanted to see again. She delved deeper, making a list of her co-workers, her neighbors. She made a list of the numbers on her phone that called strangers or went to nowhere, an empty black sound in her ear. She kept the mounted shells with her at all times, substituting a large tote bag for her purse. When, by the end of the week, she'd lost another shell, she obsessively scrolled through her now-extensive notes looking for the gaps. Nothing was missing. Which meant there was something she'd forgotten to add in the first place. It terrified her that she didn't know, would never know. She felt as though she stood on a beach staring at the horizon with waves lapping at her feet, only to look around a moment later to find the water lapping her waist. Soon it would be at her neck.

After performing a reverse phone look-up, she began spying on the woman who lived at the address associated with the number she'd seen the most in her device. She couldn't have been much older, but carried herself with a certain competence. Every time she saw the woman, some spot in the folds of her brain itched, some agony she couldn't scratch. She wore a bald spot into her scalp by rubbing at the spot over and over. The young woman soon knew where the other woman shopped for groceries, where she took her car to get it serviced, the person she dated.

One more disappeared shell relieved the young woman of her job and she only knew she'd had one from her dense, meticulous notes. She didn't miss it. She drove by the bank and felt nothing. She knew there was no way to stop the forgetting, but tried to protect herself. She read her notes every day, over and over, even when she thought half of them couldn't possibly be true. She kept enough funds in her bank account to autopay her bills for six months then withdrew the rest of her funds – $11,426 – and divided them between her bed, the ubiquitous tote bag and the glove compartment of her car.

She pored over the blog, last updated 18 months ago, looking for clues as to what had happened to its author. He'd lived in a small town where everyone knew everyone until, suddenly, no one had known him. He'd documented his life as he knew it in public, for anyone to see, hoping to be known, maybe even saved. He was full of practical advice (this was where she'd got the idea to keep her money close) and seemed accepting of his fate as soon as he'd figured out it couldn't be changed.

Not having a job freed the young woman to stalk the other woman and she found herself making extensive notes about her, too, even down to the favorite shirt she wore that made an appearance at least twice a week. One day she worked up the courage to bump into the woman at the grocery store, all apologies and helpful offers to pick up the bag of frozen vegetables she'd jostled out of her hand. The other woman was polite, but distant. The young woman stared at her, willing that she would say what they were to each other, why an electronic trail going as far back as the life of her phone said that this moment should be so much more than it was. But nothing stirred between them. They were strangers.

She thought about the one blog post the man hadn't written, one posted by his wife before she'd disappeared from his life. She'd started first by saying how much she loved this man and how good they were to each other.

I am destined to forget him, but I cannot imagine it. Every morning we stare into each other's faces and the sight fills me. We have taken to staying in the same room at all times, within sight and sound of each other. As long as I can see him and him me, we will stay in each other's memory. You cannot convince me that I will ever forget this man. Nor that he will forget me. He is the spine that holds up my body.

When she got back to her car, the young woman cried. How silly to be brought so low because someone whom she didn't know didn't know her either. But *he* still knew her… didn't he? And since he was the only person the young woman remembered, she called him and left a voicemail that sounded crazy to her even as she was saying it, but she didn't care. Maybe it would make him miss what they'd had. Maybe he would keep it, saving it over the years as he switched from phone to phone. Maybe it would become an electronic map he could follow to someday find her.

She received a reply text so quickly that there was no way he'd had a chance to listen to the message. Move on, it said. I've moved on, why can't you? And at first she was delighted at being acknowledged, known, but then the message made her angry. And embarrassed. But mostly angry.

Seething, she rushed home and then rushed to the closet to find his box. Still there, of course. Still dredging up memories, still dredging up hurt. Why, she thought, in the face of all this forgetting, should she choose to hold on to this? The box was light given all that it held. She grabbed the corkboard display on her way out as though keeping it within her sight could stop what was happening.

As she approached the dumpster, the young woman slowed. Could she really throw his things away? They were all she had left after all. No home, no car, no job. Maybe she should take the box to him. She glanced at the frame balanced on the box. The mysterious disappearing shells. Something fought to the surface, a blog she'd once read, but she couldn't pin down the details; it was an oily thing, hard to grasp.

Making a decision, the young woman carried the box towards the bus stop. By the time she reached the corner, she had tossed aside the empty frame. She didn't know where she was going. She remembered nothing, not even herself; the only thing that remained was the sensation of drowning in heartbreak.

Lesley Nneka Arimah is the author of *What It Means When A Man Falls from the Sky*, a collection of stories published by Riverhead Books (US) and Tinder Press (UK), 2017. Her work has appeared in *The New Yorker*, *Harper's*, *Per Contra* and other publications. Lesley was shortlisted for the Caine Prize for African Writing in 2016 as well as 2017.

An Unperson Stands on the Cracked Pavement Contemplating Being and Nothingness

Tendai Huchu

1. There's a Theory That Holds the Sum Total of All the Energy in the Universe Amounts to Zero

Like long summers that end, slow lifts down mineshafts, sunlight screams in pillars through the moth-eaten sky. Stand on the cracked pavement. Moss under feet and decaying sewage cables and electric pipes. Inhale the sulphate-infused fresh morning air. And shadows so long they have no end; into their cold embrace, weep. Only the rush of the two-minutes-late clock atop the high tower tells false tales of sailors lost at sea amidst the bustling commuters. Formalin in veins pumping to the one ventricle and then the other; purple fingers. The horizon glints gold in the east end. The rumbling, guttural throat that whooshes by. Hear it. And in the dizzying confines of a now crushed under the ashen avalanche past come to pass. Stand on the cracked pavement. Observe the green man walk and the red man stand. In/of the bitter bite of morning's sacred breath, through which the breeze of the first word sprung forth light unto darkness on one of the seven followed all, perturbing the empty none from which some so sprung. Cancer creeps on black soot upon the ancient city stones, heavy, scarred, bruised and battered by history. For it clings in acid rain, smouldering, that which must come down when burnt offerings to new gods are mailed. Look at them. The walls. Phantoms painted on/upon, eroding with a parasitic entropy from which nothing is safe. And yonder, the loch turned park garden/ windows block in shadows, peep. Leaf through the tiny passages between instants wherein lies the singular desire. Up tall they rise and seek. Another 500 years in which now lie these mobile-phone shops and gift shops, the scent of coffee wafting from the chains, the sleepers in their cosy hotel beds. Along which people pass through the open-and-shut door. Hands change notes with indulgences for which the soul redeems the global slain trees and rocks, poisoned rivers and baby oil inheritance spent. Harken to those streets. Yawns blow through secret corridors bouncing off walls soaked in dew. Sorry for the ghastly sight, the inconvenience of it all! To business now with the rushing leviathans of the self-same street. The invitation roars, laughter barrelling, silently, in the dopplered dark. It has cracked. Is wrecked. And the clamour aboard hears too the chime of the tram tracks trawled through tar. Slithering past flashing lights, Zeno's half long lost at the last stop. And below still, the sleigh tracks that tyres made upon that slave-whipped surface. Salve in the small scars that threaten to reveal the. Blasted by wind with each passing which unveils the strength, such force as only nature and the unnatural in matrimony can, together, muster. Stand on the cracked pavement.

2. Suicide is a Perfectly Rational Choice in a Cold World

Feel, cheek, that long-fingered bone's awful caress. Strong is the vortex that draws us to these murderous streets to revoke this great, unsolicited gift. The sky changes like a face in motion forgotten by all relations. But we recall them that flew beyond the bridge in the north onto glass. Or those from the monument down the road. The vortex grabs, seductively drawing/ for the bard's question remains unanswered. Hows and whys loiter in dry biros kissing billions of fluttering pages. The answers we seek/ lie not in the sleep-deprived faces passing.

3. We've Been Doomed Ever Since Copernicus Flung Us From Heaven

The familiar unknown. The herd clanks on the pavement. Stand on the cracked pavement and see the odour of a woman's perfume. Fine flowers in a meadow. Beyond, the fire rages in bottles that unquench thirst to blight the dustbowl. Heaven lost. And the orphan heirs wander. A bitter inheritance, all these centres of the universe. Poems no one bothers to read in obscure journals, essences bubbling over in hopes and dreams, lies and lost love. That which knows itself in the mirror. That whose contours are unknowable to itself. Whole and divided. And the buses rumble on past the red man still. Take it all in. Delay. The tall man who uses his umbrella for a cane. The white-haired man in a pinstripe suit in the lens of a camera out of frame before the shutter clicks. Lost is that immortal slice of time. A spilt cup of milk. Laws whose authors are unknown become border collies guiding lost sheep. Department stores. Banks. Hotels. Pharmacies. New buildings hastily erected, whose false exterior blends with the old city. Across the road, the nearby terminus plays videos on giant screens. Mannequins in slow queues stare at the fallen petals. Sad strings strain under the bow where seagulls feasting on carrion make rain while doves wait for olive branches to show. Low tide steals friends. Stand on the cracked pavement like Tantalus in this pool of water beneath the fruit tree. Thirteen billion years before man is born; a strange and happy accident to dissolve in.

4. It's All an Illusion: Smoke and Mirrors

It will look like something else with the camera dangling. Focus. Yashica Mat 124g twin lens (Japanese made). Behind the Berlin Wall those strings from Sarajevo haunt the square. Sweet sorrow is the ambrosia of the god-man. Let it whine as it dines on souls factory-farmed for slaughter. The maddening beauty of the conductor's empty rostrum. Women in high heels. Stockings. Cigarette butts still smouldering next to flattened pieces of gum. Jehovah's Witnesses stacking titty mags. Flesh yearning for touch even by an unsheathed blade. Exhaled breath, misty, inhaled once more and then expelled. Atoms smashing in the true emptiness neutrinos stream through. Higher and higher still, the cat flaps loose on the unhinged doors crying, squeaking for a drop of vinegar. In a large cup to take away. Trees slowly shedding their load to expose scrawny limbs hoping for blankets and mulled-wine mulch and a firm bench to sleep on. Coins clung in the beggar's bowl. Delay no more. Nothing is truly false. Unloved candyfloss sprinkled with cinnamon. A young man running, suitcase in hand, through the hedgerows and snarling branches. Bicycles breeze by hungover, the walk of shame. The fathers who absconded next to mothers who left babies in baskets. Secrets hidden behind urbane visages. Bombs in the bookstore. Ringing bells on handlebars. Different socks and clouds fall to earth. Workmen erecting traffic cones. Human signboards. Massage parlours and chiropractors dispensing sage wisdom from the Orient. Online dating profiles swiping left and right with mating sheep in the countryside for Chinese glass and magic boxes hide the path ahead, muddying thought. So say the city. To buy time lost and found in clogged drains and discount bargain bins. Court hearings postponed. Mounting debts in every pocket and rents and usury. Percussion in every chest silenced in schools and institutions. Naked children clothed, feral, the hungry fed water. And some things only a broken paintbrush can see: upturned jerry cans atop street signs pointing west. The verge, no, precipice. Castle on air of flu and minor ailments. Only blotted chimneys sweep the horizon. It's all there, except the ties that bind man to man. Each a stranger, stranger still, and estranged, strangled, mangled, doomed. Cut and cut again, the weeds grow still. Cut and cut again, the grass grows still. Statues of generals and dukes stand on bus shelters. The white and yellow lines and lane changes. Those silenced voices were once the delightful squeals of children on Ferris wheels/ delightful squeals of piglets at the abattoir/ delightful squeals of broken pianos in brothels. Faded henna plugged into headphones. At least it delights in ying-yang fish squirming on the plate, grateful for the bounty. Portraits hanging in empty spaces and empty cafés. Golden moss, sedum and echeveria. Phthisic souls entombed. And the builders and tradesmen and shop fitters whose callused hands built the air. The secretaries and lawyers and bankers. Draughtsmen and civil servants selling mind-altering cries of hear ye. The hailed turn every time like driftwood on shallow ponds. Codes written in the/ subtle shoulders drooped/ venom in kisses verging on the/ that – what? – as seen on TV and billboards/ selling desire as fiction in business columns. The late and the early, it is only an accident of the fourth-dimensional glue. Those precise accidents of birth. Snow-capped roofs run with peanut butter jelly. Invisibility and yearning. Love made on wet city streets. To the irrevocable step. Courage. Folded in the breast pocket on the left side lies a note that tells everything in a single sentence scribbled in pencil. In the far distance the street peters out. The green man strides again. Lunchboxes in leather briefcases. And those who missed champagne for breakfast. Garbage trucks trudge on for matter can neither be created nor destroyed. Conjurors sell spyglasses and periodic tables. A young woman on her way to an interview. Students' last-minute revision. To constantly undercount. Stand on the cracked pavement, there is naught else to fear, the fire has climbed up the stairs, roused from slumber. For who can truly comprehend? A minute bought on rubber cheques. And who will redeem? On this window ledge, the chips fall against the base beast within which would rather live on its knees.

5. *A Sailor Sat in an Inflatable Dinghy Reflecting on Existence*

The ocean is full of the detritus of the world. Plastic and rubbish, large as a continent, swirl and travel the world chocking and poisoning all manner of life great and small. Amidst the detritus is a sailor in an inflatable dinghy drifting through. No idea where true north or east lie, as the sky is dark and wind gentle. The sailor is parched, hasn't eaten for days, the hunger gnaws. Skin baked by merciless heat, the night is no relief. Drifting in and out of consciousness, the sailor sees only the vast emptiness and understands now just how insignificant he is in the grand scheme of it all. And if there were such a grand scheme then at least he could take comfort in it, in the fact that his small role is somehow tied to a fine silken web he cannot see except when it occasionally grazes his skin. He moves his jaw, tongue swollen, to try to give himself some relief. Cracked dry lips blister and blood cakes. He's already been sick drinking sea water water everywhere. Long gone is the hope that by some divine chance he'll happen upon a small deserted island with palm trees and maybe even a small creek. Longer still are the odds a vessel will happen by. Would not a shark fin look like a glass of cool spring water then?

6. *A Transcript of the Abjuration of 1633*

'I, Galileo Galilei, son of the late Vincenzo Galilei of Florence, aged 70 years, tried personally by this court and kneeling before You, most Eminent and Reverend

Lord Cardinals, Inquisitors-General throughout the Christian Republic against heretical depravity, having before my eyes the Most Holy Gospels and laying on them my own hands; I swear that I have always believed, I believe now, and with God's help I will in future believe all that is held, preached and taught by the Holy Catholic and Apostolic Church. But since – after having been admonished by this Holy Office entirely to abandon the false opinion that the Sun is the centre of the world and immoveable, and that the Earth is not the centre of the same and that it moves, and that I must not hold, defend nor teach in any manner whatever, either orally or in writing, the said false doctrine, and after it had been notified to me that the said doctrine was contrary to Holy Writ – I wrote and caused to be printed a book in which I treat of the said already-condemned doctrine, and bring forward arguments of much efficacy in its favour, without arriving at any solution: I have been pronounced to be under vehement suspicion of heresy, that is, of having held and believed that the Sun is the centre of the world and immoveable, and that the Earth is not the centre and moves.

'*Therefore, wishing to remove from the minds of your Eminences and all faithful Christians this vehement suspicion justly conceived against me, I abjure with a sincere heart and unfeigned faith, I curse and detest the said errors and heresies, and generally all and every error and sect contrary to the Holy Catholic Church. And I swear that for the future I will never again say nor assert in speaking or writing such things as may bring upon me similar suspicion; and if I know any heretic, or person suspected of heresy, I will denounce him to this Holy Office, or to the Inquisitor or Ordinary of the place I may be.*

'*I also swear and promise to adopt and observe entirely all the penances which have been or may be*

*imposed on me by this Holy Office. And if I contravene
any of these said promises, protest or oaths (which God
forbid!), I submit myself to all the pains and penalties
imposed and promulgated by the Sacred Canons and
other Decrees, general and particular, against such
offenders. So help me God and these His Holy Gospels,
which I touch with my own hands.'*

7. Resistance and Defiance Through Small Asymmetrical Acts of Guerrilla Warfare (I)

The black cabs and buskers. The buses aren't free. They trudge with heavy boots tethered to schedules and bells and folks boarding with correct change. They have a will of their own, much like oxen on the plough. And with a camera in the right lane, they can find themselves a furrow some such feet deep. A choice freely made is not a cup of hemlock or fine Roman nails. It's essential, self-sufficient, a closed circle entrapping its own axiom. Such a pure thing as this has no equal, unblemished and unassailable, cut diamond. Because the incontestable fact is that life itself starts without volition, from the first single-celled critter to the sweet scents of swaddled newborns in open fields in lambing season and all else, the stars and planets, great wall and all, chart their course as they must. How then can choice result from non-choice, free will from the determined? So we are forced to accede/accept because others, too, have, except for small asymmetrical acts of guerrilla warfare, acts that cannot result in victory, but necessary acts in which affirmed new elements annihilate the old. Speaking to the dark-skinned girl at a party all those years ago. She was an actuarial student whose numbers saw into the future. But they did not see the love spawned at that house party would hurt and burn sweet molasses on bare flesh and that it would seem unbreakable, until it wasn't. That which so mattered now revealed. Pressure builds up in temples on either side.

Squeezing. A vice. An awesome force. Better this than to/ the stone rolled up the hill cannot be found/ no matter the search. The copper-coloured horizon draws nearer. Beyond is dust and fog. Here in the centre of the capital city, stand on the cracked pavement. All the way brush shoulders with morning commuters. Thoroughly sober, clean and unmedicated. Take it all in. The great slope up is hidden by buildings on parade; only the winding road tears through. Viewed through the lens, the old buildings stand like old maids waiting for the flash. They have seen masters and fortunes change, and they have endured it all. In this grows stronger the copper flavour the valiant taste but once; it is still walking on upturned plugs and out bleeds a certain aching loss, for the answers we seek are not to be found in faith, power or science, nor can the questions themselves be right, removing the first rung of the ladder.

8. A Brief Digression into Native American Mythology

Up high they say there was a time, once upon, men could eat the clouds like corn for they weren't so far away/ one only had to reach up and seize. But man was wasteful and threw away that he took, which he could not eat, and so/ to punish him/ the gods commanded the clouds be raised far from his reach.

9. Resistance and Defiance Through Small Asymmetrical Acts of Guerrilla Warfare (II)

The rent sky squeezes upon itself and drifts westward. Those shafts of light have spent themselves like matches and all is gloom. Bicycles keep close to the curb. Rooftops write a sentence in the margins. Maybe this is sickness, an imbalance of the humours, perhaps even an as-yet-undiscovered germ that sits deep in the bowels, a thing that can be seen under the microscope or via x-ray even, but which feels more like the disappearance of will, that life-force that itself commands the sun to rise every morning, for without will and hope, only the night devours the... A crossed telephone line, the man saying, 'How did I get you? I was trying to call California.' And still the world turns! A woman searching for change in her purse at the bus stop. The meteor has struck, all is afire and still the corpses march on. How, without a hand gently guiding it, does it go so? A nurse walks by, tunic showing under his jumper. Up five or six storeys, sometimes only four, the buildings rise never more than eight. The elegance of the old baroque hotel. Gargoyles look down the stairs; to the railway station late commuters run. A doorman in costume stands out on his post, bowing then raising his head. And these fine pieces of the clock turn and grind upon one another, keeping the hands moving ever forward. These things and more shall pass, for they are smoke in the wind, smoke in the wind. Yet so sweet are the reminiscences of swimming on a beach in a hot and sunny climate, where palm trees drop their fruit with a thud. As real as squeaking beds. Broken lighters that flicker and die before the fag is lit. Popcorn and hotdogs with chilli sauce and mustard. Ticket stubs sweep Heaven's alleyways. It is certain, the speed with which the buses pass this point. The ones that have the next stop approach with caution, but the others fly by until they reach the next set of traffic lights. Sometimes they are slowed by a tailback that builds up, then it clears and the rhythm resumes. Farewell to football matches on pirate streaming channels. Farewell to the TENS machine. Farewell to missed appointments on duvet days. 'I was trying to call California.' A young man, only twenty and some, walls himself in earphones, eyes staring ahead, waiting for the green man. The gut tightens as though an icy hand has reached in and squeezed until goosebumps chatter the shivering mass. A pigeon flapping its wings. Courage, do not falter now and give into false rationalisations. It's been a long time coming: every conceivable counterargument's been weighed and found wanting. The matter is decided, the court has convened and ruled. There is no right of appeal. A small raised island in the middle of the road. Two teenagers holding hands. Silence. A moment please. The tunnel is dark and bats flit about the slick. To buy a few more minutes. So easy to turn back from it now. There ain't no shame in that; to say one once stood on the spot, reached into the furnace and at the very last second pulled their hand out sizzling rare. Against the baser animal roaming free within.

10. In the Multiverse Anything That Could Possibly Happen Will Happen

Fantasies of screeching brakes. A loud earthquake, thunder rolling on hammer and anvil in the smithy. Rainbow-coloured pain and green fields under the quilt. Shocked faces register alarm and calls for blue lights. The inevitable flash of smartphone cameras is the lightning after the thunder. And on the ground, beside a Yashica Mat 124g, a roll of film unspools like a ball of wool. 'That Kodak's gonna be overexposed now,' an older tourist in a hat calls out. Around his neck is a Canon which uses the same type. The drains receive with glee their red offering. A pungent odour. Frantic phone calls and messages passed. A brief mention later in a local newspaper. 'It wasn't my fault,' the bus driver says. 'Came out of nowhere. It wasn't my fault.' The lens now cracked points to nothing more substantial than a splintered black-and-white pole. Voices become muffled as if the signal's dropped behind a mountain... Those moments won't and can't exist because, without the observer, they continue as ever in the wave function of probabilistic peaks and troughs next to the cat in her box. The pictures don't form clearly. They are words blurred in mist, vague, lacking the material solidity a toe can be stubbed upon. The canvas remains pure white on the easel and dry brushes. But in them still was the essence of what could be, the same will that shaped the winding course of rivers and scarred glacial plains. Past one another in opposite directions they flow. The point is transient, no one stops, no one stares.

11. *One With An Appointment Recalls*
   'The Appointment in Samarra'

Just-felled orange plastic barricades next to a broadband street cabinet. Elder birch growing in roof gutters. Ask: can love grow in concrete while the city hems in and squeezes? And where was it to be found, here or there? Leave the cracked pavement down the road. The playful nibbly nibble of/ consequently, there was a merchant in Baghdad who sent his servant to the market for wares, but later the servant returned home, trembling, fearful and utterly distressed/ in addition, a telephone box, fallen receiver dangling/ street sweepers droning by/ heads down, eyes straight ahead/ left, right/ the people that pass by are so interchangeable, if one was swapped for the next the street would still look the same/ the sound of a jackhammer sweet as birdsong ringing out/ so the servant, wailing, told his master that while he'd been at the dusty market, he had happened across the grim figure of Death who had pointed at him/ moreover, the pavement is uneven as it rises and buckles/ squares change like Tetris/ smiling, a building being erected/ steel bars all round like railway tracks/ naked and in the air is the scent of a secret scandalous starvation/ bemused partitions set against desks, paperclips, computers, spreadsheets, shredders, and missing sandwiches in the staff canteen/ goes down as days become shorter/ conversely, the servant begged the merchant, if only he could let him have his horse so he could set off to the city of Samarra some 30 leagues away and save his life/ admittedly, jaywalkers run across the street even though what green there is shows the hardness of stone and concrete/ the very antithesis of life/ to illustrate, in America they use police/ a lot quicker/ far easier than a camera and a bus/ although right suddenly juts away, revealing a golden jubilee post-box/ high heels knocking on the pavement much like the cartoon woodpecker from all those years ago/ still buses burrow through/ beanie hats amass/ a beggar and a black dog wearing a cardigan near scaffolding wrapped in blue netting next to a sign that says, 'Don't Ignore the Workplace Pension'/ a sniffle even/ as the window cleaners' white van is parked right on the pavement/ soapy water dripping through the troughs and grooves in-between the solid blocks/ furthermore, the merchant, being a kind man who valued the service of his servant, granted the request, gave him his best stallion and bid him flee as fast as he could to Samarra, standing on the road, seeing the dust rise from the ground as the horse galloped away/ during that time tram cables overhanging and old lamps turned off, the turn of a key, an early worker opening shop as wheelie bags grumble, dragged as they are by folks heading to the station/ past gigantic flower pots littered with Styrofoam cups next to the galleries with giant Greek columns on which banners for the next exhibit are tied under the dead queen sitting atop the roof in perfect focus from the castle sitting on air from where the view sweeps to the church spires/ green lead and a flag/ many flags/ but not on the hair salons near the beeping pedestrian light, or the shiny wristwatches blinking under harsh lights to the cafe/ to buy a cup of tea to take away/ nevertheless, the merchant himself went to the market/ the first lip lacquer in a stick/ and there he indeed was startled to find the figure of Death wandering the stalls between the perfume dealers and carpet sellers from Persia and so he approached him/ as shown by the sign in bold, 'To Let: Class 1 or Class 3 use, all enquiries', next to the first-floor window/ the hiss of a halting bus/ myriad/ boards with fliers/ a lane stolen from the black tar/ however, the merchant, indignant, asked Death why he had made the threatening gesture towards his servant/ even though the point in life where the past catches up and you can trace the lines but to unthread the tapestry and find out where it all started is impossible/ men in high-vis jackets and hardhats/ Construction vehicles, delivery lorries beep as they reverse, a fire truck, black metal railings, more traffic lights/ relief/ and blunted sensations while sober: give the hot cup of tea to the beggar, drop a few coins in his hat/ a loud exhaust pipe menacing as a motorbike passes by/ expertise fresh cups a masterpiece every sip an experience/ ex-serviceman in need, please help, for the wars abroad always come home to roost/ likewise, Death replied to the merchant: 'Forgive me, I did not threaten the man, it was merely a start of surprise as I was astonished to see him here in Baghdad, for I have an appointment with him tonight in Samarra.'

12. Would You Follow This Rabbit Down the Hole?

All around the morning commuters proceed with their chaos. Garbage bins out of sight, the sea beyond. Would you follow this rabbit down the hole? To which the only answer is that only the unknown is known because questions do not correspond to answers or answers to questions like simple equations and it may well be the case that the two are wholly unrelated. Questions only lead to more questions, and answers to dead alleyways. The open-top tour bus goes in the opposite direction. Tell us what matters to you. These things and more than the heart can say as an old woman of pensionable age scurries by carrying three blue and green plastic bags. Return to the cracked pavement for the appointment. They no longer make batteries for the Yashica light meter and the best alternatives give the reading off by a fraction. Compensate. The scene is the same save for walkers passing. Slight increase in the shutter speed using the left knob and a minor adjustment for the aperture on the right. The waist-level viewfinder makes the photographer unobtrusive, just a figure on the street bowing to a little black box with silver trimming. And on the viewer, the mirrored opposite, the city appears reversed. Focus. In the periphery, when the little man turns red, the buses zoom past. And after a while the pacing of things, even that of the walkers across the street, takes on a regular, predictable hue. There are the two worlds: one in the lens, the other on the periphery. It is said that in a vacuum particles pop in and out of existence, annihilating, and everything gives back its energy to the great unknowable. A blur hurtling in from the right, out of focus. Step off the cracked pavement onto the tar. In the frame is a young man with a red backpack midstride, sharply standing out from the crowd as he rushes. A perfect moment that is obscured by the grey concrete that rises up like a fog coming out of the earth. The pleading forlorn horn of a ship in the mist, a mighty trumpet. It echoes out into the grey, trapped too on the film. Will it hurt, here on the tar? The beauty of the world drained except in the little square on the Yashica. A click. And the blur hurtles nearer to–

13. Old Clichés Carry Hints of Cosmic Truth: Everything Happens for a Reason

A hand reaches into the fog, grasps and yanks. A hand. A hand. In a whisker, danger is averted. Where steel would have met flesh, now it meets nothing more substantial than air. A hand. Startled faces on the bus look out. The klaxon recedes. A cool breeze sweeps through. 'Careful, love,' the middle-aged woman with crow's eyes says, 'no picture is worth that much.' With the green man, she crosses the road, as if nothing happened, as if she doesn't know the power in her hand to give life and her hair sways. The moment is stolen. The clock continues. And, in that moment, it is possible to see other things – maybe not love – that grow in concrete.

14. Not a Conclusion: Freedom's a Bitch

The lifting of a hydraulic press. A new lease has been signed. Shackles fall with a clang. Strange crops these. Turn the handle and feed the next frame. No. Cross the road with the green man. Quickly. Flee. Merge with the morning commuters. Descend the long, long steps, worn in the middle, that lead to the station as if to Hades itself. Past the buskers and onto the bridge under the dirty transparent roof where a train pulls into Platform 20. For your safety and security CCTV cameras operate in this train station. There at the top of the escalators is a black 42-inch flatscreen. A video plays on loop. A man in a football jersey holding his son's hand. Stand still. Stand steady. Stand clear. A woman holding onto the rail. Then how not to do it: A man running up the escalator trips and falls/ A man with an oversized bag backs up and falls/ A man walking backwards falls/ A teenager walking down an ascending escalator almost makes it, then falls/ On the loop, they fall and fall, forever falling like the morning star, falling and falling and....

Tendai Huchu is the author of *The Hairdresser of Harare* and *The Maestro, The Magistrate & The Mathematician*.

My Mother's Project

Lydia Kasese

My mother always knew the kind of woman she wanted to be. She knew the kind of life she wanted to live and how she was going to live it.

She was an artist, my mother. She did not think of herself as an artist, but I learned to refer to her in this way during introductions and questions such as 'so what do your parents do?' My mother's friends liked to tease her about the title. One of them, Ms Bonolo, loved to distinguish between artists and creatives. She insisted that these were not the same thing. A creative person isn't always an artist, but an artist is definitely a creative person. She would further add that artists were the crazy people of the world, the tolerably insane people who saw the world differently from the rest and thus often felt left out, alone and misunderstood.

I know that my mother often felt misunderstood. I am not sure if she ever felt alone, especially in our midst, but I know that in her own family, during holidays, she became someone entirely different. She looked and became small. Her movements became crippled, her speech became riddled with stammers and her usually vast vocabulary escaped her.

She grew up in a strictly religious family where prayers happened as often as meals. God was the beginning and ending of everything. And when, at the age of 15, she decided that she did not want to go to church, or to attend family worship, she had committed the worst crime in the history of their family, at least since my grandmother's sister killed her husband's lover. The crime was not just the rejection of church and worship, but she had, during a brief moment of courage, declared herself atheist, and this was the start of a life of ridicule and shame for her. Her father made it clear that the only thing keeping her in his house was the fact that she came from his seed and he had a responsibility for her.

From then on, everything that she came to do or say was seen as a result of the lack of God in her life. When, later in her teen years, she was diagnosed with depression, her mother said to the doctors that it was because her daughter did not have God in her life and that if she had kept going to church then she wouldn't be suffering from something as *white* as depression. She learned to choose silence as a response to all this, she buried herself within herself and, when at home, she came out of her room only for meals and the occasional appearances to greet her father when he came in from work.

This was not helped by the fact that she chose art for an occupation or, as she would like to put it, that art chose her. She loved the creative process but also the control she had in the outcome of the things that she made. Like how she could mould the clay and get it to bend into whatever shape that she wanted. When painting, she loved how she could make different textures with a brush, and how the outcome would always be different depending on the amount of pressure she placed on her tools.

This love of art did not make sense to her family, her father especially, who did not understand why she would opt for something as 'simple minded'. Especially after all the money he had spent sending her to the best schools.

My mother was the kind of artist that did things with her hands. She did not specialize in anything in particular, she specialized in everything. Anything her hands touched became art, whether it was painting, pottery, sculpting, gardening or even just cooking. She gave her hands the freedom she felt her mind and body might not have and they in turn gave her freedom through creation.

In the same year that she renounced religion, she developed a liking for vulnerable and broken things. She started to call out to stray cats on her way home from school, trying to lure them into coming home with her. Sometimes it worked, other times it didn't, but most times it took a bit of coaxing and weeks of bringing food to the cats before they finally allowed her to touch them.

She lived for these little wins; they gave her a sense of purpose in life. She loved the process of getting something to trust you enough to let you hold them. A friend once asked her if this need to love broken or abandoned things perhaps reflected how she herself wished she had been loved, or still wanted to be loved. She did not respond to this but instead put these questions to work in her head, eventually deciding that she did not have an answer.

So when she saw a boy, who was three years her senior in school, whispering softly and somewhat lovingly while touching the privates of a boy much younger than him in an abandoned duka, she knew that she had found her next project.

She was familiar with sexual violence – they had been taught about this in the first year of high school, this and sexual consent. This came after the government had announced in the previous year that a significant number of students had dropped out of school due to pregnancies arising out of sex that they strongly suspected had not been consensual. This lesson was only given to the girls in her stream but, being the curious person that she was, she had gone home later that day to read further about sexual-abuse cases.

In as much as she was familiar with the situation before her eyes, she was still somewhat confused. The younger boy did not look frightened; instead he had a curious and almost expectant look on his face. In her mind, sexual abuse was something that came with violence and some fight or resistance of some sort from the victim. But this was an entirely different situation and she did not know how to approach it.

As she was contemplating what to do about this situation, the younger boy noticed her presence, zipped up his pants and ran out past her. The older boy, on the other hand, froze where he was and looked at her. She smiled at him, mostly because she was not sure if either of them were ready for words. The boy, in response to her smile, came to his senses and ran out of the door, pushing her out of the way.

The following day at school, during assembly, it was announced that a boy by the name of Titus had attempted to kill himself the previous day. But, thank God, the Holy Spirit that lived within his mother had instructed her to go into the bathroom where she had found him barely conscious and oozing blood onto her white tiles.

The assembly ended with a prayer for Titus and other troubled young people who could potentially be possessed by the demon that convinces them to end their lives. By lunch time, she had put two and two together and realized that Titus was in fact the boy she had found in the abandoned duka the day before.

My mother, until then, had never met someone who had tried to kill themselves. In fact, people that had attempted suicide often never came back – they moved away, or went to live with a relative elsewhere. And for those that stayed, parents would dissuade their children from being friends with them, in case they learned bad habits from them, such as suicide.

But, being the stubborn person that my mother was, she made her way to the hospital where Titus had been hospitalized, mostly because she had decided that she had a few questions about death and the 'other side' that she wanted to know about, but also because she had a suspicion that she was the reason he had decided to take his own life.

The last person Titus was expecting to see as a visitor was my mother. She had brought with her a bottle of passion fruit juice, as is customary when someone is in hospital, and some of her old books that she did not intend to read again. He watched her warily as she approached his bed, unsure of what this visitation meant. In his head, he was already preparing the words that would beg her not to expose his shame.

Instead, my mother sat by his bedside and started talking, mostly about school, and herself, and the cats she had started bringing home that would eventually get chased away by her mother because they kept pooping in weird places of the house. He laughed a little bit when she told him of the time she got chased by the dogs in her neighbourhood and found herself up a tree and she couldn't remember how she got up there, or how to get down.

And, just like that, their friendship started. Titus was in the hospital for about a week and she went there each day. She did the talking; he mostly listened, but smiled more and laughed every now and then. The incidence in the duka was not mentioned in that first week – as with the stray cats, my mother slowly and patiently waited to earn his friendship and, eventually, his trust.

***

My father, on the other hand, was an academic. He was a very quiet man who did not speak unless spoken to. He liked to disappear in the midst of people and enjoyed sitting by himself in a room full of people. I often thought that there was a world within his head that he constantly lived in and sometimes forgot to leave.

He avoided eye and physical contact with most people. It was almost as if there were things in his body that could easily become visible to the rest of the world if he spent too much time around people. Even with us. We rarely saw him, except during meal times where ordinary, small-talk conversations would be had. This never bothered us, as he was a busy man. If he was not giving a lecture, he was locked up in his study, working.

But he was not like this in the presence of my mother. What I mean is that he did not disappear when in her presence. He came to life, smiled more, made jokes and even his posture changed. It was almost as if he became much more certain of himself in her presence.

There was something about her that drew him to her and allowed him to open up. I think more than anything they were best friends. The older my twin brother and I grew, the more we noticed this and became envious and sometimes even jealous of my mother. Of how she could somehow bring life to a lifeless man. She was also different in his presence and often we felt like an afterthought, something that they needed to have to appease their already disapproving families.

Don't get me wrong, our parents did love us; they just loved each other more. My father, despite not being available to us for most of our childhood, reached out to us when we got older. He became more involved in our lives and showed interest in things we were working on in school. He loved numbers and was really good at working with them. The only reason we passed mathematics and physics was because he helped us when we got home.

Our relationship with our extended family was a strained one. We did not stay long when visiting extended family, especially on my mother's side. Their disapproval of my father and how we lived our lives was often visible, even through their smiles. It was agreed upon, and eventually became a norm, that my father would be the person to get us out of family situations. We made sure to arrive just in time to eat, help with the dishes and leave.

Looking back, there were a lot of things that I and my brother thought were normal. We did not really question things, even in our heads, because that is how things always were. We never went for sleepovers or visited people so we did not have anything to compare our lives to. We were well aware that there were some unsaid things that lurked within our house, but we never thought to ask. Or maybe we knew not to ask. I don't even think my parents would have had the words to tell us then if we had asked.

Three years ago, my mother was diagnosed with lung cancer and it has been five months since she passed. Even though the news of the cancer came as a shock, we were not entirely surprised as she had always been a chain smoker. She had read online once that cancer was simply a result of bad luck because we all had potentially cancerous cells that could one day just decide to multiply and become cancer.

She did not believe in fighting death or life and so, when the doctors gave her the treatment options, she rejected all of them. For some reason, she just did not want to fight for her life. Instead, I believe she chose her imminent death as inspiration for the last pieces she worked on, which she eventually gave to us.

***

In the last month of her life, I moved back home. I could tell that my mother was not going to be around for much longer and Titus, my father, had now become an empty shell that mostly gave one-word answers and spent the day holding my mother's hand.

One Saturday, she called both me and my brother into her room to 'talk'. We were accustomed to these talks when we were younger and either one of us was in trouble or something in the family was not right. Most times it was the former.

With my father's hand in hers, my mother proceeded to tell us about how she and he had met. As she told us more of the story, I realized that a part of me was not surprised and it even almost made sense of the person that my father was.

In the back of my head is a faded memory that becomes

all too clear now. When I was five or six years old, I found the door to my father's study open. We were forbidden to go into it and it was always kept locked. Curious, I snuck in quietly and looked around. Right at the back of the room, underneath the table, was a gift bag that I rushed to and in my excitement poured out all its contents onto the floor. The sound of falling DVDs caught the attention of my mother who, when noticing where the sound came from, ran into the room, grabbed the DVD that was in my hands and sent me out of the room. She locked the door once again, this time with her on the inside.

I still remember what was on the cover of the DVD. It had cartoon-like figures on them and that is why it was the first one that I picked up. Two of the figures on the cover were two little girls in piggy tails that had nothing but underwear on. In between the girls was a man in underwear and a bulge in his pants.

My mother didn't say much for the rest of that day, and for a good part of the week. My father went away for two weeks after that – he had travelled for work, or so we were told. I never found the room unlocked again.

There were also other things, like how our father was barely present when we were young. He was there, he lived with us, but he avoided us. We had no memories of him bathing us, or hugging us, or even just tickling us. None of those images came to mind. There are pictures of him spoon feeding us as children, but even then we were never sitting close to him. For most of our childhood, he existed in the background of our lives, like an extra in a film.

I looked at my brother, and I could see the shock on his face. I had never told him, or anyone else for that matter, about what I had found in the study that day. My mother's reaction to finding me in the room had stunned and confused me, and the older I grew, the more it just felt like a dream that I had pushed into the back of my mind – until the talk.

***

Today is my father's funeral. And I am reminded of that day, when we had the *talk*. My mother was worried about my father: after years of behavioural interventional therapies, as well as sex-drive reduction, she was concerned that he was relapsing.

We had all cried that day, the four of us: my father for his shame, my mother for us, and us for the father we had thought we knew. I think had it been under different circumstances we might have been disgusted and possibly angry. But it was not the right moment to have the conversation about ourselves and how we felt about it, and in the last few days of my mother's life sadness and tears came more easily to us than any other emotions

My father attempted suicide again after my mother's funeral. He didn't succeed, but ended up in a coma for three months. Yesterday, after a month of intense discussions between my brother and me, as well as with the doctors, we decided to let go of my father.

My brother and I, between the two of us, have still not spoken about the day of the talk. Had my father not tried to kill himself, we might have had a discussion on the way forward, what to do, whether to continue our mother's work or report him to a mental institution. In a way, I am somewhat relieved that we did not have to make any of those decisions. I don't think either of us were made with the same courage that our mother had.

Nyachiro Lydia Kasese is a Tanzanian writer, poet and media specialist, among other things. Her first collection of poetry *Paper Dolls* was published in 2016 by the African Poetry Book Fund in their chapbook collection. Her poem 'Things That Were Lost In Our Vaginas' was shortlisted by the BNPA poetry prize in 2014 and her short story *Inside Outside* was long listed by Writivism in the same year.

This Is How the Heart Breaks into a Thousand Pieces and Then Folds into a Stone

Lidudumalingani

Two years ago, Mother took a vow of silence, choosing to communicate only in gestures. Her refusal to speak interfered with the flow of time, such that the two years felt like a few months, as if her silence were the very arms advancing time, helping it pass along at double speed. The first week of her silence, unfamiliar as it was, did not in any way upset Father, a man who can take a prank, especially one from the woman whose heartbeat is also his, but a month into it, when it became clear that it was not a prank, Father became visibly upset, telling Mother that if she did not stop her madness he was going to divorce her and find a woman who speaks to her husband. Five months into her silence – by then a NO was her head resting on her left shoulder and a YES on her right – Father reiterated his threats but Mother's response had not changed.

Mother's silence became the silent conductor of the household and we – the three of us, Father, Mother and I – were mere instruments in an orchestra, playing a long taunting silent melody that went and on. Suddenly, outside the confines of home, on the streets and on the soccer field, where I had begun to spend a bulk of my time to escape the alienation at home, it seemed as if everyone was not speaking, that, even as they moved their lips, their hands wailing in the air to emphasize their argument or to ask a teammate for a pass, no words were coming out.

When the community found out about Mother's silence, Father found it terribly embarrassing, telling Mother that she was making him the laughing stock of Imizamo Yethu, that he was being told he should perhaps wear Mother's dresses and, while he was at it, her bras and underwear. Mother tilted her head to the left, listening to Father's words at an angle instead of taking them in head on, and said nothing. When Father stormed out of the lounge into their bedroom, violently closing the cloth that formed their door, leaving it flapping about behind him, I could see his heavy body landing on the bed as he threw himself head first in frustration. Mother remained seated on the couch where she had been since morning, shuffling her feet, humming ingoma ezingcwele to praise the lord. The couch had swallowed her tiny body. The house fell into the silence that was becoming familiar. The house had always had my mother's and my sister's singing as its soundtrack. Every house has its soundtrack, bouncing on the soft couches, echoing on concrete walls, holding it together. I remember how Father would mute the TV and clap his hands as the two danced in circles in the house in the ZCC church choreography, moving in circles, up and down, their robes flowing across the floor and up, making the house feel as if it were ascending.

Mother's silence crept on us slowly, with the patience of a dammed lake that slowly fills up from light raindrops. It began with sobbing that would last till morning and then she started to say less and less, choosing to move around the house silently, dragging her feet into a rhythm. Then the blank stares followed, as if she could see something in the air. A few days before Mother went silent, while seated at the dinner table, which was squeezed tightly in the corner of the shack, Father said Mother pronounced her 'T' exactly the way my sister did and that their laughter was identical, trailing off at the end before fading out completely.

Laying the dinner table after my sister's passing has an unfamiliar feeling to it. Arranging Mother's seat to face the kitchen, Father's chair the front door that looked out into the main street, my chair on the other end of the table facing the two of them and then on the far end my sister's empty chair, facing all three of us. Father had always insisted that the family should eat together. He said that a family that eats together stays together, that even in the shack that we lived in, in which my sister and I, for most of our lives, had to alternate sleeping on the bed and the couch, eating together, regardless of what the dinner was, was a way in which we were tying our hearts into one. Even in poverty, he used to say, we will know love.

Dinner, on Monday to Thursday was at 8pm and then on Friday and Saturday, the days that father was on a night shift at the candle factory where he worked, dinner was delayed by an hour. Regardless of the day, dinner always began with my sister singing and a short prayer from me. When my sister passed away, Father's left hand and Mother's right, which would hold hers during the prayer, were left with nothing to do, until both of them stopped reaching out. There was not much to read into Father's face and, because his body hung right above the candle, his face was framed such that one could only see the edges of the sharp beard that lined up his chin, the lower lobe of his left ear and nothing else. On Mother's face the despair was clearly visible. For a year after the death I watched her hand stretching across the table to find my sister's hand in the hope that her passing was only temporary, that she would one day find her way to the table and recall the family dinner ritual. When Mother folded her hand, my sister's death confirmed by her absence, she had a look of someone whose soul had been trampled on a thousand times. I knew then that this is how the heart breaks into a thousand pieces and folds into a stone.

It was not only at the dinner table that Mother thought my sister was going to return. It was in the way she ordered me to sleep on the couch, and she would sleep on the bed, as if she had become her daughter. It was in the way that she would often go to the mall and come back with clothes for mother. Even though these clothes had not been worn, she would wash them every second week, each time folding them with great care, sorting them into colours and types. It was in the way in which she now prepared porridge the way my sister did, something the two had always argued about. My sister liked her porridge watery, arguing that porridge is not pap, while Mother liked it hard, arguing that porridge is not meant to be drunk like it is some juice. Since my sister's passing, Mother only makes watery porridge. It was in the way that she stopped seeing me.

My sister's name was never mentioned in the house and yet one could feel her spirit everywhere whilst I drifted out of sight and out of memory. The last time Mother looked at me, I had returned early from school and she must have heard my footsteps, running in between the shacks. As I reached the door she had opened it, her excitement wiped off her face by the sight of me. There were other incidents, in which I saw myself slowly drifting outside of the bounds of Mother and Father's love. It was not that I found Father's gumboots comfortable to put on and walk around the house but I had to imagine that he was me.

When Mother took up knitting again, setting her beer crate behind our house in the afternoons, sunrays filtering through the dense shacks, I did not sit next to her to watch the sunset; instead I took to playing soccer with all the passion I had. The soccer field where my team, Eleven Attackers, plays is a patch of land between the highway and the bus terminal. The forest, which stands above the rich white people's houses on the other side of the highway, is always casting carefully spread-out shadows across the field. The lines meant to divide the field have long since disappeared. They are now only carved on the hearts of the players yet so definitively that there is never a dispute about where the lines begin and end or how far the penalty spot is from the goal. At either end of the stadium, two wooden sticks stand as goalposts, firmly planted in the ground, growing roots. The ground is uneven, small mounds running horizontally on the field, interfering with the free movement of the ball and altering its intended path. It is only the exuberant spirit of the players that makes the field playable. From the soccer field, Imizamo Yethu sits on a hill, above the four-way stop, beginning with a spaza shop and then the shacks. In the evening, coming from the soccer field, Imizamo Yethu is only dots of light, scattered in the black sky, candles burning inside the shacks.

Eleven Attackers, known as an imbambo team, for we did not have a jersey and only a few of us had soccer boots, only practised from Tuesday till Friday afternoon. Winning games was great, and even the losses I did not mind, but that is not why I was there. The team had become a place of solitude for me, a place to think outside the house and where people saw me.

The death of my sister was not untimely, only the natural next step for children born in poverty, a fate that one cannot escape. You either pour your blood onto the street or leave this earth in smoke.

It was a Friday night. Mother had gone to a service with her church group and left us with Father. We would have travelled with her if it were not for Father's contention that the weekend was going to be too long if he spent it alone and that, by the time of our return on Sunday afternoon, Mother might come home to a crazy husband and that we, abantwana bakhe, might not be able to recognize our own father. Mother reluctantly agreed and told us that she would see us on Sunday, as her phone would be without signal that weekend. My sister was pleased by this, telling me that

Friday afternoon that she was tired of singing the church songs as they never end.

Father was working the night shift that Friday night but he asked a neighbour to keep an eye on us every now and then. My sister insisted that at 15 she was old enough to take care of us and so we were left on our own. My sister lit the candles and told me that she was running to the shops quickly. When she did not come back within half an hour or so I must have fallen asleep on the couch. I woke to a house on fire and found my way into the street where people were standing, watching their shacks burn while others filled buckets with water and prayer and threw it on their homes. In not more than an hour about 50 shacks had burned to the ground. My sister was nowhere to be found. It never occurred to me, or to anyone else, that she was inside the shack. It was only later, when the community gathered in the middle of the road counting the children that lived in my section, that I realized my sister was missing. Nobody wants to consider that their sister has passed away and so I convinced myself that she had not come back from the shops, that she was with friends. When one of those friends, Neliswa, showed up, having walked from another section of Imizamo Yethu after seeing the smoke, I knew then that my sister had been inside our shack during the fire. I stood amidst the panic and not a tear dropped. It occurred to me that I had watched my own sister turn into smoke or, the way I prefer to think of it now, I had seen her soul ascend to heaven.

Though my sister and I had left candles burning, one cannot say definitively where the fire had begun. The shacks are built so closely together that catching flames from another shack is unavoidable. The community tries each time to put the fires out with buckets of water but when zinc and wood are on fire, water acts like paraffin. That night was no different: under the bright yellow tinge of the fire, residents formed a chain, from the tap to the shacks, a bucket of water passed through hands and then was tossed onto a shack without much result.

It was only hours later that the fire truck arrived, with most of the shacks already burned to the ground, their owners having lost their minds. It parked at the other end of the street, too wide to squeeze into the tiny roads. It was not long before an angry mob gathered around the fire truck, demanding to know why it had arrived only after an hour, and why it had parked there and not driven in to put the fires out.

After the last fire the government had told people not to use candles, promising them that it would install electricity, but none of that had happened and nobody stays in darkness for long periods of time without going mad.

The community was up the whole of Friday night, battling flames, gathering their furniture that was burnt into charcoal. It was not so much a mission to rescue furniture as one to salvage memories. The next day, a Saturday, the community gathered their burnt zincs and nails, cleared the ground where their shack stood and built another shack.

When Mother returned on Sunday afternoon, after a weekend of praising God, unaware of what had happened, a part of her died. And since then she only exists because, when we cannot hold ourselves together, something greater than us does, until we find our spark. She blamed my father for all of it, for leaving us alone and going to work, for bringing reject candles from the factory and not buying candles from the shop like everyone else, for moving us here and not somewhere else, for not buying a house made of bricks but one built with dormant flames.

When my parents moved to Imizamo Yethu from Philipi, the government had promised to build houses in their plots in Philipi, a plot of land that stood on old train tracks and a forest. But soon after they had moved, from where their shacks had stood emerged luxury residential apartments with foundations beginning in the middle of the earth and the buildings rising high, such that, on cloudy days, the top of the buildings disappear in the sky. Mother was not happy about the move to Imizamo Yethu, then a vacant piece of land that sits above the Atlantic Ocean, and though it is not far from the affluent mansions of the rich white people who live in Hout Bay, it smells nothing like wealth, but like fish and poverty.

There had been reports shortly after we moved from Philipi that the 6-million-rand budget for housing at Philipi had been reduced to 1.6 million. The councillors, when people asked them what had happened to the money, said: 'You know these white people, they are good at hiding the money.'

One weekend I found Mother kneeling in her bedroom, her hands raised high in prayer position and tears flowing down her face. She did not hear me come in or, if she did, she made the choice to ignore me. This lasted for a few moments. She got up and slumped into her couch, pointing me to the food on the table, umngqusho nolusu. I wanted to tell her that I pray for her too, that I miss her too, that I am here. Even before my sister passed on, Mother only extended affection in short supply. When we were younger, my sister and I used to joke that Mother did not love us now but would later. We never imagined that it would turn to this, that she would choose silence over her own family.

Father grew to love the woman that Mother had become. Though the two did not speak like they used to, Mother often rested her head on Father's shoulder as they sat on the couch, brushing his hands, tracing every vein up his arm. That is love.

We spent the days after the fire sleeping at a community hall in Hout Bay, my head resting on a stranger's thigh, someone else's toenails lying next to my mouth. Father and Mother decided that it would be better for us if we moved into another informal settlement. Mother did not like the move but Father told her that she could bring my sister with her. He said: 'We are leaving. We are going to make memories elsewhere.'

The ceremony took place where our old shack used to

stand. Father banned impepho, scooped what he said were my sister's ashes and asked my ancestors to allow my sister to come with, first to the funeral in the villages and then to our new house in Kossovo, where Father had found a plot to build a new shack for us.

The new shack, Father said when we were building it, was only held together by my sister's spirit. He told me that there was also a soccer field five minutes away. It was the first time that Father had said anything about soccer to me; I did not know how he knew and I did not bother to ask.

Though the new shack was smaller, we settled in and set about making new memories. I found a soccer team, in which I played midfield and became captain, orchestrating our attacks and defence from the heart of the field, the engine of the team. A few months after we settled, our neighbours moved. Father began to make alterations to our shack, adding two more rooms. He also said that I was a man now, that a man builds a home for his family. I loved how he would shake my hand when we stood at a distance watching how the shack was shaping into the house that it ultimately became.

In the two years of Mother's silence, there were days when I felt like I was drowning in it and I contemplated suicide. But even in her silence I knew she needed me. I spent those two years waiting for Mother to see me and then at once I made the decision to step into her view. Not once did she say no when I made her tea or came home with a CD and played all her favourite gospel artists. She hummed along to the music. I knew then that my sister was listening – that we were all, as in old times, a family again.

Lidudumalingani is an award-winning writer, photographer and filmmaker from South Africa. He was awarded the Caine Prize and Miles Morland Scholarship in 2016. He is currently writing his debut novel, titled *Let Your Children Name Themselves*.

The Goddess of Mtwara

Esther Karin Mngodo

1964

No one knew where Markos Zambetakis was really from. I mean, no one. Who was he really? I knew that this would be a huge concern to my family if indeed we brought marriage up. But I knew Markos. I had walked the whole beach with him. Perhaps not exactly walking with him in the traditional sense since I was the one walking while he would drive in his Peugeot 404. Markos was not what most parents in Mtwara feared their sons-in-law would be – godless creatures ready to machete their wives once she left her father's home.

But this was 1964: you didn't just fall in love and move out of the house in Mtwara. How could I just say 'yes' to him? I could already hear my brother Peter ask. The way of the people was to send 'spies' from our clan to his to investigate. Were they witches? Were they kind? Did they have some kind of demons running in the family? Someone had to know these things before the bride was sent off. And how was that supposed to happen in this case? Were they to send some spies to Greece to see for themselves that what he claimed was true? That his father was a man of the church and his family was a noble breed?

Markos said he had a brother and sister, somewhere in the sisal plantations in Morogoro. But that wasn't enough. They were just two people who could be staged to act like family while he took me away and sold me on the black market as a slave. Yes, slavery was abolished, but we just never knew what these white people were up to. That's what my mother used to say.

It happened that I was walking home that day, through the main road near the beach. I had flip flops on dusty feet and a red *kanga* around my waist and a sack of fresh sardines in hand. Mother wouldn't let me walk that far without having well-plaited cornrows. The sky was so clear you wouldn't know that it would suddenly rain, just like the sound of trouble would suddenly catch up with me. It wasn't hard to distinguish Markos' vehicle from the rest – not that there were many vehicles to make a comparison with in our small town. Tanganyika was free now, since 1961. And in April, Mwalimu Nyerere had led the nation to new ties with the Zanzibar isles. Together, we were Tanzania, a newly born baby. And, in the new country, I became 22 in October, just a week before that walk on the beach that changed everything.

Things hadn''t changed much in the new Mtwara. It was still the Indian merchants and the British missionaries who owned vehicles. Then there were also 'the others', such as Markos. The Portuguese, Italians and the Greeks who were just another type of '*Mzungu*' if you asked my mother. The white man is still white in any tongue, she would often say. But Markos was not *really* a white man.

I had learnt to detect his heart beating for me as the sound of his car moved closer. The rattling sound of his engine was like a lion advancing on his prey, every time he drove behind me and then beside me. The fancy white car brought excitement as boys ran around it, chasing their worn-out tyres like cars of their own and cheering for us. It was the sound of freedom.

'Come on in for a ride, *mrembo*,' Markos said in Swahili, calling me beautiful, inviting me into the car. No one had ever called me beautiful before. 'Say yes, *dada* Maria,' the boys randomly shouted, others calling out '*Mzungu, mzungu*'.

Then, when I spotted my brother Baraka among them, I gave him a sharp look. He looked away and ran off.

My mother wouldn't have let me anywhere near Markos, I knew that. 'Mama *amenikataza*,' I would say to him every time, blaming my mother for yet another 'no' and tried not to let him see the longing in my eyes. I felt my mother's presence everywhere I went. The short conversations with Markos felt so wrong. Even though he spoke Swahili like a local, Markos was from a faraway land. He was from another world, another planet. He and I had no business talking to each other this way.

My mother would always send *me* to the fish market, even though my younger siblings Baraka and Neema were more eager to take the long walk to the beach. And anyway, we could always just ask Mama Suzana, our neighbour, for some food if we wanted. This was indeed my mother's way of making men see me. Although what church mothers really wanted was for their daughters to be married in the church, to good Christian men. At my age, girls like me were not only expected to be married but to be mothers as well.

At this point, our mothers would walk up to a man of God after the service and ask them openly: 'Have you seen my daughter? She is a fine young girl, able to till the land with her hands and a prayerful woman. You should come for dinner today so that you taste some of her fine cooking.' My mother had done this more often than I cared to remember. I was embarrassed when she invited Francis, the pastor's son who did not appeal to me at all.

So my walking to the fish market every other day was my mother's way of saying: 'So long my child. Go into the world. Marry handsome, marry rich, marry sons of the land of Mtwara, marry beautiful brown skin and give birth to a good number of your kind.' But my mother had made a grave mistake. Our Father and his son Jesus Christ and his mother the Virgin Mary had not heard my mother's prayer. For this one troublemaker was nowhere near the sons of God.

Even my best friend Suzana said that she had a bad feeling about Markos. 'We shouldn't talk to him,' she said. She said she had been shown in a vision while in prayer that this might be bad luck for me, especially since he was one of the colonialists. I told her that he was Greek. The colonialists were British. Huge difference. Hadn't she learnt anything in school? Still, Suzana wouldn't listen. She never listens, that *Machinga* girl.

Walking along the beach, I remember raising my head and seeing Jesca and Victoria walking in the opposite direction. They each had a child on their back and a sack of rice on their heads. Victoria was pregnant, again. It was the portrait of a real young woman in Mtwara. They pretended not to see me and seemed to be amused by something. I knew that they were talking about me.

Were they happy being married? Did marriage mean independence? Did it mean that you were worthy of love, that you were wanted and useful for something in the world? Would it mean that your mother could not control you any more? If that was not happiness, then what was it? I wanted to know.

The clouds got darker. Mother would be worried already. So I started moving in haste. 'I have to go now,' I said to Markos. But before I'd got very far, it started to drizzle. I still refused to get into his car. Yet I hadn't gone much farther before it began to pour. Markos stopped the vehicle and opened the door for me. I quickly got in. I was soaking wet. I could feel Markos staring at me. The curves of my breasts were exposed and I had to use my kanga to cover myself.

He offered to take me home; I refused. My mother would not understand, I said. So he drove away without a destination. Everything seemed to move slowly inside the car: the way he moved his hand through his hair and how he turned to look at me. Everything seemed focused on me, and on how I felt. Was I feeling cold? Did I need anything? he asked. There were no dishes to wash, no chickens to take to the den, nobody screaming at me. Someone was listening to me.

I thought that we would just drive around until the rain stopped, but was surprised to see him driving into the sisal plantations where he worked. Where are you taking me, Markos? I asked. As if I didn't already know that we were going to his house. I am taking you home, he said with a smile. Home – I liked the sound of that.

His house was in the compound somewhere. Even if someone knew that I was there, it would have taken them a long time to get there on foot. It would have been the right thing to ask him to turn around, but I didn't. I felt a certain fire being next to him. Just me and him in the car. I tried not to stare but he had hazel eyes. He had black hair and his skin was as golden as the sun. What if someone had seen us?

It was still raining when we reached the house. Markos turned off the engine and turned towards me. The sound of rain pouring and my heart beating made the silence between us too much to bear. I found myself giggling for no reason, and him doing so as well.

'I feel cold,' I said, hugging myself.

'Let's get you inside,' Markos said and smiled.

Then he started taking off his shirt. His chest was as hairy as his arms. I had never been in such closeness with a shirtless man that I was not related to. I felt hopeless in his presence. I wanted to be touched – but not this way, not here. Not unmarried either. I turned my gaze away from him, feeling embarrassed. He didn't say anything either. And before I could do or say anything, he got out of the car, ran to open the door for me and covered me with his shirt.

I was surprised to see how tall he was. I had never seen his full frame before as he had always been seated. And now I was in his house. It was a simple structure. Bigger compared to most houses belonging to *Waafrika*. But just big enough for a bachelor, or a small family. Markos brought me a towel and an electric kettle from the kitchen. I wanted to help him but he wouldn't let me. He served me lemon tea with some delicacies he had bought from an Indian shop. I had just enough time to look around the living room when he went to his room to change, though he left the door open.

Paintings hung on the wall. Familiar African carvings were everywhere in the house. A red carpet was laid on the floor. I felt like I was in a whole new world and I imagined what it would be like to live there. A photograph of Mwalimu drew me to it. 'Do you admire him?' I asked as he returned.

'Mwalimu? Who doesn't? Do you know that Mwalimu follows Plato's way of thinking? I have heard how he speaks and he reminds me of my home. Give power to the people. Leaders must be humble, that is what he says. I think you have a great leader,' he said.

'What makes you think so?'

'As we speak, this country is the leading sisal producer in the world. This country is going far economically,' he said. I loved the spark in his eye when he talked about Mwalimu. He came alive.

When Markos went to the kitchen to bring more biscuits, I picked a book from the shelf titled 'Greek gods' and found myself intrigued with the pages. I couldn't understand the things I read. Zeus? Hera? Poseidon?

'Markos, what is this?' I asked him aloud.

He came back and found me still holding the book.

'That is nothing,' he said and approached me, 'It is actually my father's. The only thing left of him that I have,' he said.

'Your father worshipped strange gods?'

'No. That is why I was surprised to find this book in his collection when he died. He is no more,' he said and wrapped his arms around me while putting away the book. His face changed and his words seemed calculated.

'And you, Markos? What do you believe?' I said to him, hoping that he would dismiss my fears. He had to be a Christian man. My parents would never approve otherwise. 'Are you a Christian?'

'Yes, Maria, I am,' he said.

'You should take your arms off me now. I need to sit down,' I said.

'Not so fast, my lady. Why do you ask, Maria Mapunda? Does it matter what I believe in for you to marry me?' he said. That was the first time he had actually said it – marry me. He said it so casually, like he was asking me for a glass of water. I smiled and turned away from him.

Then my eyes fixed on a painting. It was as if I was staring into a mirror yet, unlike how I thought of myself, the woman looking back at me was beautiful – as Markos had just whispered into my ear.

A red kanga was wrapped around her waist, radiant against her dark chocolate skin. A wide smile adorned her face.

'Took me six months to finish that. I started working on it from the very first time I saw you,' he said, wrapping his arms around my waist and kissing my cheeks. I didn't let him get further than that. I pushed myself away from him but he wouldn't let go of me. I could feel him breathing heavily, yet steadily. What was happening to me?

'Am I worthy of Her Highness?' he asked, my body pressed on his.

'You will have to ask my father,' I said, my voice strange even to myself. How can we not recognize ourselves when in love?

'Today. I want to see him today,' he said, almost in a whisper. 'I will not let you go until you say yes, O goddess of Mtwara,' he said, his eyes doing things to my body I had never felt before. But I wouldn't let myself be weak for him. I raised my head and looked into his eyes. He was serious.

'Okay,' I said, and we went.

When we reached a certain distance from my father's house, we got out of the car and walked silently side by side. I wondered what he thought he was doing. But I didn't ask. I just walked. So did he, until we reached my father's house. It was my mother that I saw first. She was sitting outside, sorting rice on a traditional sorting tray. I was getting ready for some shouting when she raised her head and her eyes and mine collided. It happened almost instantly that she dropped the *ungo* and started ululating. Suzana's mother came and joined her. My father, who was sitting outside on a stool, rose to his feet and greeted Markos like he was the President of Mtwara. Everyone was happy to see him and greeted him well.

'Eh *baba*, welcome my son, eeh. You are warmly welcomed, eeh,' my mother said and ordered that the big rooster be prepared for the guest. My younger brother and sister were both working in the kitchen while I was told to sit under a tree with Suzana, covered with kanga.

'I thought we were not talking to Markos,' Suzana said to me.

'Don't you want to know what happened?' I asked, but she did not answer.

Everyone knew that she had a gift. When Suzana told you something that she had seen in the spirit, the chances were that it would happen. It was just a matter of time.

'He is not the husband for you,' Suzana said firmly.

'How do you know that? Why can't you be happy for me? Markos is here to ask for my hand in marriage. What do you want me to do?' I asked.

'Leave him before God is forced to give you a sign,' she said.

'I love him,' I said in a low voice.

'Don't you love God?' she asked me.

Then my elder brother, Peter, stormed out of the house. I didn't know that he was in. I thought that he had already gone to the seminary. Ululations ceased and my mother gave a sharp cry. We were all alarmed at what Peter would do with the machete in his hand.

When everyone had finally calmed down, my father called for an emergency family meeting. 'How can you do this to us?' Peter asked me, like I was a traitor. Like the Apostle, he was the defender of what had to remain 'normal'.

He would defend his faith, even by the sword. Although he was just three years older than me, it sometimes felt like he was way older.

'I mean, *us*. How could you do this to all of us. *Waafrika*. Are there no men among our people? What is wrong with you, Maria?' he said.

'Son, he is a good man. A good Christian man who would provide for her. He said it so himself when he came over the other day. And he loves your sister,' my mother said, to my surprise.

'He came here? When was this? Father, how can you let this happen?' Peter asked. I also was curious about that. Since when did Mother keep secrets from him? That was almost impossible. My father looked at all of us and then pointed his finger in the other direction, causing us to turn and see what he was pointing at. 'Look at the sack of rice over there. These new sandals on my feet.'

'No father, no,' Peter shouted. I smiled.

'And the new kanga I am wearing,' Mama said.

'No! No, Mama,' Peter said.

'It is alright, my son, he is not what we thought he was,' Mama said.

'You have sold your souls to the devil,' Peter said.

'But he is not one of them, brother, he is not like that,' I said. 'And what happened to you, brother? Aren't we all God's children, O Man of God?'

'This is not love, Maria,' he said. 'And I shall not accept this marriage. How do you know that he will not hurt you?'

I looked at him and I knew that he was conflicted, as a man of God and as my brother. But we both had a choice to make. And I knew what I had decided to do.

'You are right. I do not know that. Neither did our parents when they got married. Maybe love is an act of faith, and that is the risk I want to take. Maybe love is a chance I am willing to take. I love Markos. I am willing to spend the rest of my life with him,' I said.

1967

Mathayo was still having a nap when I finished packing. He was a big baby and a heavy sleeper, especially after having some porridge in the afternoon. I used to look at him sleeping and still be lost for words. How did time fly so quickly? He was two already and had a mouth full of teeth to show for it.

I sat at the edge of my bed, holding a picture of Baba Mathayo and I on our wedding day in one hand. He was holding my hand, both of us smiling. I remembered that moment like it was yesterday. He had just whispered in my ear, '*Nakupenda Malkia*'. We looked so happy.

I had a picture of Suzana and I in my other hand. We were standing outside our garden in Morogoro. Baba Mathayo had taken the photo when she had visited us in Morogoro a few months after we got married and she had come to pray for us.

As I was watching my son in his sleep, and looking at the photographs in my hand, I recalled Suzana's visit earlier that day. When I opened the door for her, she hadn't changed one bit. I opened my arms to embrace her, telling her that I had missed her. But Suzana looked away and said she was tired. She just dropped her bags and the weight of her body on the *mkeka* mat that was outside. She had come with a young girl who carried a small child on her back. I sat opposite her as the child slept in the young girl's arms, covered with a *kitenge* cloth.

'Can I see him?' I asked.

'No, leave him alone,' she said sharply. 'Let him sleep now,' she said. I did not press her further. I tried to ask her about home, about my family, especially about Peter. I had not heard much from him since Mother had died a year before. But Suzana said she didn't know anything about their wellbeing. 'Am I their caretaker?' she asked. Our families had become estranged since she became a single mother.

'The man who did this to you should pay. It is unacceptable what we let men do to us,' I said to her, trying to show support. I cared about Suzana. A smile escaped her face, and then she looked at the boy, who was still under the *kitenge*.

'You are right,' she said and looked up at me. 'That´s why I came here to bring you something,' she said, not dropping that serious look. And what was that, I wanted to know. Suzana ordered the girl to uncover the child for me to see. He was light-skinned, like his mother. But he had curly hair. There was something else that was familiar, too.

'What is this, Suzana?' I said, fixing my gaze on her.

She looked at me and said, 'I wish there was better way for me to do this. But there isn't.'

'What is the meaning of this, Suzana?' I said, louder.

'I am sorry, but he has left me with no choice,' she said.

'What is this?' I said, even louder.

'I am tired of your husband. He stopped bringing me money to take care of his son. How does he think I would be able to care for his son on my own?' she shouted.

'What? Suzana, have you gone mad?'

'No, this is your husband's son and I am leaving him here. Didn't I warn you that Markos would bring you problems? Didn't I tell you? He was not for you,'

'And was he yours? I don't know what's going on here but this is not Baba Mathayo's son. My husband does not have a child outside of wedlock. Let alone one with *you*. You are my friend, Suzana – have you gone mad?'

'Is that what you think of him? A loyal man who sleeps with his wife and his wife only? Why don't you visit a few *Mkonge* plantations around, to know who your husband really is. You will be surprised. Thank me later, dear Maria.' Suzana smirked and got up to leave. I tried to stop her but she pushed me and kept walking away as I cried after her.

Looking at the photographs in my hand, I still wasn't sure what I was going to do with Mathayo. If I left without him, it would be easier to navigate in the big city, to get money and then come back for him later on. If Mother had been alive, I would have just gone to her. 'Oh Mama, what should I do?' I asked aloud. Alternatively, I could just go with him. I didn't know what I would do about the other boy but he was Baba Mathayo's problem, anyway. He could go back to where he came from, as far as I was concerned.

As I was thinking this, the child came into the room.

'*Njaa*,' said the boy standing in front of me while holding his tummy. I could see Markos in him. How do problems get the guts to speak? Where had I gone wrong?

'Am I your mother?' I asked him.

'Go ask your mother,' I said and walked to the kitchen where I then let myself cry. I thought of my mother and what she would have done. I wished that she was here to tell me what to do. I wished to go to her – where are you, Mama?

I had already packed my bags and was ready to go when someone knocked on the door. It was Luka, a worker at the sisal plantation. He was panting like a dog, trying to catch his breath. The day before, the Minister had announced on the radio that Mwalimu Nyerere had nationalized all *Mkonge* farms. Mwalimu had just established the Arusha Declaration, the country's socialist manifesto. We were a socialist country now, and everything belonged to everyone. It was what Markos believed. Did Markos *really* belong to everyone too? Luka told me that the workers were demanding their pay. But since they didn't know much about what had happened at the capital in Dar es Salaam, they had held my husband hostage in his office since morning. He was the plant manager.

I had to leave immediately. The neighbour stayed with the children. When I got to the plantation, there were armed men outside with machetes, sticks, spears and one even had a gun. People were screaming at the top of their voices, demanding that Baba Mathayo came out of his office. Apparently, all the other managers had left the country already.

Baba Mathayo had stayed behind, and I knew why. He loved the people here and Mwalimu had hurt him, almost personally. He hadn't slept much the previous night. 'How could Mwalimu do this?' he had complained, pacing back and forth in our bedroom. Markos believed in Tanzania, and this wasn't what he thought it would be. Did he ever believe in us? I thought he did every time he held our son in his arms at night and sang to him. Now, I wasn't sure.

As I was standing there, I heard a group of men discussing how best to kill Baba Mathayo. My feet moved faster than my thoughts, and I found myself standing on elevated ground, addressing the crowd. 'Do not kill my husband. Please, do not do this,' I said. The angry mob slowly calmed.

'People of Morogoro, please consider. Our government has made an abrupt change and we all know that it has barely been 10 years since we gained Independence. Mwalimu has good intentions and so does my husband,' I said.

'Then he should give us our money. What are we going to feed our families?' a man shouted, as another did the same.

'Please, listen,' I said on top of their voices until they rcalmed again. 'Look at all of you. There are probably a hundred of you, and only one of him. Why are you doing this? Why don't you even hold the accountant responsible. He is the one with the money, not my husband,' I said.

'Your husband is a white man. They have come to steal our land,' one shouted.

'And our money,' said another and the angry chatter began again.

'Look at those mountains,' I said, pointing at the range that surrounded us. 'The Uluguru mountains are a witness to what you are doing here. Just like the Indian Ocean is a witness to what my people do in Mtwara. We have to be patient and wait for the government to send word,' I said.

'And money,' someone shouted and the shouting continued.

My husband stayed in his office all day, leaving very late at night and returning early in the morning, hoping that the workers would calm down. I tried to convince him not to go back every day, that it was too dangerous. But he had nothing to hide, no reason to run. We were going to stay. Mwalimu could come to kick him out himself, if he wanted. This happened for three days until the police saw the seriousness of the matter and intervened. On the third day, it was chaos. And then there was order.

On the first night of this incident, I did not speak to him on our way home. He saw the boy in the living room with Mathayo and glanced at me but said nothing. And I did not ask anything. Why would I ask something that was so obvious? I did everything as if nothing had changed between us. I had dinner for him on the table, and took some water in a bucket outside for him. And I bathed him, like I always did. Although in silence this time.

Your husband is yours until you decide he is not – that is what my mother used to tell me when I was a teenager, with no thoughts of a real husband yet. When rules are laid down about an imaginary husband, about a lover you have never met, the weight of it is never the same as when the man you love rips your heart apart.

Having put Mathayo to bed, and having shown the girl where she and the other boy would sleep for the night until I figured out a permanent solution, I worked around the house until everything was completely quiet. Baba Mathayo was asleep when I finally went to bed wrapped in a *kanga* around my chest. He was on the left side of the bed, turned towards the right. I lay beside him, turning towards the right as well. I closed my eyes, although sleep was elusive. Then Mathayo spoke, in a low voice.

'Asante mke wangu mpenzi.'

I did not respond.

He had no reason to thank me.

I breathed deeply.

He slowly placed his hand on my shoulder, caressing me. Then he moved closer to me so I could feel the heat of his manhood. I could feel his heartbeat, but wasn't sure if it was beating for me any more. I didn't move. I wanted to scream.

'Thank you for what you did at the plant today. You gave me so much strength. I don't know what I would have done without you. I appreciate you so much,' he said.

'Is that all you can say, Markos?' I asked. He knew what I meant.

'I am sorry,' he said, almost in a whisper.

'Why did you do it, Markos? With her?' I asked. I felt something pressing on my chest. I was full to the brim with both words and tears, but they did not escape my heart. Not yet.

'I am sorry,' he said.

He wasn't.

'And you have a son, Markos, with *her*? Why did you keep it from me?' I said, slowly and quietly, tears rolling down my face.

'I am sorry,' he said.

Liar.

'He is almost the same age as our son. So when did this happen? When she came that time and you took photos of us in the garden? Was that when?' I wanted to scream.

'Maria...'

'Why did you do it, Markos?'

Silence.

'Answer me, Markos,' I said.

'I didn't mean to hurt you.'

'Was it on this bed, Markos?' I asked, unable to control my crying – pain finally able to escape my chest through sentences that I did not even understand. 'Am I not beautiful? Do I not satisfy you in bed? Am I not enough for you, Markos? What did I do wrong?'

'You are everything I have, Maria. Please forgive me,' he said, and I could hear his voice caressing me.

'She was my friend,' I said. 'I gave you everything Markos. Why did you do this to me?' I sobbed. The last time I cried with him around me was when Mother died. I never thought he could make me feel so in need of him in this way. He let me cry for a while before he wrapped his arm around me and started to cry with me. I had never seen this side of Markos before.

When I was finally calm, I could feel him grow behind me. He slowly removed my *kanga* to the waist and squeezed my breast. I did not resist him. He was sorry, that's what he kept saying, and that he loved me, and he kept on kissing my back and my neck, slowly pressing himself on me. I slowly opened myself to him, feeling his words on my skin, his heart deep inside me. And before long, we were slowly and rhythmically moving inside each other as we both cried.

'I love you... I am sorry,' that is all he said, like a chant, until I reached the height of my release and allowed him to do the same. He rested the weight of his body on mine.

When we finally returned home after those three days, Baba Mathayo was drained. He wouldn't speak much for days, enclosed in his own cave. He would often drink himself to sleep, and have his way with me whenever he wanted. Even without asking for my permission. Not that I had to give him permission. I was his.

I had two children after Mathayo, all boys. You would think that a man would be happy for you to give him sons. Markos was never really happy. Then, one morning in 1977, when I had come to full term and my belly was a huge pawpaw, I gave birth to a baby girl. My husband held her in his arms, and sang. He named her Christina, after his mother. He told me what it meant, follower of Christ. And then I saw it again in his eyes – the light had returned.

1999

Christina met a man 'online' – that's what she said. I wasn't sure what she meant by that but it is what she said. You see, Tina was always full of questions. When she was younger, she would ask about the kind of things that you don't always think about, like: why was the sky blue? why did zebras have stripes? why did we sleep? Things like those just are. They just are, you don't really ask about them. But when she saw her periods, and her breasts made her chest full one school break, her questions changed. She wanted to know more about her body. Hair, voice, shape, blood: everything that had structure came into question. Why and how and what now? Now, after many years of listening to Tina's questions, it was my turn to ask questions.

When the time came and I wanted to know how she had met this Prince, her Prince Charming, I had never anticipated that she would cite the internet as their meeting place. 'But what is the internet anyway?' I asked.

'Mama, it is 1999. You need to know these things. I will open a Yahoo account for you,' she said to me and went on to explain what seemed like Greek to me. Maybe Baba Mathayo would understand this child.

'But how would you know that he is genuine? Have you met any of his family on the internet?' I asked. Apparently, Prince lived in Canada and was willing to come all the way to Morogoro to meet us. He was a preacher there; that is what he told her. I wasn't so sure about this. If this internet thing was as real as my daughter explained it to me, then she wasn't safe with some stranger from there.

'Your father and I wouldn't allow that. You should marry someone we know. Isn't that right, Baba Mathayo?' I asked him.

To my question he simply responded, 'Yes, my wife,' which really meant 'don't bother me, dear, unless it's really necessary'. After years of living with him, nothing surprises me any more.

We were all in the living room, glued to the television, following the proceedings of the day. Mwalimu was dead. At some point, when Baba Mathayo had finally forgiven Mwalimu, he left the sisal plantation. We bought a small piece of land in Morogoro, where we started a farm.

Christina went on and on about Prince. 'Uncle Peter did not object when I told him,' Christina said, and added, 'We all know that Uncle Peter hears the voice of God.'

'And the rest of us don't? Your Uncle Peter knows nothing about the internet. Do you think there is internet in Peramiho? Where your dear Uncle Peter lives is Songea, not Dar es Salaam. His service unto God does not involve fancy computers,' I said. 'And besides, you are too young for marriage, dear. You are only–'

'Twenty-two. Which is how old you were when you got married, Mama,' Christina said.

But she wasn't ready for marriage. I could see how she would talk about this Prince like he was a dream come true. Christina had no idea what she was getting herself into.

'In our days, at 22, my mother was proud to send me off. You, however, are not yet done with your education. University of Dar es Salaam, that is something. I didn't go to university. You need to marry a professor or someone important, a real person. Not a person from the internet,' I said to her. But Christina would not listen to me, she would still do what she wanted to do.

'Baba Christina, please say something to your daughter. She has gone mad,' I said, turning to my husband.

'Did you say his name was Prince?' he asked Christina.

'Yes, Baba,' she replied.

'Like the American singer?' he said, and raised his head.

'My favourite.'

'You know that song "1999",' he asked, and they started singing it together. He stood up, and raised me to my feet. We danced, Markos and I, to a song I didn't even know. Christina joined us, and we danced together.

'That sounds like a really nice fella,' he said to Christina when we stopped dancing.

'Markos,' I said, with my arm on my waist. They just laughed.

How could he? He was supposed to be on my side.

'Christina, I am your mother. Don't listen to that old man, he knows nothing,' I said. But the two of them just exchanged glances, and kept on laughing.

'What seems to be funny? Share the joke, please,' I said.

'I would say, listen to your mother,' said Markos.

'Thank you,' I said.

'However, your mother – this woman that I have been married to for the past 35 years –seems to have forgotten how we met,' he said, and looked at me with those same lazy eyes that had made me say yes to him. If I had known all the things I was to go through because of those eyes, I would probably never have entered that car that day.

But I am glad that I did. Look at us now, all grown up with children and grandchildren on the way. I found myself smiling, and then laughing with Markos at the thought of us by the beach in Mtwara. The smell of sardines, the warmth of the sun on my face and the electricity that my body felt when he said he loved me: it all came back to me.

'Have you really forgotten, O goddess of Mtwara. You who have conquered the hell that I was, my queen,' he said. And with that, I let my case come to rest. I remembered. How could I forget? Love was indeed the outcome of faith. Markos shouldn't be allowed to do that to me, even at 57.

Esther Karin Mngodo has worked as a journalist in Tanzania for 12 years, which has enriched her experience as a writer. She is currently the News Editor at *The Citizen*, an English-language newspaper based in Dar es Salaam, and has written extensively on women's empowerment and human rights. When she is not writing for newspapers, Esther uses her pen to write songs, poems and short stories. She takes great pride in having been the first winner of the Ebrahim Hussein Poetry Prize in 2014, an award that promotes writings in Kiswahili.

The Storymage

Cheryl S Ntumy

The girl sits on the floor of the old dock office, hugging her knees. She has jet skin, red hair, double-lidded eyes that look past me. A circular scab on her hand tells me she's undergoing Adjusting. She must be close to complete adaptation or the Sea would have killed her already. Her documents identify her as Sechaba and the mechs call her Setch, but in the several minutes I've been here she hasn't answered to either name.

It's just the two of us in the cramped, musty space. The office has been out of use for some time now, replaced by a shinier version on the east end of the harbour. Filled with neglected crates and boxes, it stinks of mould and the ceiling has been taken over by bulbous firemoth egg sacs. The windows are closed against wind, Sea spray and prying eyes. Down here in the pit, where mechs toil day and night to keep Jalaba's ships running, anything that breaks routine attracts attention. With Adze manning street corners and cargo ships, their sticky fingers in every pie, crime is inevitable. But this is different. Anomalous, as the Law would say.

I glance at the clock on the desk. We have an hour, maybe two. Enough, I think, if I work quickly, but I've never worked a truth like this before. Fear reaches into me and scrapes my walls, great enough to hollow me out if I let it. But I won't. This is my chance.

With a deep breath, I lean forward in my chair. 'Do you remember what happened on the ferry, Sechaba?'

Silence.

'One of the other apprentices found you kneeling over the dead boy with a knife in your hand. There was blood all over your hands and clothes.'

Silence.

'Did you kill him?'

I don't expect her to answer. She hasn't spoken since she was discovered at the scene, not even to declare her innocence. The deceased was a stranger who most likely arrived on the ferry this morning. No one in the pit has any idea who he was or where he came from. Just a boy, 12, maybe 11, skin dappled with the scaly green patches associated with malaise. A junior junkie from the outskirts, the pit boys said, with unconcerned shrugs. Malaise makes you crazy. Everyone knows that. He probably did it to himself.

Setch is a good one, the mechs insisted, a natural, only a few months shy of graduating from apprentice to official. Naughty, but not crazy. Setch doesn't run around sticking knives into children. Watching her sit there, rocking back and forth, her back hitting the wall so hard it makes me wince, I'm not sure.

If it were up to the mechs, the matter would be closed already. Setch is one of their own and the child was a stranger. But someone called the Law, who wheedled and threatened and coaxed while Sechaba sat there, slamming her shoulder blades into the wall. The Law did what they're required to do in anomalous situations. They sent for Counsel.

Counsel is strong and certain, steady steps on firm ground, clear thinking and clever theories. He makes order out of chaos. He smooths things over. He's not known for making catatonic possible-murderers confess, but if anyone could, I suppose it would be him. They sent for Counsel, not for me. When the message came to the Great Hall, Counsel was out, the senior apprentices were nowhere in sight and I... Well, I was desperate. Five months I've been in seclusion. Five months, after a year in his service, learning a trade that didn't call me, living as a shadow until I could exist again.

A dead boy. A mute witness. The messenger must have said something about justice and clarity and settling things once and for all, but that's not what I heard. What I heard was… fuel. Food for my story-starved soul. Five months is a long time to go hungry.

I didn't pass the message on to Counsel. I knew what he'd say. 'This work is not yours to do. You have yet to find your place.' He says it often, as though repetition will make it true. There is no place for me and we both know it. I am a thing that once was, ceased to be and has become again. I must make my own place, and so, instead of calling Counsel, or running to fetch one of the seniors, I broke the rules. I asked the messenger to lead the way.

I'd been high up in the towers of the Great Hall for so long that I had forgotten what the world looked like, but when I stepped out I remembered. The sky, always roiling with dark clouds. The sour Sea tang in the air; the high, narrow streets above a maze of canals; the jostling. When we reached the dock, I longed to stop and gaze out past the ferries and subs. I missed the Sea. I missed the world. But not nearly as much as I missed stories.

'Sechaba, if you say nothing, the Law will take you away. Do you understand?'

Silence.

My gaze slides to the clock once more and I know I don't have the luxury of waiting any longer. Setch won't talk to me, so I must talk to her. I inch the chair to the left until I'm directly opposite her, staring into her blank eyes, and then I wait for the tale to turn me.

My craft is an old one. I know this in my bones, and from fragmented legends about times past. It comes slowly as always, beginning with an itch behind the ears, a tentative knock on the inside of my skull. Querying, testing the waters, wondering whether I'll let it in. Yes, old friend. The door is open. I part my lips and let the words come.

It's a simple tale, an old-fashioned 'A long time ago' story, the kind my own grandparents might have told me as a child. It's a maybe-folktale that sounds like the history of a people, a tale that warms the belly in the telling, a comforting, familiar balm. The words don't matter. It's a strange thing, because one would think it was the words that held the power, but it's not. The words are merely vessels. The story lies beneath them, inside them, hidden in the folds. The true listener must read between the lines.

Sechaba stops rocking. Her eyes flicker, and then focus on my mouth. I sense her longing, almost lecherous in its intensity, and slowly her limbs unfold and she crawls across the floor until she reaches my feet. She won't speak, not yet. This is a small tale, a key to turn the lock. I'm knocking on her door as the tale knocked on mine, and she is considering opening up to let me in.

The tale ends. She looks at me, eyes wide with expectation. I look back.

'If you want another one, you must ask for it.'

Her tongue slides over her lips and her eyes dart left and right. She reaches out to place one hand over my feet, her touch cold against the exposed skin between the sandal straps.

'Again.' Her voice is a raspy whisper. 'Again.'

And so I tell another tale, another innocent story of a girl who opened a box she was told to leave alone. A warning tale, like many she has heard before, no doubt. This one feels different, though. It evokes a vague anxiety, the sense that something is not quite right.

Sechaba gasps. 'I was only going to look at the engine,' she says.

It is here that my story ends and hers begins. As the words spill out of her I see things as she saw them. Sechaba snuck onto the boat to examine its inner workings, the heart of the job she was almost trained enough to do. It was a brand new ferry, the latest model. She was curious. She had waited until all the passengers were off, or so she thought.

She found the boy, crazed and desperate, in the cabin of the abandoned ferry. Standing there, where he was not supposed to be. Panting, spittle running down his jaw. Clutching a very big, very rusty knife.

'I saw him stick the blade in,' she says. 'But he didn't see me, not till I screamed. He fell and I took the blade out, but that made it worse.' She shakes her head. 'Blood everywhere, just kept coming. I wanted to run but my mind went funny, couldn't think, couldn't move.'

She speaks the truth, and yet I sense that a lie lurks somewhere inside this story.

'Malaise makes people crazy,' Sechaba whispers.

I see it then. The lie. I see the dying boy on the floor of the ferry cabin, with his malaise-stained skin, and I know it wasn't the drug that took him. I see his eyes, sightless now in the shimmer of Sechaba's recollection. In that instant I know what killed him. I see beyond his gaze into his fading mind. There was a secret. Someone else's secret, something the boy sought out and thought he could use to his advantage. But in our world there is a price to be paid by those who take what was not meant for them. The dead boy didn't understand this, and in that ignorance he's not alone.

Leaping to my feet, I rush to the office door and throw it open. A boy jumps out of the way. He looks at me in panic and I see his tale before he has time to think to tell it. He is the one who found Sechaba at the scene, and instead of waiting to hear her account before the Law, he crept to the door and eavesdropped on my sacred, secret stories.

'What have you done?' I grab him by the shoulders and shake him, terror filling my consciousness until spots dance before my eyes. 'Why are you standing out here, *listening*?'

'I'm sorry! I wanted to know...'

'Those stories were not for your ears!' I release him. There is still time. The tale might not have taken hold yet. 'Come inside. I'll fix it.'

But he turns and flees, and it takes me a moment to recover

enough to give chase. I'm no match for a mech apprentice, though, and before I reach the other end of the dock he has vanished. My fear sharpens as I turn back towards the old office. I did what I set out to do. I used what called to me and uncovered the truth. But I also made matters worse, unravelling the thin thread that holds everything together. There will be more death, more scandal, unless I find the boy. I can fix it. I'm sure I can. But I can't hide from Counsel.

When I reach the office Setch is standing in the doorway.

'That boy,' I ask, 'do you know him well?' She nods. 'Where would he run to? If he was scared. Where would he go?'

'I...' She shakes her head, her mind still trapped in the cobweb remnants of my tales. 'He likes the water.'

Water? Which water? Our whole world is water. Swallowing my panic, I wait for her thoughts to coalesce. There are no quiet, contemplative spaces in Jalaba, no corner that doesn't bustle with boats and bodies. The apprentice won't return to work. He'll seek sanctuary. But where?

'The cliffs,' says Sechaba at last. 'We go there sometimes. Kranes drop all kinds of scrap on the rocks; you can find good parts if you look hard enough. Juju says it's the best place in town.'

I look towards the north. Mist hides the better part of the cliffs.

'He likes to climb.'

She almost whispers the words, her gaze lowered. The rocks are jagged and slick with krane oil. Not even Adze would attempt to scale those cliffs.

'You've seen him do it?'

She shakes her head. 'He told me. He says you can get all the way to the top if you know where to put your feet.'

'Ai! She speaks!'

The voice comes from behind me. I turn to see that mechs have gathered in their greasy overalls, hands and faces streaked with grime.

'Yes, she speaks,' I reply, eager to leave. 'Tell the Law she's ready to give her account. I'm sorry; I must go.'

'Your credit!' one of the mechs calls out as I hurry past, but I can't stop, not even to claim the fee.

I have to return to the Great Hall and tell Counsel what I've done.

*** * ***

He's waiting when I burst into the Hall. Standing in the middle of the room, hands clasped behind his back, head tipped backwards. Contemplating the ceiling, maybe. More likely despairing of ever instilling proper discipline in his junior apprentice.

'Counsel, sir.'

He lowers his head.

I'm short of breath and dishevelled, which is never wise in Counsel's presence. 'I'm sorry. I was–'

'I know where you were. What I don't know is why.'

He refuses to face me, and I feel the heat of shame as my thoughts spin in a desperate effort to justify my actions. Why did I answer the call? Why do you think, Counsel? Because you've locked me in this glorious temple for the last five months, your prisoner, your prize. Intense study, you called it, as though it were a reward. Because you've drained me with tests and notes and constitutional trivia. Because I was wasting away while you took your time deciding what to do with me, where to place me, how to use me to your advantage. Because, Counsel, *sir*, I was starving.

The words collect in my head and remain there, clanging against each other. At last Counsel deigns to look at me.

'You had no right.'

'I'm sorry, sir.'

'You're no Counsel,' he says. 'Not even close. I have had to bend you to make you fit into this mould but even as an apprentice you're a disappointment. You're too flighty, governed by your emotions, by that monstrous chasm in your soul that cries out for stories like a suckling child. I thought intense study might finally change you, but look. Look what you've done now! Will you ever learn to control yourself?'

Swallowing my humiliation, I whisper, 'I try, sir.'

'You try? I have never seen you try! You are constantly giving in to your primitive urge and there is no place for that sort of thing in this world. As for running off to answer a call in my absence...' He grunts in disgust. 'I risked my work, my standing, to save you from alienation and you thank me by spitting in my face! The Law depends on Counsel to find answers where others have failed. How can you do that without discipline?'

There is no answer I can give that would satisfy him, no way to reassure him that I'm worth the sacrifices he's made for me. I have no affinity for any of the accepted crafts. I waited for years, watching children my age and younger find their callings and take their places as apprentices. By the time I was three years past apprentice assignment, the only thing that moved me was stories. But stories are not a calling, not any more, and the Placement Committee would have exiled me if Counsel hadn't stepped in.

I know I should be grateful. He broke our most sacred rule to save me. He lied to the Committee, told them he'd witnessed my call to counselcraft one afternoon in the Great Hall courtyard. He told them I was a late-blooming natural. Now his words wash over me, words he has uttered so many times I know them all by heart. I'm tired. Less hungry after Sechaba, but so tired.

And then I remember the reason I came back here. The boy, Juju. The cliffs.

'I did the work, sir.'

Counsel falls silent, stunned by my interruption.

'I shouldn't have answered your call, but I worked the truth and I found the answers, all by myself.' Now that I've begun, the words come quickly. 'The girl, Sechaba, she didn't kill the stranger. She found him on the ferry and he killed himself in front of her. She thought it was malaise. It looked like malaise, but it wasn't. It was a calling curse. I saw it in his eyes as he died, in the girl's memories. He took in secrets crafted for the ears of another and they turned him the wrong way. That's when I realized that there was someone outside, eavesdropping, and I –'

'Your skills aren't advanced enough for that kind of work,' Counsel cuts in.

'I didn't use counselcraft. When I got there the entire syllabus left me and I used my own... my *primitive* urge.'

His lips curl in a snarl. 'Impossible.'

'I tried to tell you before, sir. Stories are medicine–'

He strikes me with the back of his hand, so hard I almost lose my balance. 'Heresy!'

My cheek burns and I fear his ring might have torn the skin, but there's no time to nurse it.

'Counsel, please. The boy who overheard has run away. I need your help to find him.'

'My help?' he bellows, and then bursts into bitter laughter. 'After your insubordination? After flaunting your superstition in public and tarnishing the name of this Hall? Now you want me to help you clean up your mess?'

'It's only...' I hesitate. 'He went to the cliffs, I think. I would have followed him on my own before returning here, but the kranes...'

Downturned lips, narrowed eyes. Counsel's disdain is palpable.

'Please, sir. The tales I told to make Sechaba talk weren't made for other ears. The apprentice who heard me, Juju....'

'Then go and fix it.'

'The kranes.' I bite my lip, embarrassed by my weakness.

'A whole apprentice, afraid of birds?' His features have shifted now, settling into an almost-smile. Maybe he's revelling in my torment. 'Assuming your speculation is correct, you'd better find your eavesdropper before the curse claims him. If you run you might be able to make it back for evening study.'

He means it. He's not going to help me. As soon as this becomes clear I flee, terrified that I might already be too late. Through the crowded streets, into the market, dodging bio-chip vendors and metal drums filled with plucked waterfowl and writhing tentacled beasts. Hawkers sidle up to me, opening their coats to reveal illicit tech, and I don't even stop long enough to shake my head.

I glance down at the motors in the canals below, their engines screaming as they pull out of designated stops, spraying the pavement with green Seawater. Maybe it would be faster to take one. No – traffic is too slow and there is no time for haggling over fares. I head up the Hundred Steps, past the consortium, weaving my way through the queue outside the main Conservator bank.

By the time I'm back at the dock a light drizzle has started. Past the ferries. Around the executive harbour. Almost colliding with two tall Adze in bright wax print shirts so crisp they must be new. One reaches for the stunner at his hip before realizing that I'm only a harmless girl, and moving away with a grunt.

Then comes the beach, thronged with vendors and tourists. I avoid it by taking the hiking trail. A small private yacht club, another market, and then the cliff and rocks, crammed together along the coastline. I hear the kranes before I see them. Their guttural call is aggressive, almost malevolent, and I keep my head down to avoid attracting their gaze.

It is said that they don't like us. Not just Counsels, but Sanguines and Creators, too. They don't like anyone who looks too deeply, or thinks too hard, or knows what others wish to hide. No one says how they feel about people like me, because people like me no longer exist. The words they used to call us have faded away and language closed over the gaps the way the ocean covers sunken ships.

I slip and trip over the rocks until I'm almost out of earshot of the market, then look up. In all honesty, I don't expect to see Juju, yet there he is, climbing like Sechaba said. My breath catches for a moment, but he moves with purpose and skill.

He's too far away to hear me call, so I continue my slow journey. A clutch of kranes has perched a short distance away. There aren't many, less than ten, but the smallest is as big as a man, rubbery wings large enough to engulf me. I swallow my panic and watch them out of the corner of my eye. Their long grey bodies squat on the rocks, glistening with oil, wings folded back, angular heads bowed as their skinny arms pick through the treasure they've brought up from the sea. Suddenly one of them turns to face me. Its blue eyes narrow and it bares a row of sharp black teeth, hissing, alerting the others to my presence.

Heart racing, I bow my head to show them I mean no harm. I'm not here for them. They don't respond, and it's an agonizing eternity before they stop staring. Another krane flies overhead, casting a vast shadow, and I duck instinctively although it's far above me.

I'm at the foot of the cliff now. I reach out to test the rock. My hand slides over the rough surface and comes away slick with oil. How did Juju make it up there? I focus my gaze on the rock, seeking. Stories can do many things, but they require a level of reciprocity. The rock must yield, and I don't have enough experience to know whether it will.

The water pounds against the rocks behind me, washing up all the way to my feet, drenching the hem of my skirt before I have a chance to snatch it out of harm's way. The silky trim isn't Seaproof; I watch the fabric curl in on itself and harden. I've taken to dressing for libraries and gilded staircases rather than the streets. Counsel apprentices aren't meant to go clambering over rocks. They are made for sedate conversations in quiet rooms. But I'm not a true apprentice.

I wait for the tale to come. It takes time to find a connection here, the rock too old, too solid. Maybe I'm naïve to think I can work truth out of a cliff, but Juju left a trail and the stories might be able to follow that. Words come to me. It's a tale so ephemeral I'm afraid I'll lose it. As I speak the words I realise it's not a tale at all, but more of a proverb.

It's not enough, but fate is on my side today. I look up to see Juju descending and the fear leaves my body. I sink to the ground, waiting for him to reach me.

'Why d'you follow?' he demands, a moment before he jumps to the ground. 'I said sorry. Didn't I? What else?'

I get to my feet. 'What you did was dangerous.'

'I know, I know! Bad luck to eavesdrop. Might hear Adze secrets, curse you so you go to the water and drink till you die.' He scratches his arm, and the back of his neck, and the top of his head. 'Not the truth. Truth is bigger than that. I know. Other things, not just Adze curses. Story things, eh? I know. It's why the blade, that kid. Saw or heard something he wasn't supposed to, made his mind go funny, then the blade. I know. I see it. I see everything.'

It's raining properly now, but neither of us makes any move to seek shelter.

'What do you see, Juju?'

He shivers and doesn't answer. Instead he says: 'Special places for your feet. On the cliff; that's how I get up. Special places, safe and you don't slip because the oil's mixed with the lichen and thickened. Kranes showed me. Clever things, eh, kranes. Like mechs. Pick things up, pull them apart, put them back together. Not like you. You break things, can't fix them. Broke that kid with your stories, now trying to break me. I see it. I see everything.'

Indignation fills me. 'I had nothing to do with what happened to that child!'

'Someone like you, then.'

'There is no one like me. It was a calling curse. He should have known better. So should you.'

Juju shakes his head. 'Told mechs not to let you work Setch, but...' He shrugs. 'Wanted it over. Counsel sent her, they said. Sent *you*? Girl without a calling for so long, not even a senior apprentice? Mechs called for your father, not you. Why d'you come? Don't you know your place?'

The world feels close all at once, tight and unyielding, and I find it hard to breathe. Where is the story? I'm waiting and waiting but it seems to be lost. Where is the tale that will keep this boy safe from the consequences of his curiosity? That's why I came here, to fix what I broke. To redeem myself. Why is he so ungrateful?

Maybe it's this place. Maybe it's the kranes, watching me with their beady blue eyes, scaring my stories away.

'Let's go back to the dock,' I shout over the rain. 'You'll get in trouble for being away so long. By the time we get back all of this will be sorted out.' I say it like I'm certain.

'Not going back to work.'

'But –'

'Not going.'

I shift position, trying to meet his gaze. Stories are medicine, but… He looks at me, and I can see the change in his eyes. They're rolling around in the sockets, too bright, too wide, bulging and red. Old friend, where are you? Come and help me, please.

'What are you?' Juju cries out.

'What do you mean? I'm a junior apprentice Counsel.'

'No. What are you?'

Ah, yes. He sees everything. 'I don't know,' I confess. 'Something…old. Something bad.'

'Find out.' He's starting to sway on his feet. 'Can't do your work if you don't know what to call it.' A sudden sharp cry escapes his lips. 'Oh, it hurts!' He begins scratching again, clawing at his skin as though trying to get under it.

'Juju, stop!' I look into his spinning eyes, searching for my story in vain.

He drops to his knees and begins to bang his forehead against the rocks.

Where is it? Where is the story? I fling myself at the boy and wrap my arms around his shoulders, straining to hold him upright. He's crying now, a loud, drawn-out sound that culminates in a choked gasp before starting up again. My grip slackens a little and he forces his torso forward, breaking free. His head hits the rock and when I pull him up, he's bleeding.

Something grabs my foot. I kick hard before turning to see my assailant. The kranes have come to rescue their mech friend from the wicked apprentice Counsel.

'I'm trying to help him!' I tell them, as he pulls us both downward with strength a boy smaller than me shouldn't possess.

His head slams against the rock once more. The kranes hiss and jab their bony fingers at me.

'Stupid creatures! I'm trying to save him!'

They grab my feet and pull my hair, hissing through the rain.

I jerk and curse, but refuse to let go. 'Go away! This has nothing to do with you!'

But they don't leave.

'Stop it, stupid things! This isn't your place!'

And then... oh! I see it. The glaring obstruction in my path, the reason the tales haven't come to me in the moment I most need them. Like Juju I see everything now, and for a moment I'm too astonished to move, paralyzed by my stupidity. When the shock fades, I release him and crawl backwards, allowing the kranes to gather around his thrashing form. They cover him with their slippery lithe bodies, hiding him from view. The crying stops.

They remain in that position for some time, and then roll away like waves. Juju is still kneeling, shoulders heaving, but he is no longer trying to break his skull open.

'What did you do?' I call out to the kranes.

They ignore me, instead focusing their attention on their patient. They speak to him in a crooning sibilant tongue, touching his face and shoulders tenderly as though checking for wounds.

The rain has turned back into a drizzle. Juju looks at me.

'Kranes got a word for people like you.' He sounds weak but calm, as though nothing untoward has happened, as though we've been sitting here chatting all this time. 'Say our language has holes, theirs doesn't. Maybe why you can be something old. Language left a hole and nobody filled it, people like you get lost, go around answering the wrong calls.'

I swallow, still shaken. 'What did they do?'

His shoulders lift in a careless shrug. 'Went inside my head, took the bad thing out. Wasn't really a bad thing, more like a thing that was fine before but inside got all twisted up and strange, didn't work properly. Thing you made to fix Setch. Story thing.'

Yes, the story thing. It stirs within me, liberated now that the ignorance that bound it is gone. My primitive urge, a craft so old my people forgot what to call it.

'I'm sorry, what I said before.' Juju gets to his feet, then reaches out to help me up. 'About you breaking things. Wasn't me, understand? Twisted-up story thing. Made my mind go funny like that kid. Really was a junkie, eh? Saw his skin. Curse or no curse, that kid was full of mal.'

I nod.

'Should go back to work. Have to tell a big fancy lie so they don't whip me for serious. Ai! Especially Six. Man got a temper like a Catavan storm. So, you coming or what?'

With a glance at the kranes, I say 'I'll catch up.'

Juju looks at me, eyebrows raised. 'Not hissing any more doesn't mean you're friends, eh? Kranes still don't like your kind.'

I laugh, surprising myself. 'Thanks for the advice.'

He shrugs again and starts off across the rocks, as sure-footed as one of his oily grey comrades. I turn towards them.

'Thank you.'

They stare at me in silence.

'I didn't understand. I thought you were confused about what was happening. I thought…' I sigh. 'I didn't understand.'

There is a tale that must be told when I return to the Great

Hall. Somehow, I must find a way to sit Counsel down and tell it so he hears me. He has always been immune to this medicine of mine, and I thought it was because he is so stubborn, so righteous. I thought maybe it was all superstition and emotion and something wrong inside me, but today I worked a truth and helped a girl and now I know what's real.

The kranes haven't moved. They seem to know what I want from them, but they won't offer it. If I want it, I must ask. Their language, like my stories, requires reciprocity.

'You have a word...'

I falter, afraid they'll turn me down, then remember that I have nothing to lose. What else is there? Another five months of intense study under Counsel's thumb? Five years? A lifetime? No. No, never. I was hungry and now I've tasted stories and must have more. I must be fed until I'm strong enough to work harder truths than traumatized silences, until I'm brave enough, wise enough to fix what I break.

I begin again. 'You have a word for people like me. Will you tell me what it is? My people... we need words. Like Counsel and mech and apprentice. We need names to know who we are, and there is no name for what I am. There hasn't been for a long, long time. I'm not supposed to exist, you see. People like me... we're not real. I want to be real.'

Silence.

'I know you don't like me, but maybe one day I can return the favour. Will you share your word with me? Please.'

The kranes exchange glances. They stretch their wings and roll their necks and whisper amongst themselves. Then one of them beckons. I go to kneel before it.

A long time ago, there was a girl who opened a box she had been instructed to leave alone... I didn't know my place. I think of all the years I spent waiting for a call I could answer, and then I let the thoughts go, pebbles worn smooth over time, too smooth to serve me now.

The krane leans in to whisper in my ear, a word in its tongue that has no parallel in mine. But it's enough. I smile with my whole being, and I know I will never be hungry again. Inside me the story wakes, knocking on the door. Yes, old friend. The door is open.

Cheryl Ntumy is a Ghanaian writer based in Botswana. Her short stories have appeared in *Lemon Tea and Other Stories from Botswana* and *Mapping Me: A Landscape of Women's Stories*. Her longer work includes the Conyza Bennett trilogy: *Entwined*, *Unravelled* and *Crowned*; the paranormal novella *Crossing*; and several romance novels published by Sapphire Press. She is currently working on another young-adult trilogy.

Five Is Not Half of Ten

Daniel Rafiki

I knew I would have to be the early bird on some days.

What no one told me was that, on other days, I would be the worm. The unsuspecting worm whose only misdeed was having a body too long to be concealed from sight. Or, sometimes, simply not burrowing into the earth fast enough.

You see, most earthworms can re-grow lost segments, assuming the damage to the rest of the worm isn't too grave. But being a policewoman had taken more parts of me than I could ever re-grow. I looked strong. There were times I even felt strong. There were also times I wouldn't let anyone near me, afraid I would cut someone with all the pieces of my shattered self.

It was Thursday.

Thursdays often reminded me of Kui. Perhaps it was because our official first date had been on a Thursday. Because I was tired of Mama's perennial rice cooking, we ate at Hashmi's that night. We had what in my opinion was the single worst pizza ever made. The crust was as crunchy as shortbread biscuits, so friable that it cracked noisily when you tried to break off a slice. Or rather, a block, which is what we called those slices for the rest of that night. Neither of us whined about the food. We ate in silence. Served us right for the amount of money we were paying for the meal. Talk, like our meal, was cheap.

Or maybe it was because, on our way back to the dorms that night, she picked a fight with our taxi driver, whose name, fortuitously, was Friday James. I thought it was a silly name too. I just knew not to say it out loud. We were kicked out ten minutes after our pick-up. I had rolled my eyes at her, peeved at how unnecessary their argument had been. It was just after midnight.

At least Friday got us to Friday, Kui said.

We both laughed.

I have a quiet laugh but when something tickled Kui she had an explosive laugh and she came crashing into me; taking advantage of our proximity to tag onto my hijab and ease it behind my right ear, till I could feel the hand of its chiffon fabric against the back of my ear lobe. She liked it that way. Kui did what she liked.

It was the way she appeared to know exactly what decisions I needed to make. That is how I fell for her. How unbelievably strong-willed she was, too. It happened slowly, as though she was playing a flute that charmed me out of a basket. It wasn't one of those clumsy, leg-buckling, thud-making type of falls. It felt like I was gently tripped; that in the seconds it would take me to reach the ground my world froze and she was the only one in it. It was also how perfect she looked under the sun and on that night, how much greater she looked under the moonlight.

When she curled her fingers around my wrist and pulled me into a kiss, it was the first of countless moonlight kisses we would share. I remember hesitating. It was hard to suppress the dyed-in-the-wool traditionalist in me that wouldn't be caught dead kissing a girl on the street. It was harder to resist Kui.

That was 10 years ago.

I haven't seen Kui since The Split – the new order the then government of Musanze instituted. I came from a people that had survived graft, greed and power-hungry officials for decades, but when The Split restructured an entire society, it was a new low. The ruthless manner in which it was implemented, coupled with the inherent naivety of the poor people of Musanze, now *Fives*, meant a terrifying new way of life, re-living in the exact moments of history long thought to be forgotten.

I haven't seen most of the people I went to school with since The Split. I still used to go to Hashmi's sometimes. Not in the hope that I would run into her. Bumping into her at our favourite restaurant would never happen. Walking through that glass front double door would only bring me grief, and I was done feeling that.

Besides, only Fives could go to Hashmi's. Actually, the whole of Lisami Street, where the old restaurant building defiantly stood a decade later, was a street for Fives.

***

When the doorbell rang, I sprang up from bed – for the second time, since I had already been up to perform Fajr. I wore a hijab, lest it was a man at the door. I thought it seemed particularly warm for April, as I walked past the scattered clothes in my living room to get to the door. Living alone for that long meant I had stopped noticing a lot of things, the heap on my floor being one of them.

It didn't take me very long to get to my door because no Five lived in a house that big anyway. I closed my fingers around the door handle, twisted it and began to swing it ajar. It scratched against the floor, and forcing it open made it sound like a bad DJ record, the result of years of water damage.

On that day, the parcel was delivered by Faiza. They were particularly careful about who they sent to deliver the weekly posting to my house. Almost always a woman. Always a Muslim. The police force was too scared to create a circumstance that would trigger The Violation Clause, a scenario that in turn, granted precedent for a court hearing that could lead to a change of status for the afflicted party, from a Five to a Ten.

Faiza hardly spoke. If there were any traces left of the woman she was before she joined the force, you could only see them in the way she wore her uniform. Tight trousers, just long enough; perfectly tailored shirts and a subtle tilt in the way she wore her cap. Our uniforms definitely did not come like that. She either had a flawless tailor, or an excellent body. This is for you, she said, hand delivering my assignment for the week as was the norm, and was quickly on her way.

I would be stationed at The Tower for the week. Good news.

* * *

Musanze had always been a city of the haves and the have-nots. Different parts of it showed you different things. Whenever I visited Kiyovu and The Beach Bay, I saw people that lived in semi-palaces and drove the newest cars. Their daughters wore silver bracelets, their sons wore dreadlocks cleaner than their sneakers, listened to online radio, celebrated Black History Month, and had turkey for Thanksgiving. Kui was from The Beach Bay.

Their children's children would live the same, if not a better life. They would have bigger houses and even bigger egos. Their disregard for the people that lived on the other end of the city would be worse. They would walk with a bounce that came from the entitlement they thought their birth certificate gave them. It was biological privilege. Family wealth wasn't the sort of thing that you lost in Musanze. Being born in that part of town was like having a get-out-of-jail-free card. Not that actual jail would ever be an option.

Behind her father's back, sometimes Kui came across town, to Bugogo, where I was from. Her father was the Minister of Justice, and ran a chain of hotels, which were all presently areas for Tens. She would come here to have her hair done into braids or to shop for bangles. Occasionally, she would visit me, against my will.

In Bugogo, the rain rained harder and the sun shone hotter, almost as if nature were an accomplice punishing the people here for their plebeian position in the food chain. When people that weren't from here had to get things from this side of town, they wore different clothes, carried less money and brought their spare phone, the Kadudu that WandaTel sold for 400 francs and whose exhaustive list of specs included making and receiving phone calls.

They also always had to leave in a rush. You couldn't be around Bugogo for too long – God forbid you catch a cold or some poverty. The people that lived on this side of town were natural hard workers. Having three meals a day had long been a luxury and what most people considered as too skinny was acceptable here.

I was born in Bugogo. I attended high school on scholarship and, when I had to leave home, it seemed like an upgrade from the place where I had spent my entire childhood. Constant food. Hot baths. A mini-heaven. Growing up without a father was one of those things I did not obsess about until I picked up a few books and met a few other girls in high school, both of which made it a big deal. Maybe it was just the fact that they had fathers. My immediate neighbour was a single mother, and the neighbour of that neighbour was a single mother. When I look back, it does strike me as odd that our whole community was made up of single mothers. How did they all find each other? What was wrong with our fathers? Was it the same man? What a man! Was it the same bunch of men? How did you prove you were a single mother? Did it count if you were just pregnant? Would they ever send away some single mothers? Why did no one speak about it?

I never found the courage to ask Mama all these questions. Mama never said much and there was an air of imperturbability to her that gave the impression that she was complete, a finality to her that made her the kind of person that you didn't question, particularly about a man. I was close to Mama Kip, whose son was my age and was the first person to notice my growing breasts, and who remained a huge fan of them as I grew a fuller chest. I asked Mama Kip once about all the mothers. There are some things that you can only learn in a storm, Yasmin, she said.

The monthly Sunday meetings that all our mothers attended are my most vivid childhood memory. They were always held outside Mama Kalisa's house because she had the biggest stove. She also didn't have any children that I had seen. She was just Mama. No one asked about Kalisa. Mama Kip made enough black tea to last the community a week. Mama Unal brought extra white plastic chairs from her small chair rental business. On meeting Sundays she made sure she rented out only some of her chairs, so she could provide some for use by the women. When there was plenty, they ate plenty. Most times they only had tea. When Mama Chiraghdin made *viazi karai*, my mother would make the accompanying tamarind sauce.

I am not sure what they discussed. It was likely they encouraged each other. Kui once joked that it was probably an admissions meeting deciding on the fate of new single mothers wanting to join the community, and that they discussed their secret plan to cut off all men's penises – sentiments that offended me but that I still smirked at.

Mama would come home from the meetings seemingly happier. But this would only last the night. She would return to her usual stern self by the next morning, as if the load of happiness was too heavy for her to bear. As if the load tipped her stability scale over to joy and she couldn't have that. Most of the women of the community were like this. Mama would go about her business, lifeless still.

I had no siblings. So when Mama died two years after The Split, I would never forgive her for a lifetime spent not opening up to the one person she had.

***

The Tower was a half-hour ride away from my house on MZ 9 ST. I straightened my badge before I grabbed my bike keys to leave for my station for the week. It was shortly after 8am. LAW ENFORCEMENT: THE TOWER, my badge read. Yusuf Yasmin was the order in which my name appeared. I preferred that Yasmin came first. The reverse made it seem like a man's name.

My motorcycle ride was a ritual. Helmet firmly in place, I rode to work. I was a little late and hardly felt all the little bumps and potholes in my road that were typical of any Five street. This week would be important. I was hopeful that all the months of planning wouldn't come undone.

Crossing over onto Avenue de la Paix meant a change in environment that worsened my anger at the system. The people were different. A Ten Street. I rode over perfect roads whose yellow lines were aggressively repainted every month. No Ten would ever have the displeasure of interacting with a Five here. Unless of course, they were a police officer or a guard.

The Tower was at the end of Avenue de la Paix. The building was essentially a symbol of The Split, having been the first building used to implement it. Which was upsetting, because everyone had seen the building being innocently erected before then. The Minister of Justice had announced it to be the new legal headquarters. No one had seen this coming. Actually, no one that cared had seen this coming. It was made of grey, smooth stone and the word TOWER was visible outside the 26th floor, in bold black. It was lazily named, but it was the only structure you could see from most parts of Musanze. Who puts up a building and calls it BUILDING?

Tomorrow would mark a decade since The Split, a milestone that no one really needed to be reminded of because every second of your life was a stark reminder.

* * *

When the announcement came, 10 years ago, I had four days of high school left. I don't remember exactly what I was doing but the state of emergency was announced on the evening news, and I only heard about it a few hours later as a consequence of one of Kui's and my evening escapades. Getting back to the campus had to be done tactfully, but on that day when we returned there was just something about people that marked a change.

'Are they allowed to do this?' someone asked.

I eventually saw the announcement and understood it all: the silence, what this meant for Kui and me; what it meant for Mama and the other mothers; everything. The announcement played over and over. When you thought you couldn't possibly hear it one more time, they repeated it again. Regular programming was interrupted for two days to allow for the repetition and, by the end of those two days, it was stuck in your head like a catchy tune.

The re-evaluation and re-registration of each family was to be done at The Tower, two days from then. All citizen records were also to be stored there. The government was very clear about its demands. There would be split roles, split amenities, split relationships and split spaces. Your social status would be re-evaluated bi-annually. Some Tens became Fives. Very few went the other way. Mama Unal had been doing well for herself with the chair rental. Four years after the split, she was re-evaluated as a Ten. She would never have to see Bugogo again – in fact she couldn't by law.

It was obvious what this meant for Kui and me; there was no point crying over spilt milk. What was done was done. Our split was brisk. I wrote her a note I knew she would remember.

> You and I were made of glass, we'd never last
> Meant to die, we moved fast and then we crashed
> You and I were made of glass, we'd never last

She did not respond.

When high school came to an end, after those four days, I had few options to explore that were better than being a policewoman. The new state of things sealed my fate.

Why she didn't write back became a void that I struggled to fill. Occupying myself with as much distraction as I could get my hands on barely did the trick.

***

My work day moved quickly. All I did at The Tower was walk around the data centre. It pained me that I had to protect the structure that had left me so vulnerable. This was where they kept all the records, and all our identification was linked to the giant computers the Chinese had built into this room. There was one Chinese engineer with me; here for routine maintenance. He knew not to talk to me, as if even he, a goddamned foreigner, had been integrated as a Ten.

I surveyed the room with a keener eye, taking note of the door and the distances between the computers. I would need to relay this information to Manzi at the meeting later today. Considering how important it was, the data centre was in a fairly small room. It relied too heavily on the triple-grill door that was 'foolproof'. Those damned Chinese again.

I thought about Kui some more.

On some days I wished I could talk to her. I wanted to tell her about my bad days. Kui would know what to say. She had a way of simplifying things, of making anyone that was in her company feel every inch relaxed.

I would tell her about the four weeks I was stationed at the new market in Bugogo. That Mama Chiraghdin still sold *viazi karai* and how it completely broke me to have to collect half of her daily earnings to pay her daily Five tax. I had to collect this tax from a large number of the same women who shaped my childhood. And no one knew how much I cried that week – I cried so much that my tears ran out and my whole body started to hurt. And when that happened I started to scream because the hurt just would not stop.

I would tell her about Kip, who had grown into a sturdy young man who rode a bicycle, running people's errands. When he shoved a policeman for demanding unfair license fees, we arrested him and I hadn't seen him since. I had contemplated sneaking a picture of my bare breasts to him in prison because I was sure those would at least make him smile.

I could also tell her about my first week in the force, when the wound from our separation had barely formed a scab and I was thrown into a world that I had worked so hard to escape. That was also the week when Abdul with the big head tried to kiss me on one of the training nights. I almost broke his rib trying to punch him away. I am still irritated by the mere thought of a man. And when Abdul then spread the rumour that I swung for the other side, I walked around with my head held high because no one would ever question me. I was taking after Mama after all.

Mama died six years ago because St Hannah's, the Five hospital she went to for her leukaemia treatment, ran out of chemotherapy drugs. I took a week off from the force after that.

There were weeks when I worked on Ten streets. I tried hard to ignore how unbothered Kui and her fellow Tens were. No one that lived at The Beach Bay ever had their houses randomly searched in case they 'seemed suspicious'. On my days at the RCT mall, I wondered if she would ever come to see a movie. She didn't. I would get angry at myself for thinking about Kui yet again and swear to myself that it was the last time I would ever do it.

***

When I finished work at The Tower I got on my bike and rode to Hashmi's, which is where we held all our Resurgence meetings.

I arrived last. Everyone had ordered their meal and Eva had ordered me the usual. We were tense. This final meeting was only supposed to happen when two people who were part of the Resurgence were stationed at The Tower. It had to be done then or we would miss this priceless window. I briefed Manzi on the detail of the data centre. He was stationed at The Tower with me. Karan gave the final instructions about shorting the fuse and which wires Manzi would have to pull. It was pointless detail to me. I knew my role.

I barely slept that night but morning came fast.

It took me a little longer than usual to get ready because of all the uncertainty I felt about today. I was late for work but I rode steadily, thinking about how fast I would have to act for our plan to work. After parking the motorcycle, I walked through the main vault equally fast, ignoring Manzi, who was outside the vault. He seemed relieved. I figured that my late arrival meant he had started to suspect that I had bailed out.

The walk up the stairs was easy. It was a short carpeted staircase like those in most urban homes, which meant that I didn't to have to lift my leg too high with each step. A total contrast from the ones in the houses on MZ 9 ST which were irregularly built; making each individual stair a separate mental calculation. I had a deep hate for the building. I could still remember seeing it as part of the announcement 10 years ago, and it had not changed, while obviously profiting from tireless maintenance and renovation.

Time moved slowly. As I walked about the data centre, I could see a horde of people here for their scheduled bi-annual re-evaluation. The process didn't take very long. When they took your fingerprint, it would be linked to your financial records and movement co-ordinates. Re-evaluation took into account how 'good' a citizen you had been, along with your social and financial links. Some Fives were hopeful. Most Tens were anxious, naturally. Getting downgraded was a certain path to depression.

12.30pm. This was my cue. I left to attend Jumu'ah prayers, as had been the plan. I wasn't guilty that prayer was my alibi. The way I saw it, God wasn't guilty that he had forsaken me. It seemed fair. Little suspicion would be raised by a petite Muslim woman leaving her station for prayer past noon on a Friday. That part was easy.

Leaving the entrance door open was dangerous. Manzi would have to get up there very fast and I cued him with a nod once I left The Tower. Getting to the mosque that was on a Five street would have taken half the time on my motorcycle but I chose to walk.

I thought about Mama all the way to the mosque. How nonchalant she would have been if she had found out what we had planned. How she would still have set the table and served *ibitoki* like nothing had just happened. It made me sad that I never found out what moved her, that all she saw was in such plain colours.

The frenzy began just as I was leaving the mosque. As the sirens became louder, I could see everyone rushing towards The Tower. Enough, was all the announcement said. People knew where to go. The smoke was getting carried to the right by the wind, over The Beach Bay, like a cloud that was about to bring a new kind of rain onto the land.

Television videos of building fires looked so little like the real thing. The fire burned for days, red flames tearing down layer after layer of this dreaded symbol of our schism. By the time the fire was contained, The Tower had been razed to the ground along with The Split.

Weeks passed and people settled into their new, old lives. I stayed on MZ9 ST. It seemed like the right place to call home. I would get dinner at The Manor soon; have a Ten-course meal perhaps.

There was hope again. Five was equal to ten.

And it's tough for me to shelve it, it's you I see myself with, was the text message I got several weeks after the fire.

I stared at it, recognizing the response I expected to get ten years ago.

But that was a void I had already filled.

Daniel Rafiki is a Rwandan writer and general maker of bad puns. His short story 'Versus' won the Huza Press Prize for Fiction 2015. He is currently based in Nairobi, Kenya where he splits his time unequally between writing and medical school. He describes himself as a closet writer who finds the art thoroughly fulfilling and hopes that his passion for literature, Africa and science will soon come together nicely.

That Little House in the Village

Zaka Riwa

Mike and Mo arrive at the wooden gate in their tinted 4x4 around 17.15 and stop. From their windscreen, they see the bigger part of the sky covered by tall trees and their intertwining branches. On the other side of the gate, they see a small farm filled with banana and coffee trees. It is getting darker and harder to differentiate one from the other.

'Holy shit, it's nice!'

Mike replies, 'Darkness comes early down here.'

Mike, who sits in the driver's seat, draws out a bundle of keys from his trouser pocket and hands them over to Mo. Without asking or waiting for explanation, Mo grabs them, opens the door and jumps out. He proceeds to the gate with quickening steps as he looks around. He slips his hands into the space between the narrow wooden bars of the gate, to get a better handle on it, and inserts the key. After a minute of fumbling with the lock, it opens. He pushes the left side of the gate as he walks the other half of it to the opposite side. It swings with such force that it bounces all the way back at the same speed. A thin and long, grassy driveway leads to a small house at the other end of a compound, with two lines of mud where tyres have left evidence of their passage the day before.

Mo places a stone in front of the right foot of the gate to block it, and it obeys him. As Mike finishes parking close to the kitchen door, Mo sees a man approaching. He emerges from the neighbour's field on the opposite side, coming straight towards him, with a long stick in his hand. He has a hard face and the intensity of his stare worries Mo. Mo immediately calls out Mike's name. Mike from his rear-view mirror can see that it is Babu Nduu. He switches on the car radio and turns the volume up. He steps out, closes the door and follows them. Babu Nduu, seeing Mike approaching, increases his pace to meet him halfway. They are both smiling to each other as they shake hands. Babu Nduu's smile is much wider and more genuine than Mike's. Mike throws a quick glance at Mo and then back at Babu, saying, 'Baabuuuu, how are you doing, Baabuuu?'

Babu replies with equal excitement, 'Now that I've seen you, my boss, I'll be doing great'. Mike bursts out laughing and shakes Babu Nduu's hand vigorously as if wanting to prove how strong he still is. He says, 'Baaabuuuu, I've told you I'm fine. You don't have to be coming here every time. Don't leave your wife for my sake.' He points at Mo. 'Have you seen my friend here? I've come with him and we have some work we need to do in quiet.'

Babu chuckles and lets go of Mike's hand. He brushes his palm softly as if to release the sweatiness of Mike's hand, saying, 'Yeah, you know, I heard the sound of the car from there,' pointing to the direction he came from. Then laughs as he looks at Mike, 'and I had to come to check to see if it was you or someone else, you know'.

'Yeah, I know,' Mike interrupts. 'But I'm here now, and for the next two months, remember? I won't need your service until the end of the week. So I don't expect disturbances of someone tilling out there or cutting branches, right?'

'As you wish,' Babu replies politely, looking around. 'Now that I know it's you, I'll go. If you need me, you know where to find me.'

'Yes I know, Babu, don't worry, just relax. You see, I came with my friend this time. He can help me out if I need a hand with something. Unless it's something serious, which I know won't happen, you can rest, okay?'

Babu nods and smiles at the same time. He waves his hand in agreement, turns around and starts walking away with his stick. Mike salutes him with a polite hand gesture, 'Goodnight, Babu.' Babu raises up his stick and, without turning his head, shouts back, 'Goodnight, boss.' He disappears just as he came, through the neighbour's banana field, into a pathway that goes straight down to a local bar.

Mike closes the wooden gate and walks back to the house. Looking through the kitchen window, he sees that Mo has already offloaded most of the stuff they came with. He looks inside the car and sees that only one thing remains. The music is still playing, but turned down a bit from when Babu was around. Inside on the kitchen floor there are two crates of beer, an ice-cooler box, a heap of folded plastic bags, a bar of soap, four kitchen knives, a stove and a sack of charcoal, the 50kg size with wire mesh on top.

Mo asks, 'Should we bring him in?'

'It's her, not him.'

'Whatever! Should we bring her in or wait until everything is set?'

'We need to prepare the space properly. Give me the knife; I am going to bring banana leaves that we'll put on top of that plastic sheet as a carpet.' Mo hands him a small knife and he walks out.

Mo starts clearing a space at the centre of the sitting room. He unwraps a huge plastic sheet and places it on the floor. He then puts the stove at the corner and some charcoal in it. He brings some rough papers from the kitchen dustbin and lights the fire, filling the room with smoke. Mike comes back with a dozen banana leaves from the farm behind the house and is surprised to see smoke coming from inside the house. 'Mo, what are you doing?' he shouts. 'Take the stove outside! You want to kill yourself or you just want to burn the house down?'

After a series of coughs, Mo replies: 'It's fine, I know what I am doing. Just come in.' Mike enters carrying his banana leaves and sees the room filled with smoke.

'Do you know how many people die from carbon monoxide in their sleep, every year?'

Mo is still blowing up the charcoal to get the fire going. Mike lays down the leaves in a parallel arrangement on top of the plastic sheet. 'It's more than these leaves here.' He opens the windows to let out the smoke.

He takes out a photograph from his shirt pocket and looks at it before showing it to Mo.

'This is how it's done.' Mo looks at it and then compares it to the leaf arrangement Mike has made. He returns the picture to him.

'Yeah, we are good to go.' The fire in the stove is gradually heating up.

He rises up and walks out. 'Let's do this. Let's bring her in. Let's begin our offerings.'

They go to the car, open it and Mike pulls the rope that ties her. She resists and starts making a noise. Mo turns up the volume of the car radio to drown her cries. He then gets into the back cabin and pushes her out by holding her rear feet up. They bring her inside the house in haste, shortening the rope to her neck. They grab both of her feet, pull them closer and tie them together on to her neck so that it is harder for her to shake or stretch herself. She lies down on her side surrounded by banana leaves, still making noises continuously with her mouth. After making sure that she is tightly tied and there is no way she can loosen herself, they step aside. Mike looks at her and then says: 'Let's do it quick: her noises will soon cause us trouble. Lock the door and bring those knives. It's time.'

Mo comes back with two sharp knives. He hands one over to Mike, looking him in the eye as if he is having some doubts. Mike raises his eyebrows, like someone who has forgotten or missed something obvious, 'You want to do it?'

Mo shakes his head in refusal, 'YOU should do it!' with the emphasis on 'you' aimed to give reassurance. Mike laughs.

He looks at the picture again before kneeling behind the goat's neck with his long knife and says: 'Go to that side and hold down her feet and torso with all your strength. Make sure she doesn't move. You never know these things.' Mo silently obeys Mike's instructions. But her continuous bleating disturbs him.

Mike grabs her lower jaw tightly as he presses her neck against his thighs, and forcefully starts slicing her throat after a count to four. Mo doesn't understand why he counts to four. Most of the time people only count to three. He wants to ask him about it but there is no time. The moment her skin is sliced, the goat starts convulsing rapidly. She shakes uncontrollably and bleats a distorted sound that worries Mo. But Mike does not hesitate. He lets go of the jaw and instead holds the neck tighter. He holds the neck just a few centimetres from where he is still cutting. He continues to press the knife's blade to and fro with as much force as he can, until he reaches a jugular vein and cuts it open. Blood starts gushing out profusely in all directions. It shocks Mo, who suddenly releases his hold of the goat's torso and limbs, after a spray of blood lands on his hands, chest and parts of his lower face. He starts spitting continually as if he had swallowed a poison accidentally.

After Mo releases his hold on the dying goat, the convulsion increases and she throws her body around, making it harder for Mike to continue cutting the neck without more blood flying into his face. The goat's neck twists sideways as she jerks up and down, throwing kicks. She sprays blood all over the place. Mike is thrown backwards and lands on his ass. They watch in disbelief as the goat continues to convulse, releasing a strange sound from her sliced throat that only gradually recedes.

Mo starts, 'Man, look at all that blood!'

There is blood everywhere. On the plastic sheet and banana

leaves, and it even reaches the areas of the floor that they didn't cover. The half-lit stove in the corner and the wall next to it have red marks streaming downwards, and now a thick bright red line is running across the floor towards the door.

'And what were you doing?' shouts Mike, in an angry tone.

'What do you mean?'

'If you hadn't let go, none of this mess would've happened! All of this is your fault!'

'I think I've swallowed some. Have you ever tasted fresh blood?'

'You were smiling, what did you expect?'

'I wasn't smiling, you fool! I wanted to tell you to stop and before I said it... it got in.'

They watch the animal's last kicks and tremors as life leaves her body. The more blood drains out of her, the weaker her kicks and tremors become. Finally the convulsions stop. The goat lies still, motionless, surrounded by blood. But blood continues to come out of its sliced neck, slowly, slowly. Mo rushes to the kitchen and comes back with a duster, trying to catch the running blood before it reaches the door. The duster is quickly soaked and he has to go back looking for another, which happens to be Mike's towel. When Mike realizes it is his towel, it is too late. It has already swallowed too much blood.

'What are you doing? That's my towel!'

'There's nothing else to stop this blood going out, unless you want to drink it'

'Oh God, look at all this mess now.'

Mike's hand feels sticky on the knife's handle. He puts it down and smells his bloody hands only to pull back in revulsion. He then goes to the kitchen and comes back with a bowl of water and a handkerchief. He dips it in and starts washing off bloodstains from the wall. He sees the stains coming out, 'Ahaa, it's coming out, see. They aren't permanent stains. Nothing to worry about, then, let's just do our thing. Cleaning can wait.'

Mo sits down on a wooden stool close to the outer door, observing the drying blood that was once bright but is now turning dark red. It looks sticky and thick, like oil paint.

'It tastes funny, you know, a bit salty.' Mo says.

Mike turns to him and replies: 'We have now passed the point of no return, my friend. We are now murderers. We've spilt the blood of a healthy being and cut its life short.'

Mo raises his shoulders up and down, dismissively. 'You killed her, not me! It was you who held the knife and sliced her throat. It was you who took a life.'

'And it was you who held her tight for me. We are equal sinners, my friend. Look at all that blood splattered around here. If you'd done your job right, maybe we could have been pardoned. But instead we've committed a mortal sin in a very sloppy way. Even the devil is disgusted with us. All because of you!'

Mike's words set Mo thinking. He is not sure if what he has done is equal to what Mike has done. 'How can it be? I just help a friend do what he thought was right. How can I be counted in the same way and bear the same weight as him? If I help my boss write a report or finish a project, I don't get the same credit and am not held as responsible as he is. How can this rationale be accepted in sins but not in wealth?' He wonders how responsible a man is for an act, just by being present at the scene and not by the extent of his involvement in the actual deed? 'Can I be held responsible just because I used to know a murderer? Or because we've spent a night drinking together? Can a wife be condemned for having a murderous husband? Does it count if she knew it or not? Is there any valid connection between him and Mike's sins?'

'Mike, what if someone comes in now and finds us in this mess?'

Mike politely and seriously replies, 'You locked the door, didn't you?'

'I thought you did.'

Mike quickly walks to the kitchen and finds the outside

door unlocked. The keys are still outside. He takes them out of the lock and looks around. The evening is quiet and the air fresh and cold, but the music from the car stereo is still playing. He opens the car door, switches off the music, locks the car and comes back in.

'The keys were outside, just imagine…'

'But who will dare to come here, anyway… no one knows us here.'

Mike takes out the photograph and inspects it once again. He put it down, grabs the knife and proceeds to cut the remaining parts of the neck up to the bone. 'Meeen, slaughtering is quite hard work!'

Mo, who is now untying the rope from the goat's feet, replies: 'Heartless, ruthless, sinfully regrettable hard work! But now we've finally broken our seals, we aren't virgins any more. We have a front seat in hell's hall.' He throws the rope into the corner, brings two beer cans, and hands one to Mike. They open them, cheer and each takes one long sip. Mo burps and says, 'The perfect way to wash away the blood of the sacrifice. For sure, it tastes nice.'

Mike smiles. 'Let's go outside for a bit of fresh air. We've soaked too much blood into our system in here. Let's not turn ourselves into vampires before we've even tasted that meat.' Mike looks at the stove. The charcoal is now red hot with heat. 'Look, the fire is ready. We can't rest now. Come on, grab a knife, we need to cut his belly up first and peel the skin off.'

Mike takes the knife he used to cut the throat and starts cutting a long line through the goat's chest all the way down until he reaches four tiny teats at her lower belly. He then pulls the skin off the flesh. It comes off very slowly – she was a young goat.

As Mo pulls the skin off the meat, Mike thrusts his knife deep into her belly and pulls it down with force. He cuts across the goat's lower abdomen and opens up below her rib cage. The goat's long and folded intestines slide out, leaving a hollow space between the ribs. Mo is surprised.

'Geez, what's that?'

'A hose,' Mike laughs. 'That's how your belly looks like from the inside.'

Then he squeezes it at one point and watches it bulge out at another. He repeats this with other sections and watches the result with a smile. It looks shiny and spongy and playful. Mo tries once and quickly draws back, 'What's inside?'

'It's shit!' Mike laughs.

'So why are we mixing it with the meat we're gonna eat?'

'The shit hose is also meat. People used to eat this. They ate everything back then.'

'Are we gonna eat that too?'

Mike pulls the whole folded intestine out and separates it from the goat's back. He does that after cutting the oesophagus and the other section that attaches itself to the rear end.

'No. Bring me one big plastic bag. We'll throw this out when we leave or maybe we should bury it somewhere in that banana field.'

'And what if they find out?'

'Who'll find out? There's no one here and, besides, we'll be gone by then.' As Mike lifts that shiny, folded thing into the plastic bag, some half-digested, greenish stuff spews out onto the plastic sheet below. He stops.

'Come on, put it down and help me out here.' Mo helps him pushing it around, by rolling the spongy gut into the black plastic bag. They shove it to the farthest corner of the room.

They each come back with a knife and start cutting off chunks of meat from the chest and the ribs. They chop these off the bones they are attached to, without breaking any.

'Let's do it quick, we are wasting all this charcoal now.'

They place three large pieces of meat onto the wire mesh on top of the stove. The heat is high; the meat starts dripping blood into the hot charcoal, making a continuous hissing sound.

'Are you sure that's how it's done?' Mo asks.

Mike looks at the meat on the hot mesh and then back to Mo and says, 'That's how they did it. Now let's go chill outside for a while.'

'But how long does it take to cook? I want to taste it first.'

'I read somewhere it takes around half an hour or so. The one I tasted was dry and a bit darker in colour. Not like this.'

Mo with a high-pitched voice: 'What? You've tasted it before... where?'

'Overseas.'

'When? You mean last year when you went on a trip with your boss? Shit, did your boss know?'

'No, he didn't. He was always in the hotel. He never went anywhere. It was the locals that introduced me to it. I was at the bar with this guy and we started chatting and you know, one thing led to another.'

'Weren't you afraid?' Without waiting for an answer, Mo asks another question, 'How was it?'

'At first I didn't like it. It tasted so strange. It was like chewing a rubber band, a bit slippery. But then later, the taste of it, the juice in it, was kind of nice and unique.'

'Was it in the open? Isn't it illegal there?'

'It is, but, you know, there's always someone who knows where you can find stuff.'

'And why didn't you tell me? All that time, you came back and you just kept quiet? Why?'

Mike looks at him hard and long and then back to the meat on the stove. He turns it upside down to let the other side get the heat. The meat continues dripping into the fire, creating another hissing sound. Mo continues with his enquiry, 'Did you think I'd snitch on you?'

'Nooo!'

'So, why didn't you tell me until now? We've talked about this before. How we wanted to one day try it. But you go out and do it, and keep it a secret from me? I'm hurt, seriously.'

'Listen, man, it was a one-time thing and I wasn't so sure about it. Not that I thought you'd snitch on me, but someone in the office would've suspected something if I'd told you back then. I know you, Mo.'

'Fuck what you know! You don't know shit about me! You've insulted me so much today. You need to apologize right now!'

'You see, this is what I am talking about. You'd have been this much excited and people would've known. This idea didn't come to me until some months later, after I came back from Beno's funeral. You remember Beno? Do you know he was buried not far from here?'

'I know, you've told me!'

'That's when I learned of these rented houses for tourists and backpackers who come here to climb the mountain and so on. So, I asked this guy how it works and they told me, if I want to come and chill for a holiday, it's cheaper during the low season. Months later, after I'd quit the job, that's when I had an epiphany. The idea of coming back here to do it started creeping up on me.'

Mo is pacing up and down as if he is troubled or unconvinced by Mike's explanation. But Mike continues, 'But anyway, now you know and we are here doing it, end of story.'

He takes a piece of banana leaf and starts fanning flies away. He chases them to the window but they keep evading him. He wonders where they are coming from and how they know there is something here. He gets tired and stops.

'Come on, let's try this.' He picks up one piece from the wire mesh and puts it on a plate. It's still hot to touch with bare hands. The colour of it has turned darker than the original and its edges are now harder and sharper. A little burnt.

He cuts a small piece and gives it to Mo then cuts another piece, throws it in his mouth and starts chewing. Mo watches him closely, waiting for him to spit it out. He sees Mike's smile emerging as if his expectations have been confirmed. Then he cuts another piece and eats it. Mo's reluctance wanes and he licks it twice to gauge the taste before chewing. It isn't so bad. He then throws the whole piece in and starts chewing carefully, like someone who's chewing rice with sand in it or waiting for a bomb to explode. Something spongy is dancing between his teeth. He isn't sure if he's supposed to go on chewing or spit it out. He stands by the window, pushing the curtain aside, as he prepares.

Mike sees it and barks at him, 'Aaah aaaah' shaking his head sideways: 'Do not spit it out, under any circumstances. Keep chewing… keep chewing…' He cuts another small piece and gives it to Mo. He places the rest back on to the fire, as it is still bloody inside.

Mike fans the flies again, trying to chase them out through the window, but in vain.

Mo points to the plastic bag on the corner. 'Shouldn't we throw this stuff out, 'cause it's bringing a lot of flies in here. We can't close the window with the stove inside.'

Mike turns the meat over again.

'Fifteen minutes more, they'll all be ready.'

'Now let's go chill outside. We've tasted blood and it's great. We are vampires now.'

They grab the plastic bag with the intestinal guts and take it outside. Mike's shoes, t-shirt and part of his trousers have blood stains, as do Mo's. But Mike's stains are more visible because his trousers are khaki and Mo's dark blue. They come out to the fresh, cold night air of the night, the plastic bag between them.

'We'll need a shovel or a hoe.'

'I know where he keeps them.' They put it down and Mike goes for a shovel before proceeding into the banana field. They dig a shallow hole between four banana trees, bury the plastic bag and cover it up with sand. It is dark.

Mike goes back in and returns with two beer cans. The wide smile on his face is like a permanent feature, revealing his excitement to the world. As he steps out, he wants to scream so loud that his grandfather in his grave would hear him and smile back with pride. Filled with satisfaction in knowing that he has finally fulfilled his dutiful ritual and has become a proper man now. A man who has slaughtered a goat with his bare hands, drunk its blood and eaten its meat. A rite of passage for all men in their clan that has now been banned by law and by popular beliefs, ever since they started to turn the whole country into an animal-worshipping state. He wants to scream so loud, to terrify all those men in their sleep who made this illegal and suppressed it ruthlessly. It was once a proud undertaking, performed outside during the day, in the shade of banana trees, with neighbours and friends around sipping *mbege* and telling jokes. Now it's illegal and sinful even to talk about it. A valuable communal gathering lost to history. It saddens Mike somehow and he'd always felt guilty for being part of that. But now, at this moment, he has surpassed it and he is proud of himself and his friend, Mo. He hands him his beer.

After a couple of rounds and alternating moments of silence between them, Mo asks, 'But how did we end up like this?'

'What do you mean, "like this"?'

'If your grandpa did it, then when did this ban start?'

Mike looks at Mo for a moment, rests his head back against the wall, facing the night sky. He sighs.

'No one knew where it originated. Some say from the west and some say from the east. One solid fact we know is that it came from somewhere else and swept this whole region like a perfect storm.'

He takes the photo from his pocket again and turns it upside down. He looks at the inscriptions on it before giving it to Mo. 'They used to call it the era of the turmoil. You see, that's why he wrote that at the back.' Mo looks at it and sees the inscriptions, even though he can't read them properly.

'Is this your great grandpa's handwriting?' Mike assents and Mo continues, 'How do you know for sure?'

Mike adjusts himself before starting to speak. 'Let me tell you what happened back then. After many years of dramatic changes and political unrest, finally a leader emerged. A charismatic, evangelical leader who rallied the larger population at the most crucial period in our history and, with the force of the tired but determined masses behind him, he assumed office.' He took another long sip before continuing. 'Back then it was not like today. And since he had the support of the majority who were desperate for peace, especially the evangelical missionaries who had helped him gain power, once in power he started a parallel secret mission on their behalf. And he considered that mission as his personal divine duty.'

'What mission?'

'He started supporting these strange beliefs so they spread and took root, secretly financing their operations from the state's coffers. Anyone who questioned him was dealt with accordingly. Twenty years down the line, the mission and its agents had mushroomed into all corners of the state and engulfed the whole region. The majority of citizens agreed to it because they were tired of chaos and just wanted peace. Any peace was fine to them.'

He took a long sip, 'Then they passed laws to institutionalize those beliefs, which meant enforcing them as a way of consolidating their hold and crushing all remaining pockets of resistance.'

'How?'

He puts his can down, steps aside and starts peeing on the flower bed, next to the wall. After he finishes he comes back and continues with his narration, this time with active hand gestures.

'They went in simultaneously, on all fronts, militarily and culturally. They rewrote history books and cultural programmes. They banned a lot of stuff. Monitoring conversations and dictating what belief is or isn't appropriate. The rebels, as they were called back then, couldn't stand that sustained pressure from the state and its agents. Remember, the evangelicals were in bed with the state.'

'Wait a minute, who were these evangelicals? How do you know all these stuff?'

'Where do you think I got that photo? Back then, only humans had rights. Look now, even the goddamn trees, bananas, ants and beasts have the same rights as you. We are so lost! Shouldn't rights come with responsibilities?' Silence, and then he continues: 'So, after 50 years of noble resistance by people like my grandpa, they were eventually squashed. Then it was followed by another 50 years of peace and quiet. The tradition died.'

Mo interrupts again, 'You mean, the peace and quiet we have now?'

'But as you know, even the worst of droughts can't turn all seeds into extinction. Nature is nature and it only needs one good rain to take its course again, to repeat itself again. Nature is more powerful than me and you, Mo. Nature is more powerful than our will, we are just too stubborn to acknowledge that. That's what happened.'

A moment of silence passes by. Mo stares at Mike's face without a word, and then says, 'Yoo Mike, is this the meat thing or the drink thing? You've turned into a philosopher all of a sudden, talking sensible shit there, back to back. No wonder they ban it.' He then stretches out his can to cheer. Mike ignores him; instead he takes a long sip and swallows it at once with a frowning face.

They sit down on the edge of the kitchen stairs and stretch out their legs, watching the moon rushing across the dark sky, as it gets swallowed by one cloud and then another and moves one branch to the other. They know it is a momentous night for both of them that they will remember for the rest of their lives.

*** * ***

Mo wakes up to the sounds of people talking and walking

outside. He is not sure if it is a dream or not. Gradually he becomes aware that there is unusual activity going on outside. He goes to the window that faces the backyard, pulls the curtain out and is shocked to see so many people standing outside in groups of five or ten. He immediately closes it. He rushes to the sitting room and looks out of the window facing the opposite direction. There are even more people gathering on that side. It is like the whole village has descended on this place. He rushes to wake Mike up with a whisper, 'Mike, Mike...wake up!'

'Mnnnh.'

'Shhhhh.' He covers his mouth with his index finger as he points outside with his left hand. Mike is not awake yet and can't understand what Mo is up to. He thinks it is one of those silly games that Mo used to play when they were back in boarding school. He pulls the sheet up to cover himself completely. But before it covers him, Mo pulls it off and throws it down. He bends over the bed and whispers to his face again: 'They've come. The whole village is here. Wake up! We are in trouble, I'm not kidding, Mike!'

This time Mike sees the terror in Mo's eyes and can also hear people walking past their window, talking to each other in a language he did not understand. They are the coarse and confident voices of men who seem to be in an argument. They pass on and disappear to the other side. Mike leaps out of bed and stands at the window to get a better view. He is shocked at what he sees and immediately draws back the curtain.

'What's going on, Mo?'

'I don't know.'

'When did they come?'

'I just woke up now and realized we are surrounded.'

'Shit, we are screwed!'

Mike quickly pulls his trousers up, finds his phone and scrolls up to Babu Nduu's number, but before he can dial it, something hits him and he stops. 'Mo, have you seen Babu Nduu outside among them?'

'Who?'

'Babu Nduu, the old man who came here yesterday when we arrived. I was talking to him, remember?'

'Aaah, him. No! I don't know, maybe he is around. I haven't looked into people's faces. Why?'

'We need him now. He is our saviour here.'

'Do you think they've discovered us?'

'I don't know. Why else would they be here?'

Mike kneels on the edge of a window and starts scouting the faces outside for Babu Nduu. He can't see anyone who resembles him. Some people are coming from the banana field and others are going to it. He is not sure what they are up to. He can't clearly see the whole view of the banana field from his window. Then he hears the sound of people coming towards the kitchen door. They are arguing loudly in a strange language that he does not understand. But he's heard it before. It is the local language.

And then his heart almost bursts out of his chest when he hears someone shouting his name from the other side of the kitchen door, 'Mike! Mike! Mike!' The sound is so loud that you would be able to hear it from the other side of the house. The doorknob turns violently five times, followed by another shout. This time he can hear the person calling, who is walking towards his bedroom window. The sound ends up behind that bedroom window with three bangs, before another argument erupts between them. Mo is hiding in the corner of the room, a few centimetres below that window, squatting and shaking.

'Mike, are you in there? Mike, wake up! Mike!' The shouting stops.

Mike turns to Mo and asks in a whisper, 'Should I answer?'

Mo shakes his head vigorously. 'No! Soon they'll get tired of it and go away.'

'But we don't even know what's going on?'

'Whatever it is, it's not worth opening that door. Have you forgotten what we have in here? They'll lynch us without blinking.'

Mike thinks about it for a moment and says, 'You are right.' But somehow the fumbling with the doorknob becomes more frantic. Mike crawls across to the sitting-room window and takes a look outside. He sees a police officer and two village men alongside him arriving with an axe and a tool box. He realizes they are going to break down the door. He rushes back to the bedroom to Mo.

'Hey, they are breaking down the door. Dress up and get ready to fight. Hide your IDs and your money. They are coming. Where are the knives?'

Mo is busy going through his bags and putting his IDs in a plastic bag. He starts looking around for a safe place to hide them. He stops for a moment and looks up. He whispers to Mike, 'Heey, why don't we hide up on the roof?'

Mike thinks for a moment and says: 'No, you hide. I am going to open that door. Whatever happens happens, damnit!' Like a man who has suddenly been hit by a reasonable fate, he walks straight to the kitchen door. He can hear someone banging the door's hinges. He turns the keys slowly to open it. He notices that the fumbling noises from outside have stopped. He opens the door with a surprised look on his face, like a man who has just emerged from a deep sleep. The first face he sees is Babu Nduu's. He shouts at him, 'Heeey, what's going on?'

'Ooh my God, Mike? We knocked at your door 50 times. We called you out like ten times, even from your window. Were you just sleeping?'

Smiles fill many people's faces when they see the door opening. But then those smiles turn into surprise when they see bloodstains on Mike's trousers. Babu Nduu and the officer see them too, and he is the first to ask, 'Where is your friend?'

Mike is puzzled and doesn't answer. He looks around again

and asks Babu Nduu, 'Why there are so many people here? What's going on?'

The police officer pushes the door in slowly. He asks Mike, 'Can I come in?' It is more of an order than a request. Mike has no choice but to step aside and let the officer enter, followed by Babu Nduu and two other village men. Mike closes the door behind him and turns the key to lock it. He then follows behind the men to the sitting room. He hears a shocked exclamation from there, 'Whooouu, whooouuu, whooouu!!'

Mike enters the room. He encounters four mean, shocked faces staring back at him. Their horrified faces turn to a slaughtered goat at the centre of the room. Then to the blood splattered on the floor, to the stove and then back to him. 'What... what is happening here?!' Someone rushes to support himself by leaning against the wall. Dizziness suddenly engulfs him.

Before Mike can answer, the officer jumps at him and slams him against the wall, and they both go down together like a heavy sack of sand. He is like a passing ball caught in mid-air. The officer is proud of his catch. Even though he has a slightly bulging belly, it looks nice on him to the eyes of the other two village men. He is still as fit and strong as any young officer can ever be. He's at the top of his game. They'll go out telling everyone what happened inside that strange little house in the middle of the village. He knows, when all is settled, that the story will be passed around during dinners and he will be pleased. Some will offer him nice smiles and some free beers, he's sure of that.

He draws out his silver cuffs from his side pocket and locks both of Mike's hands behind his back. He grabs his trousers from the waist and pulls him up roughly. He then lets him sit against the wall that has blood stains on it running down to the floor.

'You are a filthy, sinful, worthless cannibal! You are not a human. You are worse than a wild animal.'

He spits thick, elongated phlegm onto Mike's face as he says it. The phlegm lands on Mike's left eye and he has no way of wiping it off his face. He just shakes his head and tries to use his shoulder and upper arm. He doesn't succeed.

'Look, just look there, he even had a stove,' a village man cries out, pointing to the few pieces that are left on the wire mesh from the previous night. 'You see? He cooked some!'

The man turns to Mike and shouts: 'We are going to burn you alive today! I swear, I will bring the petrol myself!'

The other man fails to restrain himself and starts vomiting in the corner. After he finishes spitting, he then comes and stamps hard on Mike's neck with his right foot, before the officer intervenes.

'Heey, listen. No one is burning anyone here. Not on my watch. He is going to the police station! Do you hear me? Now you…' pointing to Babu Nduu, 'Go to the station now and tell them to come here quickly, before they burn this house down with this man. If word gets out to these men outside, then there is nothing I myself can do. Besides, why did you rent a house to cannibals?'

Babu Nduu wants to say something, but before any words can come out of his mouth, the officer insists: 'Now, go! And do not let anyone know about this. Go straight to the station and come back with them. If you tell anyone, it'll all be on you. Do you understand?'

Babu Nduu immediately answers, 'Yes, yes.'

The man who has just vomited opens the door for Babu Nduu to leave and then closes it immediately behind him. Those on the outside do not understand what is going on inside.

After a few minutes of silence, Mike reluctantly and politely asks the police officer. 'May I ask why there are so many people gathering outside?' Everyone looks at him in a puzzled way. No one answers. He changes his question. 'If they don't know what's inside, why are they there in the first place?'

The officer looks at him long and hard and says: 'A man discovered parts of intestines that were being eaten by dogs this morning, as he was going to his farm. He thought maybe someone was eaten alive at night by a lion or leopard or something. No one was sure what had happened last night. No one heard anything unusual. So they assumed it was you, that it was your guts out there.'

'Ahaaa.'

'Babu said you came with your friend yesterday, that you weren't alone. Where is your friend?'

Mike hesitates for a moment. 'He left before dark, yesterday. He didn't stay.'

'On foot?'

'Yes.'

'Does he know his way out?'

'Yes.'

'Are you sure?'

Mike nods his head, agreeing. The officer looks at him sternly, interrogating his eyes without saying another word. He shifts his gaze first to the two village men and then to the floor. The officer then starts looking around the room carefully, starting with the dead goat and then investigating the kitchen before coming back. 'I don't see where this goat's intestines are. I assume that was what we saw out there. Was it?'

Mike doesn't answer; he just looks at him. The officer starts to walk around the house and slowly pushes open the door of the bedroom. He waits for a moment to pass before he enters, cautiously. He looks around and sees no sign of another man. He goes back to the sitting room.

The police pick-up truck arrives and two officers jump out, followed by Babu Nduu. One holds a camera on his chest with a strap around his neck. They walk slowly, ordering people to stand at a distance. They reach the door and knock. It opens and they enter.

After 15 minutes, Mike is escorted out by two police officers who throw him in the back of their car. He lands roughly on his neck. The whole compound is covered with men, women and children standing in groups, their murmuring rising and falling. The villagers are not sure why he is being cuffed and taken away by police. They are confused as to why the police would treat a man who has lost a friend in such a horrifying manner with no sympathy. They start to speculate that maybe he is the one who killed his friend and threw his body to be eaten by wild beasts outside in the dark of the night. Who is he anyway? Where is he from? No one could answer any of their questions. Babu Nduu is also taken by police along with Mike. They sit at the back, side by side. The police car leaves at high speed, leaving one officer and two village men still inside the house.

The officer comes out and gathers the people around. He says: 'Listen everyone, we are grateful to you all for your co-operation and information. It has helped us to come here quickly and follow up this matter that has caused many of you here such concern. Our village is a quiet one, with nice and loving people. Its reputation is known everywhere, and that's why we get visitors from all over the world. These guests are providing us with good income here and we have benefited from them for many years. Now let's not start spreading rumours that might tarnish that long reputation. A reputation that was built over many years, from our fathers' and grandfathers' times.'

He pauses for a moment to gauge the people's reaction. Many have no clue where he is going with his speech. He sounds more like a politician than a police officer. The whole village has been struck by fear from the moment this day started. And no one has gone to the farms or to the market, because no one is sure that there is not a wild predator out on the loose. They all remain at home.

The police officer continues: 'Now that we are here and we have looked into this matter, the preliminary statement we can make to you all is that there is no predator on the loose in our village as we had thought there might be. And what we saw earlier is not a human intestine or anything like that. No one has been murdered or attacked, as far as we know. So you can all go home in peace and continue your activities. But from now on, this house is closed for further investigations. No one is allowed to wander around here, because that may interfere in our evidence collection and investigation. Thank you and have a good and productive afternoon. You may disperse.' He then opens the door and walks back in.

Mo hears the officer's speech from his hiding place up in the roof. He can also hear a few murmurs from those standing outside. He doesn't move a muscle. He waits and waits and waits until all is quiet.

His watch shows that it is 1.36am. He carefully climbs down from the stillness and darkness of the roof to the room below. He looks around Mike's pillow and suitcase, but can't find any keys. He walks to the sitting room and looks around without turning on any lights. Still can't find any keys. He then goes to the kitchen and steps on the car keys behind the beer crate. He picks them up, walks to the gate and opens it quietly. He comes back, gets into the car and switches it on. He misses the gate post by inches in reversing. The neighbours come out to hear the engine's roar. They can't figure out what has just happened, because there are no flames or headlights to be seen anywhere in that total darkness. It is a miracle that nothing is broken and the 4x4 is gone.

Zaka Riwa lives and works in Dar es Salaam, Tanzania. He works as a freelance copy writer and graphic designer to advertising agencies, blogs and online publications. Currently, he is working on his first graphic novel of a historical nature, written in Swahili. When he is not writing or designing, he is painting his neo expressionist art on canvases. You can see some of his works at zakart.co.tz

Family Ties

Darla Rudakubana

Tesi

It was Papa's younger sister, Jeanne, who told me about it. I was the first one she had told, she explained, because I would know exactly what to do. She didn't trust anyone else. She often called me to ask for money or would invite herself to my house to give me updates on everyone and eventually ask for money. I didn't mind. It was just like Papa's family, always evading responsibility. I was calm when I received the news, almost like I had expected it and had been preparing for it without knowing. We needed to have a family meeting to think things through.

Ineza

I woke up to Tesi's dark frame standing over me and mumbling something I couldn't quite catch. It was a scary sight, I tell you. Something had definitely happened because she had woken up an hour too early and would not leave my bedside. She spoke so quietly that it took me some time to register that it was Papa. He was dead. Her calmness kept me calm, although my heart was beating at an unhealthy pace. I imagined she could hear it so I pulled the sheets up over my shoulders as she revealed her plan. We needed to have a meeting. We needed to get Dona.

Dona

'Papa is dead. We're coming to pick you up. We need to start preparing,' Tesi's voice said calmly on the other end of the line. It was 5am in the morning. I was usually awake at this time, unable to sleep at night, but had been overwhelmed with sleep lately. I must have heard the phone ringing in my dreams and picked up automatically before I realized that the conversation was real.

'Papa is dead?' I asked myself again, repeating Tesi's words over and over in my head.

***

Tesi

Dona's screams woke me up an hour too early. I leaned over to the window to see what was happening, only to find his bald cone head bobbing up and down as his screams morphed into a wild laughter.

'Look, Tesi. Look.' He stared up at me through the window.

'What, Dona? What?' I responded angrily to his high-pitched shrieks.

'The eagle – it took the meat right from my hand!'

'What?' My heart stopped. I jumped off the top bunk of our bed and ran barefoot through our dark corridor, through the nearly empty living room and out to the courtyard. Fuming, I was prepared to slap the boy so hard that it would knock his teeth right out of his mouth. They were rotten anyway. I would be doing him a favour but, even if he was only my half-brother, I couldn't do any sort of damage and expect to get away with it.

He pounced on me before I could act on my intentions, wrapped his little fingers around my arm and pulled me to the middle of the courtyard.

'Look,' he shouted, pointing his thin forefinger to the roof of our kitchen. 'Can you see it? Can you see it?'

Yes, I could see it. I yanked my arm from his hand, almost throwing his little frame to the ground.

'Stupid child,' I hissed, kissing my teeth and walking to the kitchen. There she was, my other half-sibling, the other stupid child with her dirty small shorts and oversized black Hard Rock Café t-shirt, sitting at the entrance of the kitchen, one foot crossed over the other. A tin pan with cubes of beef in it was placed defenceless beside her.

'So you're the one giving him meat to throw away?' I shouted at her. She squinted up at me as if staring at the sun, then quickly looked down at her toes. I kicked the pan. She jolted but did not lift her head.

'So in your mother's house you have so much meat that you give it away to wild animals? What kind of girl are you? Is it animals first in your household?'

'Look at me, Ineza,' I commanded. She slowly turned her face towards me and held my gaze. She seemed angrier than I was, which surprised me. 'Do you have money to buy more meat?'

'No,' she said through her pulled lips.

Satisfied, I stormed into the kitchen and there I fought with pans, plates, knives and forks loudly so that both Dona and Ineza, and the world outside for that matter, would know that I was truly angry. Papa would be back for lunch soon expecting a hearty meal from the little food that he bought from the market. Roti ikiro, imitega ikiro, inyanya ikiro, ibitunguru ikiro, poivron ebyiri, sauce tomate agakopo. Cubed beef, one kilo; green beans, one kilo; tomatoes, one kilo; onions, one kilo; green peppers, two; sauce tomate, one tin. The only thing he committed to and bought in bulk was a full sack of aromatic rice from Tanzania. The rest of his money was always saved for the evening outing to the local bar, his daily pack of Intore cigarettes and those useless Krishna wax matches. All that money spent on nothing important.

Ineza

Tesi is shouting again. She wakes up shouting and goes to sleep shouting, I tell you.

The only time she doesn't shout is when Papa is home and she's practising what to say to him in her mind. We are lucky that she can't think and shout at the same time. There would be no moments of peace for us, I tell you. You know, those moments for Dona and Papa to laugh like crazy people, as they like to do over everything and nothing.

I think maybe she hates being here with Papa more than anything and that's why she is always shouting. Papa can be scary sometimes but it's good for her because she likes to scare us too. I hate being here too but I do not shout just because of it. Anyway, how will shouting help us? We cannot say no to our mothers when they ask us to spend the whole holiday with Papa. We are just children.

Today started off badly, I tell you. She caught us feeding the eagles and almost threw Dona to the ground. I was laughing until she came after me. Shouting and shouting and kicking pans until I grew tired of listening to her. I would have given her a hot slap Steven Seagal style but I forgave her out of respect. She is my older sister, after all, and I think I understand why she is unhappy all the time. She has to cook and clean and wash our dirty clothes while we play all day because Papa doesn't have a maid. I would help her if I knew how to but I don't know how to cook or clean properly yet. I try to clean our room as much as I can. I fold my clothes and help Dona with his. I put the soap in the basin for her when she is washing and I help her set the table when she has cooked, but it is never enough to keep her from shouting. Papa needs to invest in a serious amount of cotton wool if we are to save our eardrums.

If I could, I would not travel for hours in the sky and more hours on the road just to sit in this courtyard all day. If I had a choice I would stay home and go to Kariba Dam or Victoria Falls with my friends and do all the muzungu things with their exciting families. My mother always says that it's important to go home and get to know our people. By people she means the people in the village, the grandparents and their neighbours and their neighbours' neighbours. You know, the ones that serve you cup after cup of warm milk in cups the size of jerry cans. Apparently you can't say no when someone offers you a drink around there because it's considered rude. So you have to drink up and get diarrhoea.

Although it's fun at first, it gets boring because, truthfully, people grow tired of you. They grow tired of making up English Kinyarwanda words because your Kinyarwanda isn't that great – like you're supposed to magically learn the language by osmosis as soon as you land in the village. They grow tired of having to pick you up because you don't have owl eyes like they do and are always tripping and falling on the dark paths home. They grow tired of taking you along on their daily duties, like herding cows, because they can't trust you with the calves. A calf doesn't suddenly respect a thin girl with a stick. Those things are small and cute but evil and fast I tell you. It is hard to fit in there, no matter how much you try.

With Papa it's different because he never gets tired of us. It's the opposite for him. He would rather skip the village experience and have us sit in his courtyard throughout our holidays. It's tiring and difficult, I tell you, because, to be honest, when he is around we always have to have stories to share and a reason to laugh. Who laughs all the time if they are not crazy? Anyway, I fit in here by necessity. I fit in with Dona and with Tesi, without explanation and without a choice.

Dona

'Is Tesi mad at us again?' I asked Ineza, who sat staring at her toes for a little too long.

'Did you see how she kicked that pan? Yes, of course she is.'

'I didn't mean to make her mad. I thought she would be amazed to see us making friends with eagles. The other day she was sad about us trapping bats. Remember?'

'Yes, I remember,' Ineza said. 'But why did you call her? You know she doesn't like playing with us.'

'Yes, I do. I just thought maybe...'

'I have a plan to make her forgive us,' she revealed, 'and it's not your silly songs or your made-up stories this time.'

'Fine, let's hear it.'

Tesi was not too happy and had lectured us for almost a whole hour when she found us trapping bats that had escaped from the holes in our ceiling in the night. She went on and on about causing harm to others, even if the others were animals, because 'you never know what they are going through'. That day I sang the national anthem to her as best as I could. She laughed and laughed and then started crying. I didn't know why she was crying, but Tesi was never happy for too long. I had to tell her funny stories from my school so she would laugh again. She didn't laugh but she stopped crying.

'We have to help her with the cooking today,' Ineza revealed.

'Cooking? But I can't cook, Ineza, and last I remember you were not so good at it either.'

'I said washing, Dona, washing. You have too much wax in your ears, I tell you,' she responded. I listened harder this time. 'We will wash the tomatoes, the onions, green pepper and prepare the green beans. Go get them from the kitchen.'

'No way am I going in there. Haven't you heard what's going on in there? She will break my bones like she's doing to those pots and pans and you know I can't run, Ineza. You go.'

'Dona, I can't. Look, my bones are smaller than yours. She will just look at me and I will break.'

'Okay, fine.' I believed her. 'I will go in there singing loudly to distract her so you can grab the sack and run back outside.' Tesi loved my singing – I was sure we could pull it off.

'Rwanda nziza gihugu cyanjye...' I marched into the kitchen singing as loudly as I could, leaving enough room for Ineza to grab the sack from behind the kitchen door and drag it outside. We set up our workstation in full view at the entrance of the kitchen – two small basins, one with water for the

washing and the other to place the washed vegetables in.

Ineza and I huddled around the washing basin and got busy washing dirt-ridden tomatoes, onions, green peppers and green beans. When Tesi walked out and sat next to us with a pan of soaked rice on her lap, our efforts doubled, me almost kneeling on the ground to dip my hands deeper into the shallow basin and Ineza wiping her forehead too many times to clean off invisible sweat. Tesi was calm. Quietly washing rice. Not looking at us. The silence was overwhelming so I decided to sing again.

'*Uyu mugati wamanuste mu iguru...*' Before I could sing the next line, Ineza burst out laughing and got me laughing uncontrollably too. Tesi giggled but did not look up from her pan of soaked rice.

For people like Tesi you have to always find ways to keep them happy or they can change the colour of the clouds. I know this because she is just like my mama. My mama cries easily and feels like she is always alone even when she is not. She says we don't have people because it is only the three of us: her, myself and Bibi, my grandmother. Sometimes I believe her and then I change my mind when I am with Tesi, Ineza and Papa. They are my people too and, even if we are only four, it feels like there are a hundred of us sometimes.

It is hard to believe that Papa doesn't love me – he is always happy to see me when I come for the holidays. Mama thinks he doesn't and always says that he is not on our side. It is hard to believe that Ineza is not on my side. I told her about the bad kids at school who trip me in the dining hall and make me drop my food almost every day. She always says that she wishes she were there with me so she could sneak up on them and round kick them like Jean-Claude Van Damme. I am not so sure if girls can round kick but I believed her. The other day Tesi saved my life. She told me never to eat at Mama Kadogo's house because she would poison me. Apparently Papa Kadogo is not really our Papa's friend. He just pretends.

Tesi

When Papa came home for lunch, we had already set the food on the small coffee table and were waiting quietly on the only sofa in the living room. I was so caught up in how I was going to bring it up that I didn't hear his car pull into the front yard and him fumbling with the door handle. Dona jumped up to receive him, waking me up from my daydream. Ineza followed behind him almost reluctantly and I got up to join them, pushing her forward.

'Nshuti Nzanjye,' he greeted us, to Dona's amusement. 'How was your day?'

'We fed eagles, Papa,' Dona blurted out. Papa laughed his usual loud laugh, throwing his head back and stroking Dona's bald cone head. Ineza stood frozen in front of me, resisting my pushing. I somehow understood why. I reached for her chin and turned it up towards me. 'Go outside and get a chair for Papa to sit on,' I instructed. She hurried past Papa and Dona and out the door, her head fixed on the ground, and half dragged a wooden chair from the balcony to place it across the sofa, on the other side of the coffee table.

Papa and Dona had already taken their positions on the sofa, Dona sitting too close to Papa. I motioned for Ineza to join them on the sofa so I could sit facing them on the chair she had brought in. She obeyed. I zoned out again, biting my nails, thinking of how to start.

'Papa, I need school fees,' I managed to say, disrupting Dona's story about eagles and bats and not causing harm to animals. The house fell silent; all three sets of eyes looked at me.

'Mum hasn't been able to raise enough for this coming term and we are not so sure what to do,' I mumbled, suddenly afraid of what his response would be and hating my mum for putting me in this position.

'The food is getting cold, let's eat,' Papa announced after staring at me, searching my eyes, for what felt like too long a time. I was not sure what to add so I watched him uncover the serving dishes and pile food on his plate. Dona followed, serving only what Papa had taken and only eating when he did. I looked over to Ineza, who was looking me almost afraid, unable to serve herself. I handed her a plate and nodded for her to start serving. I leaned back on my chair, biting more nails, unable to eat. I was lost in thought until I was startled by the sound of Papa dropping his plate on the coffee table. Dona did the same and also stood up when Papa stood up.

'How much do you need?'

'Eighty thousand – and maybe some additional money for transport.'

He reached into his back pocket and pulled out a thin black wallet. He took out two 5,000-franc notes and reached across the coffee table to hand them to me. I took them from him and stared at them as if I could not count. By the time I looked back up he was out the door and his car was reversing out of the front yard.

Ten thousand francs, I thought to myself. What am I supposed to do with 10,000 francs? Would he give me more later? Was this the additional sum for transport? I was furious but determined still to get my school fees from this so-called father of mine by any means necessary.

My final plan involved Ineza and Dona and they seemed eager to join in. Dona agreed because he enjoys taking part in anything that sounds like a game and Ineza maybe because she was afraid for me. The plan was to save and collect as much money as we could from Papa, especially from our evening outings to the local bar. Ineza volunteered to buy Papa's cigarettes, only to come back with a few sticks, complaining that they were not selling full packets that day. Dona told a story about the cubed beef giving him diarrhoea and begged for Papa to consider buying chicken, which never made it out of the market let alone to our plates. I complained about Ineza's sudden fever and stomach aches and got some extra money to go to the chemist. Every day was a different story and a different strategy. By the end of the holiday we had saved 50,000 francs. Not enough but pretty good.

***

Ineza

Papa is sick. I think it's serious this time. Let me know when you are in Kigali. I would like us to go see him together. Tesi's Facebook message had been the main reason I had planned my trip back to Rwanda. It had been 15 whole years since we last saw each other. If I had known that the last time we were together for the holidays would be the last, I would have prepared a touching goodbye speech, I tell you. By the time the following holiday came round, my mother was more inclined to let me do what I wanted. I of course opted to do muzungu things with my friends and the routine, being less hostile and much more fun, stuck.

Tesi and I had been keeping in touch via Facebook since she sent me a friend request a year before. She was married now with a baby. She was a housewife and soon to be a part-time student at the National University of Rwanda in Kigali studying something or other. At first I responded to her messages out of obligation but the more we exchanged the more I enjoyed talking to her. She presented a rare opportunity for me to share what was going on in my life. I exaggerated most events, crouching tiger hidden dragon style, but only at first. I loved to see pictures of her baby. I thought she looked like me but with softer-looking hair – her curls had it all together, unlike mine, I tell you.

When I got to Kigali, Tesi picked me up from the airport in her rickety Mitsubishi Turbo. She still looked like the 15-year-old I remembered except that she had replaced her braids with a long silky weave and had on long red gel nails. She talked a little too much, but it was okay, it saved me from saying much. I watched the road while she drove aggressively, breaking a few traffic rules I'm sure, to get us into town and to her house. I managed to get in a few words in when got to her place. 'Where is the bathroom? Where is our baby?'

Tesi's baby was even cuter in real life, I tell you. Oblivious to the world and the people around, her chubby legs and arms, suspended in front of her, were her main source of entertainment, while Tesi and I talked about time lost and events missed. Tesi told me about how she flunked high school and could not make it to university straight away. The switch from French to English just five years ago really set a lot of people back, she explained. I wasn't sure about that, though I would definitely pick English over French any time. Too many unnecessary complications in the French language, I tell you.

She told me about how she met her husband, a successful doctor who had studied in South Africa and had come back to Rwanda looking for a homegrown wife. Tesi obviously fitted the description – you know, Brazilian weave and artificial nails and all – and was quickly hooked up by her high-school friend. She told me about her wedding that was not really a wedding because Papa didn't attend and banned anyone in his family from attending. Apparently they had a disagreement on how the dowry should be used. Tesi wanted to use it to buy her wedding dress and save some for her household. She had no real money at the time. Papa thought it was rightfully his, as tradition dictated, and thought it extremely disrespectful even to consider using it for anything else outside of his plans. In the end Tesi's mum decided the wedding would not take place at Papa's house to cut down on transport costs. So Papa decided not to go.

Tesi planned to start university the following year. Her husband had agreed and would help her pay for it. So all wasn't too bad except she hadn't been in touch with Papa or anyone from his family until two months ago when she got news of his deteriorating health. Tesi lectured me about forgiveness and the importance of being there for people even if they were not there for us. Although I think she was trying more to convince herself and I felt like it was her way of getting me to agree with her plan to visit Papa. I didn't mind, I wanted to see Papa anyway; I needed to make up for all the missed holidays and the unexplained silences on my part. I was never a talker, though, so I wondered how it would all go down.

'What about Dona? Is he coming with us?' I assumed she had reached out to him too and that they had already had this conversation.

'I haven't seen or spoken to Dona in a long time,' she replied. 'I heard his bibi passed away but I didn't know how to reach him and I didn't even have the money to send to his mother.'

'He changed his surname on Facebook,' I revealed. 'It took me a while to find him. He never responds to my messages, though.'

We decided to hunt him down and break the news to him of our trip to see Papa. He had to come with us because we had a responsibility to look after our father, Tesi concluded. After several calls to people Tesi thought would be useful, we landed on Dona's university classmate who told us that he was planning Dona's surprise graduation party, which was to take place the next day. He asked if we would like to attend. It was then or never, Tesi confirmed, so we took the details and he agreed to signal us when the time was right.

Our secret American Ninja mission turned out to be more embarrassing than anything, I tell you. We walked into the party late, although it was more of a meeting around a plastic table than a party, to be honest. Dona, standing on the other side of the table in an oversized black blazer, was giving a thank-you speech. With little choice, we walked right in front of him, disrupting the event as people on either side of the table shuffled and passed down plastic chairs just to accommodate us. I was suddenly scared. What if he didn't want us there? What if we ruined his party and he would announce it and kick us out during his speech?

Dona hesitated when he saw us walking in but continued to speak as if we were meant to be there. It was only after his speech that the MC of the event, his friend, requested that we introduce ourselves since everyone in the room already knew each other. Tesi went first.

'My name is Tesi and I am Dona's sister.'

'My name is Ineza and I am also Dona's sister.'

My heart was beating. I looked across at Dona to see his reaction but the mumbling from the people around us distracted me. The MC spoke again in an attempt to make up for the short introductions and perhaps to silence the whispers around the table.

'I see the resemblance now,' he announced. 'It's a testament to what kind of person Dona is when not only his friends are here to celebrate his achievements, but his close family is here too... although none of us knew he had sisters... but that's a story for another occasion.'

This was going to be interesting, I tell you. It was sad to know that Dona hadn't told his friends about us. I wondered if he had told them about Papa? I wondered how it would have been if we had kept in touch over the years and had helped him to organize his graduation party. Between Tesi's love for the expensive and my Pinterest-inspired design skills, we could have blown his graduation party out of the water, I tell you. This was not the time for such regrets; I wanted to hear it all from Dona. So when the speeches were done and Tesi wanted to wrap things up, we pulled Dona aside and quickly told him about our plan to visit Papa. Unlike my plan to grill him, I couldn't speak and left the talking to Tesi. He simply nodded and smiled, not saying much more than 'thank you for coming, I will be in touch'. Tesi and I drove back to her house in silence.

'Do you think he will come with us?' Tesi finally asked when we got to her house.

'I'm not sure.'

Dona

I hadn't recognized Tesi with her long hair and short dress until I saw Ineza following close behind her with her head to the ground. My heart skipped and I lost my train of thought for a moment but had to continue with the speech I had practised. I would figure out how they found out about this later on; I didn't want to cause an unnecessary scene.

It was the usual kind of party, speeches followed by Fanta and brochette for the guests. I was surrounded by people who could not even begin to understand my reasons for not revealing I had sisters and had changed my surname. With a father who was never in the picture and a mother who constantly tested my loyalty to her side of the family, changing my surname was the best way to clearly show whose side I was on. With my father's name dropped, my half-sisters no longer had a significant part to play in my story, especially the uncomplicated story that I preferred to tell. It was easier this way. The less you share, the less you feel. The less you feel, the less you care.

Standing in front of my sisters in my rented suit, I decided they didn't deserve any special attention. It had been too long and they had missed many opportunities to reach out to me, despite Ineza's empty Facebook messages that I felt did not deserve responses. When Tesi told me about Papa being sick, I didn't react in any particular way, even though it hurt. It was a little too late, I thought, to be feeling for each other, especially for Papa. So many things had happened. So many things I had had to deal with by myself.

When Tesi sent me a text with the details of our visit to Papa, I was thinking about Papa and the girls. I wondered what man, if not a cruel one, would have fathered children only to abandon them. Mama had told me about their short-lived relationship and his family's refusal to acknowledge us as part of them because he was still married to Ineza's mother. She told me about the pain and embarrassment he had caused her amongst her family and how she could not forgive him for promising to marry her, only to leave her hanging. She often told me to pick a side when I questioned her about Papa and his family.

When Bibi died, she changed the clouds. Mama cried all the time and wanted me to be close to her all the time too. When I stepped out to visit friends she thought I had snuck off to visit Papa and would shout at me for picking him over her. It would have been less painful for me if it was true, but I had not seen him since my last attempt just before university. He was cold and quiet most of the time and only became friendly when he wanted money for cigarettes and matches. I vowed never to go visit him again. I did not want to cause my mother any more pain. I owed it to her to be the person she needed me to be. Considering also that not many people called us or helped us with Bibi's funeral, it was an easy thing to do. At least I thought so until I got Tesi's text. The desire to hear Papa's side of the story and be in the company of Tesi and Ineza once again seemed a much lighter load than that of protecting Mama's feelings and mourning Bibi. I responded confirming that I would join them. The days leading up to the visit seemed to zoom by.

The silence in the car was masked by Tesi's non-stop storytelling. She had updates on everyone and anyone. Some we knew and others we pretended to know. Ineza let out an occasional 'ah okay', or 'really, that happened', to fill in the gaps and I laughed out loud when I couldn't hold it in any longer. As the buildings whizzing past us started to get familiar, memories of our last holiday at Papa's house flooded my mind and had me smiling to myself. I couldn't muster the courage to ask Ineza if she remembered some of the funny scenes so I looked on silently as we got closer and closer to Papa's house.

Tesi

Papa was sitting on a wooden chair on his balcony when we drove into the front yard. He didn't seem to recognize any of us until I stepped out of the car and called out to him. He wiggled to the edge of the chair and pulled himself up with the help of a wooden stick.

'Nshuti zanjye,' he greeted us in a tired voice. I gave him a quick hug and made way for the others to greet him too. Dona did more patting on the back than hugging and Ineza gave him a side hug, right shoulder first. Papa laughed and laughed and attempted to skip into the house – something that would have had Dona in stitches years ago. Dona did not laugh. He simply followed Papa into the house. I motioned for Ineza to go ahead of me as we followed close behind.

Nothing had changed. All was as it was the last time we were here, except the house was darker, more solemn. It looked like it had been a long time since it was cleaned and seemed to have had more non-human visitors than anything.

'What can I get you?' Papa asked as we shuffled in single file to sit on the sofa.

'Papa, we just got here,' I was embarrassed that we had come empty-handed and would now have to depend on whatever little he had. Papa had been retrenched two years before when the trucking company he worked for had downsized and moved most of its resources to Uganda. Too proud, or too old in his view, to look for other work, he had been depending on handouts from family members and friends of the family. These had become less frequent as the months had gone by, according to my sources.

'Nonsense, you must be thirsty. Tell me what you want to drink,' he insisted. Two cold citrons and a coke for me.

'Dona, go next door to Mama Kadogo's and ask Kadogo to get your drinks. I will pay him when he brings them,' Papa instructed.

Dona quickly disappeared and returned as quickly as he had left to join us in the silence. I looked around the house, from wall to wall, corner to corner, passing time, thinking of what to say and when to say it.

'How are you feeling?' Ineza surprised me with her

question to Papa. I looked at him, waiting for his response.

'I'm just limping through life,' he laughed, throwing his head back and then looked down at his knees. 'My legs get affected the most, especially when it's cold. I can hardly walk. It's not too bad now, though.' Ineza had done her part so I took it from there.

'Are you taking any medicine? Should we go to the chemist later on?'

'Yes, the medicine is endless. I think they are trying to cure me of things I am not even sick of,' he laughed. Dona didn't budge or show any sign that he was going to talk any time soon. 'I hope you are taking them religiously,' I quickly filled in the gap. 'It's important if you want to get better quickly.'

'Ah, it's up to God now. I am an old man, nshuti.'

'Have you eaten lunch? What do you have in the kitchen,' I got up to go to the courtyard. I was starting to suffocate on the sofa looking at his frail frame. I needed to get out of there.

'Mama Kadogo does my shopping now. You know, the usual,' Papa said, unmoved by my rush to the kitchen.

I dashed through the courtyard and into the dark kitchen but could not find anything. I rushed back into the house to report my findings but Papa cut me off as if reading my mind.

'Today is a special day. We will have Fanta and brochette,' he said out loud. 'What do you say, Dona?'

Dona nodded and Ineza did so too, looking at me in a way that said sit down and calm down. I obeyed and instead started biting my nails. Silence.

'Why didn't you come to Bibi's funeral?' Dona asked, butchering the silence. Ineza and I looked at him, unable to look at Papa for fear of his reaction.

'You didn't ask me to come.'

His response must have angered Dona because he clenched his jaw. Kadogo interrupted our thoughts with a loud bang on the door. This time Ineza jumped up to receive him. His wide smile shrank as soon as he walked into the house and was met by an uncomfortable silence.

'Citron zikonge na coka imwe,' he said placing the sweating bottles on the coffee table.

Papa patted down his right trouser pocket and then his left. 'How much is it again, Kadogo?'

'It's 1,200, mzee.'

'Do any of you have a 1,000?' he turned to us, looking each one in the eye.

'I'll pay for it,' Ineza offered and got up to hand Kadogo a 5,000-franc note. 'Prepare a brochette and a plate of chips for each of us with the rest of the money. Please make it quick,' she said, almost pushing him out of the door.

'It will be ready now now,' Kadogo assured her before half jogging across the front yard.

I got up before Ineza could sit down and motioned for her to follow me to the courtyard. She silently followed, understanding that we needed to give Dona and Papa time to talk. In what felt like less than five minutes, Dona stormed into the courtyard where Ineza and I were sitting at the kitchen entrance.

'He is still the same hard-headed, selfish man,' he said through clenched jaws. 'I regret coming here. Please let's make this quick. I want to go home.'

Papa had lectured Dona about the responsibility of children to their parents, in particular their fathers. Overriding Dona's argument that Papa was the elder and should have come looking for him and should have tried to play a bigger role in his life while he was growing up, Papa was determined to get the point across that children must respect their fathers and look after them when they were in need. Where was his contribution to his health care? he had asked. When was the last time he had called in to check if he had eaten or let alone check that he was still alive? Dona could not understand why Papa would still try to push us away even if we were the only people who reached out to him. He concluded that we were wasting our time – that Papa would never change.

Ineza was next but her nervousness told me that it would

not go so well for her either. As I predicted, their interaction lasted an even shorter time. Kadogo with the brochettes and chips was her saving grace. She too wanted to go home as soon as possible and showed it by wolfing down her food. It was silent again as everyone busied themselves with eating.

'I was thinking of bringing the baby to visit you...' Papa cut me off before I could finish my sentence.

'It's not a good time right now, Tesi.'

I looked back down at my plate and pushed a few more fleshy chips into my mouth. It was indeed time to go. I needed to get back to my baby. I needed to get back to my life in general.

'Do any of you have any money?' he asked, as if feeling the end of our visit was near. 'I need to pay Mama Kadogo for all the food she's been bringing otherwise she will stop feeding me. You don't want me to die of starvation, do you?'

We all looked at him. I was not certain about the others but I wished he would die.

***

Ineza

When Papa died, we had to move into his house for three weeks. Tesi, Dona and I tasked ourselves with preparing for the funeral, calling all his family members, hosting fundraising meetings and hosting the many visitors that flowed in and out of his house without a schedule or a structure. It was a difficult thing to do, I tell you, planning for things we had never planned for before and meeting with people we had long forgotten or wanted to forget.

My mother, of course, couldn't make it. She had some important meeting in Europe that couldn't wait and couldn't be postponed. I didn't mind. The only true skill she had at this point was to check her phone for messages and emails every minute. It was easier this way, I tell you. I was pissed off more than I was sad, to be honest. Papa had basically thrown a smoke bomb and disappeared before I really got to know him and could ask him those grown-up questions. For some reason I believed that talking to him would help me come up with a rebuttal for Mum's ever-winning argument that she had to be 'both a mother and a father and it's not fun'. As I watched the last person walk out of Papa's house, I was somehow envious of them – soon to forget their tie to him and to continue to lead perfectly uncomplicated lives. I wished that could have been me. I wished I could just walk out and not feel a thing.

Dona

Mama and Tesi's mum joined us on the first day of the funeral. Mama stayed long enough to make sure meals were prepared and Mama Kadogo had given us a sufficient supply of soft drinks and beer for the guests. Her most important job was to overfeed us so none of us would faint and maybe follow Papa to the grave. Mama Tesi only talked to Tesi, telling her to do this and that, clean this and that, say this and that. She flashed her teeth at Ineza and me in what we agreed was a smile only when we caught her staring or approached her for advice on what to do.

I felt unburdened, although little was taken off my shoulder and my mind. Papa's passing brought me more peace than a generous sprinkle of holy water from my mother's pastor. I had no living reason to be angry any more so I let my angry thoughts drift out of the door, one by one, with each leaving visitor. Having Ineza and Tesi by my side, I felt like things would be okay, given that we could now support each other through the loss of our father. Forgiveness, I'm sure, would take a little longer.

Tesi

The house was finally empty. As the three of us sat on the sofa, surrounded by a sea of plastic chairs, I regretted that Papa never met his only grandchild – that he never knew her and she would never know him. Although I had a few more years before I needed to explain this to my daughter, I needed to make genuine bonds that soared beyond my own need for survival. Ineza and Dona were a good start and I would make sure that they would know my daughter and be part of her life.

Darla Rudakubana is a short-story writer based in Kigali, Rwanda. She won the Huza Press Prize for Fiction in 2015 for her story 'The Exit of Fear and Guilt'. Darla is also a communication consultant and trained journalist – she has written for and worked with various publications in Rwanda and the region including *The Accelerator*, *Inzozi* and *Eve Girl* magazines.

The Caine Prize rules of entry

The Caine Prize is awarded annually to a short story by an African writer published in English, whether in Africa or elsewhere. The prize has become a benchmark for excellence in African writing.

An 'African writer' is taken to mean someone who was born in Africa, or who is a national of an African country, or who has a parent who is African by birth or nationality.

The indicative length is between 3,000 and 10,000 words.

There is a cash prize of £10,000 for the winning author, £500 for each shortlisted writer and a travel award for each of the shortlisted candidates (up to five in all).

For practical reasons, unpublished work and work in other languages is not eligible. Works translated into English from other languages are not excluded, provided they have been published in translation and, should such a work win, a proportion of the prize would be awarded to the translator.

The award is made in July each year, the deadline for submissions being 31 January. The shortlist is selected from work published in the five years preceding the submissions deadline and not previously considered for a Caine Prize. Submissions, including those from online journals, should be made by publishers and will need to be accompanied by six original published copies of the work for consideration, sent to the address below. There is no application form.

Every effort is made to publicize the work of the shortlisted authors through broadcast, online and printed media.

Winning and shortlisted authors will be invited to participate in writers' workshops in Africa and elsewhere as resources permit.

The above rules may be modified in the light of experience.

The Caine Prize
Menier Chocolate Factory
51 Southwark Street
London, SE1 1RU, UK
Telephone: +44 (0)20 7378 6234
Email: info@caineprize.com
Website: caineprize.com
Find us on Facebook, Twitter @caineprize and Instagram.